To all of us starting our adventures later in life—just because it took a while doesn't mean it won't still be amazing. Also, to all my fellow bisexual disasters.

CONTENT NOTES AND TROPES

S pace for More is a spicy alien romance featuring a human and two aliens. It includes consensual, open-door sex scenes including: FFM, FF, and FM pairings, alien genitalia, oral sex, anal sex, dp, dvp, knotting, lots of fancy cum, using said fancy cum in creative ways, and public sex.

There are mentions of body shaming (for plus size alien MMC), trauma from upbringing (both alien MCs), worries about not being enough for their partners (alien MMC and human FMC), repressing emotions (both alien MCs), and sexual inexperience/loss of virginity (human FMC).

Throughout the book, there are mentions of medical topics including use of needles (once, human FMC), costs of medical care, obstetrics, high-risk pregnancy (past, patient of human FMC), and nausea/vomiting from anxiety (alien FMC).

Some tropes included in Space for More are fated mates, second chance, hurt/comfort, hidden motives and deception, fake spy nonsense, and grumpy x sunshine x feral gremlin.

If you have any questions or need more details about the content of the book before diving in, please feel free to reach out me at emilyantoinetteauthor@gmail.com.

TRANSLATION TECHNOLOGY

In Space for More, all characters use a neural implant that provides translations of languages they don't speak/read. When a word or phrase doesn't have a direct corollary in another language, the translator will either provide the closest equivalent or the untranslated word from the source language.

The level of translation for idioms also depends on the individual's experience communicating with other alien species. For example, Mezli understands and uses human idioms because she has a human best friend. Mezli and Phelix's curses translate directly to human ones both because of their exposure to/research on humans, and the prevalence of nexxit in the Xi Consortium making their language database more robust (in comparison to seladin like Maerlon).

GLOSSARY

Aespians (ay-spee-ans): An insectoid, bipedal species with a chitinous hide that covers most of the body and long legs that bend much more prominently than humans. Aespians have vestigial translucent wings and large, prominent eyes, thin noses, and antennae-like protrusions on their foreheads.

Ankites (an-kites): A humanoid changeling-like species that can alter their features to look similar to other alien races. When not catering their appearance to look more appealing/welcoming to other alien races, their forms are more amorphous, with less defined features. They can't change their limb configurations or skin shade. They are typically slender and tall, though they can become more or less curvaceous or angular as desired. Ankites don't have hair, but can make a facsimile of it that looks like tentacles or a solid drape coming from their head.

Coalition: The main human governing force formed from the various human colonies and starships.

Cycle: One full day. On Spire, the artificial environmental systems create a day-night cycle that lasts 26 galactic standard hours.

Esh'et: Seladin curse, closest human curse is "shit".

Europa 3: A remote farming colony inhabited by elderly humans.

Fa-shar: Seladin curse, closest human curse is "damn".

Flesstra: A large rodent commonly kept as a pet in the Xi Consortium.

L'thris a talla: Seladin term (antiquated), translates to "most beloved" or "keeper of my heart".

Mslep: A cabbage-like, sickly gray vegetable eaten by nexxit.

Nexxit (neck-sit): A humanoid species that has four arms. Their skin ranges from dark pink to light pink skin. Nexxit tend to have black hair, large dark eyes, thin noses, and pointed ears that rest flat against their heads. Most nexxit have a slight build and they are shorter than humans.

Nexxa Itat (neck-sah ee-tot): The nexxit homeworld.

Seladin (cell-ah-din): A humanoid species characterized by their dark gray or midnight blue skin, glowing pupilless eyes, and luminescent skin markings. They have long pointed ears, sharp angular facial features, large noses, and sharp, fanged teeth. Typically, they have white or gray hair and brow ridges with skin markings instead of eyebrows. Their bodies are tall and broad shouldered, with long arms and legs.

Shikzeth (shik-zeth): A humanoid species with volcanic, magma-colored skin under rougher slate-colored outer skin/plating. They are typically broad and muscular, with large, blunt features and narrow eyes. They have horns and either no hair or coarse red, black, or orange hair. Some Shikzeth wear a breathing apparatus to allow them to breathe oxygen, however most that leave their home-world have respiratory implants.

Skrllpt: Am extremely spicy Shikzeth dish that looks like mashed potatoes.

Spire Station: The largest and most technologically advanced space station created by the Xi Consortium. The station is broken into three habitation rings/districts—Orion, Sagittarius, and Perseus. Often shortened to Spire.

Vuloi (voo-loy): A humanoid species characterized by their hulk-ing, muscular bodies. Vuloi have dark green skin with a lizard-like texture. They have two rows of eyes, with the top row smaller than the bottom row.

Xala: Nexxit equivalent for woman.

Xalar: Nexxit equivalent for man.

Xi Consortium: The united governing force for Xi space, which borders humanity's local sector of the galaxy. Comprised by representatives from each of the Consortium species—aespians, ankites, nexxit, seladin, shikzeth, and vuloi.

Yesle: A fruit from the nexxit homeworld that tastes like a mixture of oranges and peaches, and becomes sickly sweet when overripe.

Y'thir: Seladin social class of second-born seladin those who leave the seladin colony ships or Sela 2 to learn from other cultures and provide for their families.

PRONUNCIATION GUIDE

Eden Mori (ee-den mo-ri)

Phelix val Nafar (feh-licks val nah-far)

Mezli val Frye (mez-lee val fry)

Ashlath (ash-lath)

Tysea (tie-see)

Hadrell (had-rell)

Fina (fee-nah)

Breks (brehks)

Maerlon (mare-laan)

1

✦EDEN✦

"All incoming passengers must submit to decontamination and a routine inspection of their bags. Please see a dock attendant if you have questions about this procedure." A glowing hologram of a lithe, androgynous ankite with a ponytail made of solid, ooze-like matter smiles with programmed cheer as it gestures toward an interminably long, snaking line of people trying to leave the docks. People that are all *aliens*.

I can't believe it. I'm actually on Spire. And surrounded by aliens! Not that I wasn't surrounded by aliens on the multiple days-long transit ships I took to get here, but I was confined to cramped passenger cabins most of that time. But now? Gods, this place...it's beyond anything I could have ever imagined. I only wish my cabin had a viewport, so I could've seen Spire as we approached the massive city-sized space station. Though when I managed to look through a viewport leaving the last transit hub, I felt lightheaded and queasy at the vastness of space. Who even knew space sickness was a thing? This whole trip has been mind-boggling, and now that I'm here, it feels like my life is ready to begin. It feels like—

A chittering curse behind me is the only warning I get before I'm unceremoniously shoved by an aespian with enormous glittering eyes, knocked off balance as their hard yellow carapace collides with my shoulder. I stumble to the side and directly through the hologram, which flashes a bright warning light. "Please refrain from standing on the holo platform," it says calmly.

I scramble off of it, my cheeks flushing as I notice a crowd of aliens gathering to watch the bumbling human spectacle I must be right now. I swallow down my embarrassment and push my glasses back up my nose, smiling as big as I can and waving at the aliens staring at me. A pair of dragon-like, scaled green aliens just a few inches shorter than me wave back and smile, showing off rows of pointed teeth. One of them points at my chest and giggles to the other, and I realize my loose top got tugged down enough to be almost indecent in my tumble. The flush on my cheeks creeps down my neck as I right the neckline. A much larger alien of their same species—a vuloi, I think—shakes their head at them with a chastising grumble and tugs them away toward the exit queue. The rest of the aliens that were gawking at me seem put off by my open acknowledgement, turning away as well, though I don't miss a few lingering looks at my chest.

Of course the first thing aliens would notice about me are my big tits. That's what most humans notice about me, but they're polite enough not to stare for too long. The alien species that popu-late the Xi Consortium either don't have breasts or they're much smaller than mine, so I must look like an oddity to them. I make a mental note to skip wearing any low cut tops while I'm here to reduce the amount of potential gawking.

I make my way over to the exit line with my bags in tow, heart fluttering with excitement as I slowly wind my way toward the security checkpoint and decontamination scanners. I still can barely process that I'm here. The bruise forming on my arm from where the aespian collided with me helps me stay grounded in reality, so I'm oddly thankful for the encounter.

When I applied for a sponsorship to the annual medical conference on Spire, I had zero expectations. After all, the Xi Consortium was only sponsoring the expenses of one human to attend. There was no chance in the universe that they'd pick me. Sure, I padded my resume with some exaggerations and embellishments—it seemed only fair for someone who's been stuck on a backwater colony her whole life and not afforded the opportunities of other doctors. But even with my creative liberties, the odds were infinitesimal.

And yet, here I am. When I got the comm telling me I'd been selected for the sponsorship, I screamed so loud that my mom thought I'd hurt myself. My parents were filled with trepidation about me taking this journey halfway across the galaxy, since I've never even gone off colony before. But by the time I left the spaceport on Europa 3, I think they were glad to have a break from me babbling about the conference and all the sightseeing I wanted to do on Spire. Even Dad's placid demeanor cracked to show a hint of annoyance as I told him about my sightseeing itinerary for the hundredth time.

Mind abuzz with thoughts of whether I should visit the massive golden arboretum in Orion district, or go to the neon-soaked nightclubs in Sagittarius district first, the hour wait in the security and decontamination queue feels like nothing. When I'm not considering my itinerary, I'm glancing at everyone around me and trying to recall what species they are and all the facts I'd memorized about them prior to the journey. The ankite in front of me keeps looking back over their shoulder at me, and though they pretend to be looking elsewhere, I notice their features shift to resemble mine each time they look, their broad eyes growing closer together and narrowing, their lips plumping and widening, and the solid drape of gelatinous matter hanging from their head shaping into an approximation of my chin length curly hair. I desperately want to talk to them, but since their observations of me are surreptitious, I resist the urge.

I've heard that ankites are considered the most universally appealing species out of all the Xi Consortium aliens, due in no small part to their ability to alter their features. But out of all the aliens I've seen so far, the pretty pink nexxit with their beautiful large eyes and four—yes, *four*—arms intrigue me the most. Just think of what a partner with four arms, and hands to match, could do.

Not that I'd know what a partner with just two hands is like.

Visiting Sagittarius district goes to the head of my list of activities, as I consider that depressing thought. I'm thirty years old and I've barely even kissed someone, let alone done more than that. Impossible, right? A cute, smart girl like me with massive tits, a decent personality, and a libido the size of this space station couldn't be a virgin. But alas, it's true. One of the many downsides to growing up as the "miracle" baby to older parents on a retirement farming colony was the lack of eligible partners. Unless I wanted to date someone at least twice my age and even then...

I shudder as I recall the time I tried flirting with my widowed neighbor, Artem. He was strong and handsome for a man his age and my dumbass twenty-five-year-old self thought my interest would flatter him. Too many age gap romance novels and not enough practical romantic experience combined to make me bold. Instead of sweeping me up into a lust-fueled, forbidden affair, Artem took one look at me, laughed, and then told me to go home because it was "past my bedtime." And not in a sexy way. More of an exasperated, somewhat revolted way.

Yes, a brothel in Sagittarius district is stop number one tonight after I check into my hotel. I've already done some research into which places to go. I considered going to a pleasure simulation, but I'll be damned if my first time is with a holosim. I want to feel some sexy alien's body pressing against mine, and feel their muscles tense beneath my hands as they hold me. I want to taste—

"Either keep moving or get out of my way, human," a terse voice grumbles behind me as two pink hands land on my shoulders to move me to the side. I snap out of my heated thoughts and scurry to the security agent that's waving me forward with an impatient frown, throwing an apologetic look over my shoulder at the nexxit behind me.

I really need to pay more attention to my surroundings. And get laid ASAP, judging by the tingles I feel when the vuloi dock officer winks his column of eyes and tells me I don't need to undress to use the decontamination pod. They should really have a sign or something, how was I supposed to know?

When I finally exit the security checkpoint, I barely have a moment to take in the dazzling sight of the artificial blue and pink sky and the sprawling maze of walkways and multistory buildings filling Orion district's massive habitation ring before I hear someone call out my name.

Shit, did I leave something back at the checkpoint? I spin around in place to find the source of the voice.

"Over here, Dr. Mori!"

I turn to see a pale green ankite in a fitted gray suit waving at me, holding a datapad with "Dr. Eden Mori" written on the display in universal. I didn't know I'd have someone picking me up when I arrived. How thoughtful! I smile and head over to the ankite, who returns my smile.

"Glad I caught you before you wandered off. It's surprisingly difficult to spot the sole human in a crowd due to your height."

I laugh as they look down at me and run a nervous hand through my hair. "Ah, sorry about that!" I apologize, despite not doing anything wrong—a bad habit I'm trying to break.

They nod. "If you'll follow me, we've arranged a private air taxi to take you to your hotel for the week."

"Apologies. I didn't know that I'd have someone waiting on me out here." Shit, I did it again. "While I appreciate the greeting, I'd like to take some time to explore before I head to my hotel."

"I fear I must be the one to apologize, Dr. Mori." They reach inside their suit jacket and pull out a badge, then hold it out to me. There's a holo image of them on it, along with the name "Agent Tysea" and the symbol of the Xi Consortium. "Things have changed since we extended our sponsorship to attend the conference this week. It was meant to be a charitable offering to extend the good-will of the Consortium to our new human allies, however..." They pause and look around, taking a step closer to me before speaking so only I can hear. "We require your assistance in return on a covert mission of grave importance."

"You need a doctor?" I ask, confused why they'd need me when the station is crawling with far more qualified medics.

"We need the full array of skills you mentioned in your application for the conference sponsorship, not just your medical knowledge."

"W-what?" My eyebrows shoot up as I startle at their statement. "I think I may have given you the wrong impression." I search my memory, trying to recall what I wrote in my resume. I may have lied a lot, but I didn't mention anything about being able to work on "covert missions of grave importance." Unless that part where I said I had years of experience uncovering mysteries and getting to the bottom of problems was misleading. I meant figuring out that Mrs. Greene had a rare allergy to spriskroot-based medications, not actual sleuthing.

I clear my throat and give Agent Tysea an apologetic smile. "I'm just a medic. I don't have any..." I lower my voice to a whisper, "secret agent type skills."

"Yes, that's becoming evident now that I've met you. Nonetheless, you're who we have to work with. Please follow me." This time it doesn't sound like a request despite their light tone.

So much for a trip to have some fun and get rid of my v-card. What the hell have I gotten myself into?

2

✦PHELIX✦

"Apologies for disturbing your rest, Lord Nafar. Docking will commence soon and disembarkment will occur in a quarter hour. The time on Spire is currently 17:23." An artificially pleasant and even voice speaks over the comm into my ship quarters, stirring me awake.

"Right. Thank you," I reply groggily, sitting up slowly from my bunk, making sure to not bump my head on the frame of the sleeping alcove. The cheaply made covers slide to my waist and I scratch absently at where the fabric has irritated my skin.

So much for so-called "luxury" space travel. After the past week aboard this subpar vessel, I won't be using this company's services again. Especially not at their exorbitant rates. I could've bought my own ship and flown here for only twice the cost of this trip from Nexxa Itat to Spire Station.

"Please let me know if you need any assistance with your departure. Do you require luggage transfer to your residence on Spire or a guide for your time on the station?" the VI asks cheerily.

"That won't be necessary." I don't trust them not to lose my bags, and some of what I've brought is too important to risk. The one benefit of arriving on a GalaxyVenture ship is that all my belongings have been pre-checked by station customs, and I get a private decontamination chamber, so I won't have to spend hours waiting in line to leave the docks. Which is good, since my arrival time is already cutting it close—there are only two hours until I'm expected at the medical conference's welcoming event.

I've already packed my bags in anticipation of a quick unboarding, eager to get off of this junk heap of a vessel. With quick, studied motions, I dress in my travel suit and comb my sleep-mussed hair.

Goddess, I look rough. My reflection in the slightly warped hygiene room mirror shows dark pink circles staining my under-eyes and the telltale hint of a contact rash on my neck. Wonderful. I'll need to shower as soon as I get to my accommodations or I'll end up wanting to scratch my skin off the rest of the night.

That won't do. It's imperative that I make a good impression on my colleagues. The most renowned medics and researchers from across the Xi Consortium have gathered for their annual conference on Spire Station and it's my first time attending. I intend to put their skepticism toward me to rest. To my face they call me bright-eyed and optimistic. Behind closed doors, I'm sure they're more likely to say I'm a precocious upstart without the experience to back up my ambitions. Or, even worse, they don't talk about me at all. This conference is my chance to prove myself to the greater medical community, as well as my chance to make some other meaningful...contributions.

My hand reflexively goes to the datapad in my satchel, checking to make sure it's still there. Professional pride and ego may be one factor in my attending the conference, but it's not the only one.

A concerning clunk followed by a hiss fills the room through the ship's subpar sound dampener as the docking clamps lock onto the vessel. The floor shakes violently and I have to brace myself against the wall with my upper hands to not topple over.

Yes, it's definitely time for me to get my own ship. I send a comm to the Nafar family retainer to arrange the purchase and crew procurement in time for my departure in a week. Mother won't be pleased, but I have enough in my trust to cover it even if she protests. It frustrates her to no end that Father set aside a large chunk of his fortune for his children. Such an extravagant purchase will remind her that she can't exert financial control over me anymore, which brings me a whisper of satisfaction.

Disembarking is thankfully fast since I'm let off before the other passengers. Normally, I'd feel guilty about the special treatment my noble status affords me and insist that families and the elderly deboard first, but tonight's schedule doesn't permit any such niceties. The private transport to my hotel is waiting and makes good time, despite the bustle of station traffic. The shuttle whizzes above garish neon signs, the lights blending together into a kaleidoscope of color.

How long has it been since I've visited Spire? At least a few years. The last time being when Mivael, my older brother, chartered a cruiser to the station for his 40th name day celebration. Most of my memories from that trip are drowned in the liquor-soaked debauchery of the weekend. I was feeling rather sorry for myself— how could I not after not only ending a years-long relationship, but having my true mate run away from me after our first meeting? Alcohol may have numbed the pain to a dull haze, but the horrific hangover and resurgence of anguish in the wake of that bender was bad enough that I haven't let myself get out of control since then.

Will Spire Station be more enjoyable through sober eyes? Or was the partying and alcohol the glossy veneer which made it tolerable? I suppose I'll find out soon enough.

The shuttle pulls up at my hotel for my stay on Spire, and a white-gloved aespian attendant immediately races to open the door for me. This place has all the trappings of an overpriced, pretentious place that Mother would adore. Which tracks, since she's the one that insisted that I stay here. I would have been fine to seek out a modest apartment for a week's rental, but no, appearances must be maintained.

The hotel staff buzz around me like courteous flies, seeking to aid me in return for my goodwill. Or better yet, my credits. Father taught me to be generous with tipping—no doubt they can smell that on me. I'm swept into the lobby and up a gilded lift to the penthouse suite, the attendants chattering the whole time about the various services the hotel offers. It's all I can do to maintain my placid veneer and refrain from scratching at my irritated skin until I shake them off once they deposit my luggage inside my rooms, locking the door behind me with a sigh.

Goddess, this place is ridiculous. A gaudy seladin crystal chandelier hangs over a two story sitting area. The whole back wall of the space is mirrored, though they're the type that can be made transparent so I can have a view of the district. There's a fully furnished kitchen, pristine and probably never used since anyone who stays here wouldn't deign to cook their own food. No food synthesizer, unsurprisingly. Goddess forbid I'd want to eat a replicated meal. The bedchamber and hygiene room are up an impractical, spiraling staircase. They're just as annoyingly posh as the rest of the place. The whole suite looks like it was designed to impress others rather than provide functional comforts. It's far more than I need. I'll spend most of the week at the conference hall and certainly have no plans for company.

Less than five minutes after I've arrived in the suite, the chime of an incoming comm through the suite's audio system goes off. With a sigh, I ignore it and set the system so that I won't be disturbed. No, I don't need their help unpacking or finding my way around the suite. No, I don't need a guided tour of the district. They'd probably offer to wash my slit for me if I asked. The joys of being part of the second house of Nexxa Itat.

I know I sound like a pompous ass. People would kill to spend a night in this kind of luxury. My frustration comes not from my access to such privilege, but from the expectation that I want to indulge in it. There are far better causes and efforts to invest my credits in than wasting them on a place like this, when something far simpler would suffice. But no, I have to uphold the appearance befitting someone of my status.

My grumpy thoughts fade somewhat after a cool shower that soothes my irritated skin. Alright, I admit it's nice to have such a large bathing chamber. I'd love to linger in it for an hour or two, but time is slipping away. Once I've unpacked and sent my suit for the conference through the auto-presser, I dress and finish my final preparations. The giant mirrors in the living area reflect back my appearance, which is...unimpressive.

I'll be the first to admit that I'll never be chosen as a representative for nexxit beauty. To start, I'm taller and broader than the willowy ideal for all nexxit. Mother would tell me to try to obscure some of my figure with more traditional, loose fitting robes, but I look like a shapeless lump in them. My neck is fine and my skin's particular shade of pink is tolerable and fairly smooth, thanks to the endless skin resurfacing treatments I've endured. My too large nose and odd green eye color cap off my lackluster appearance.

Vanity isn't an indulgence of mine, but Mother's criticisms ring in my ears despite my best attempts to ignore them. My body is functional. It allows me to do my work, care for patients, and move through this galaxy. Why should I care if it's not small enough to be deemed good? Right, because being different is bad and standing out makes me an imperfect scion of the estimable Nafar house.

I absentmindedly smooth the front of my charcoal jacket where it pulls at the fasteners with a frown. Attempting to wipe away Mother's criticisms is a futile effort. They're a persistent stain on my mind. Shifting the damage she's incurred on my psyche into the recesses of my mind only means it will spill out again at the least opportune times. Better to look at myself in the mirror, let my mind recall her words, and recognize my deficits wholeheartedly. And consider buying a looser-fitting jacket.

I pull my focus away from my reflection and gather my data-pads, rearranging them in my bag and checking each one multiple times. There's no way I'm leaving them unattended in this suite— I'm sure some nosy cleaner will be in here the moment I leave to find out what kind of undergarments a nexxit noble wears. When I'm satisfied everything in my satchel is present and in order, I center myself with a deep breath and head to the conference hall.

3

✦ MEZLI ✦

Damn, that date was a bust.

With a slight wince, I down the rest of my too-hot tea and set the mug on the cleaning pad. The spicy-sweet flavor is meant to be savored, but my date didn't last long enough for the liquid to cool. I shouldn't have waited for them to arrive. At least then I wouldn't have completely wasted the twenty minutes that passed until they deigned to show up.

Not only did they get there late, but then the ankite jerk said a total of two complete sentences. They didn't even interact when I asked some of my best first date questions.

On top of everything, my appearance obviously didn't impress them. I don't give a shit what some stuck up ankite thinks about me, but at least attempt to be polite!

Goddess. When they left after barely ten minutes with the excuse of an "emergency", I didn't bother to fight it. What a waste of time. Plus, they didn't even offer to pay for my tea.

Honestly, it shouldn't surprise me. At least they looked like their profile pics. The last few dates I've gone on ended up being totally different people than shown online. I've even had a few scam bots. But no matter how pretty my date today was, it doesn't make up for a lack of chemistry and basic manners. I'd much rather meet someone who looks like shredded *mlesp* but who can banter with me than one who looks pretty but is like talking to a VI—and not a particularly well-programmed one, either.

Ugh, that's what I get for going on a tea date instead of out for drinks. If we meet at a club and the person is a dud, I can find someone else to have fun with. And having fun is the whole reason I've made Spire my home. There's no end to places to explore and clubs to dance your cares away in, and I know all the best spots.

My comm makes a twinkling chirp, letting me know I've received a message. I roll my eyes when I see who it's from. Ugh, Paul, come on. This is the fourth message he's sent today reminding me of the time, location, and dress code for tonight's event, urging me to not be late. A spiteful part of me feels tempted to show up late just to mess with him. I know he's super stressed, but damn, I got it after the second message.

Paul's lucky I'm willing to give up a prime weekend night to be his date to the human embassy opening. I doubt there will be any fun singles there, just a bunch of nervous humans and people there to gawk at them. I'd take it as a challenge to seduce one of the humans, but Paul made me swear not to. Something about not traumatizing his coworkers. None of the non-humans will spare a second glance for me, no matter how hot I look. They'll be there for the crop of exotic new arrivals.

All this cuteness is totally wasted. Unless...

Maybe tonight's the night that I finally make a move on Paul. When we're not at each other's throats, we're flirting. I know he's attracted to me, even if he pretends otherwise. He's certainly appealing, with his smooth, light brown skin and his dark eyes. I bet he'd look even better tied up in my bed while I torture him until he begs for me. The cocky ones are always the ones that beg the most.

Plus, I can't resist the appeal of trying something new. Humans are definitely unexplored territory. He's only the second I've met in person. The other is my long-time human best friend, Fina. I've held off on propositioning Paul because of his shitty history with Fina—breaking her heart when he dumped her a few years back. But now that he's finally admitted how much he mishandled their relationship, my horniness outweighs my vengeful nature. I know he's curious about alien sex, but has had no luck on the Syzygy dating app. What better night to experience all the Xi Consortium has to offer than the celebration of the human embassy opening? And now that Fina's firmly entrenched in her romance with Maerlon, I don't feel bad about getting with her ex.

We could make something casual work as long as it's clear that it's just physical. That's what I tell all my dates—I'm up for fun and pleasure, but have zero interest in something serious. People get too attached if you don't set boundaries, and my "no relationships" one has been firmly in place since I left Nexxa Itat to start a new life here.

The more I think about this idea, the more I like it. Perhaps I can salvage today after all.

I tread my well-worn path on the walkways of Orion district

back to my apartment, mind filled with potential seduction tactics. The lame ankite from earlier is already ancient history.

Once home, I don't waste any time. I put on my favorite dress—the one I save for special occasions that hugs my body perfectly, with semi-translucent, shimmering fabric. It's just daring enough to be sexy without being indecent. I pin my hair up to show off my long neck, and paint all twenty of my nails to match the dress, sharpening them to blunted points. When I look at myself in the mirror, I give myself a little shimmy and a wink. Damn, Paul's one lucky human. He won't know what hit him.

A dull thump from the sitting area of my apartment snaps my attention away from my dazzling reflection. Dammit, did the neighbor's flesstra sneak in when I came in earlier? That little shit is always trying to get in my loft and chew my shoes. If it wasn't so cute, I'd call station pest control on it.

"Shaila! Come here, you rascal. I know you're in there. Quit messing with my stuff!" I call out into the sitting area, poking my head out the door to scan the space for the pesky flesstra.

A heavy hand clasps over my mouth. I squeal against it in surprise, but the hand muffles the sound. Another hand grabs two of my wrists and pins them behind my back. I scratch out wildly with my lower hands and the intruder grunts in pain, but holds tight.

Fuck! My mind frantically tries to recall the self-defense training course I took years ago, but nothing but blinding panic and adrenaline comes forth. My attempts to twist out of this assailant's grasp are futile, and when I try to stomp on one of their feet, they easily avoid it.

The intruder makes a frustrated huff and holds me tighter. "Calm down! I'm not here to harm you. I just need to talk." Their voice is even, like they're trying to soothe a wild beast.

"Fuck you, you broke into my home! Let me go!" I shout point-lessly against the large hand over my mouth. I scrape my sharp teeth against their palm and in their moment of surprised pain, I twist around to look back over my shoulder at the person holding me.

Goddess, preserve me. My eyes widen in surprise and my panicked pulse races even more. It's the ankite from my tea date. Did they follow me home?!

Fuck, Fina keeps telling me I should be more careful. Now it's too late and I'm going to get murdered by some creepy asshole. Please, Goddess, or anyone who's listening—I promise I'll stop being so reckless. Just let me get out of this alive.

Angry, bewildered tears stream down my face as I continue to struggle, feeling what little strength I have utterly fail me.

"Please. I just need to talk. If you calm yourself, I can explain. Well, we can explain," the ankite says smoothly. They look over toward my living area and, with dread, I notice two other people sitting on my couch. Another ankite and a...*human*? What the fuck is going on?

I might be able to fight off one person, if I could still my mind enough to be smart about it. But three? I stop struggling, sagging in their grip in defeat.

"You're scaring her! I thought we were here for her—" The human calls out in shock, only to be cut off by a stern glare from the ankite sitting next to them.

The jerk restraining me keeps their bruising hold. "Are you going to listen?"

I can't even remember their name, they said so little during our date. What kind of fucked up game are they playing? I nod as much as I can in their grip. If I can distract them and get them to talk long enough, maybe I can get a message out to Paul or Fina.

As if reading my mind, my stalker yanks the comm device off my wrist and shoves it into their pocket. The muffled, angry noise that escapes my mouth earns a tighter grip on my wrists, and they shake their head in warning.

I force myself to be still again and am surprised when they release their grip. I shove away from their grasp with a gasping curse, tempted to scream out for help.

It's useless. By the time anyone came to see what the commotion was, I'd probably already be dead.

"What the fuck are you doing here? Why did you follow me?" I hiss at the intruders, rubbing my wrists and backing away from my assailant.

"We needed to speak with you, Mezli. Or should I say Princeps Mezlitrasta val Frye?"

My heart stops when I hear my full name. Who the hell are these guys and how do they know who I am?

When I ran away from home to Spire, I was terrified and naive, but I'd at least had enough forethought to use a fake name. The second a docking official heard the name Frye, I'd have been flagged in the station's system as a "visiting diplomat" and my chances at a fresh start and freedom would've vanished. So I spent the majority of the credits I'd brought with me to convince a shady seladin on my transport to sell me a fake ID. I've been Mezli val Grisa since. At least until these people showed up at my home.

"That's not my name," I say, attempting to keep my tone even despite the shock. Are they here to take me home? I'd thought my mothers would've accepted my leaving years ago, but maybe I underestimated their need to have me under their thumbs.

"Lies aren't necessary, Princeps Frye," the pale green ankite sitting on my couch says. "As my colleague here said, we're not here to harm you."

"I suppose you can't damage the goods, my mothers might dock your pay," I say, my heavy sigh fluttering my bangs.

"Your mothers have no bearing on this conversation, Princeps Frye," the asshole ankite behind me says, their orange skin flushed red from the exertion of restraining me.

"Then why the hell are you here? Because I'm not going back!" The thought of being whisked back to a life of playing the perfect, placid princeps makes my stomach roil and a panicked sweat bead on my neck.

My terrible date rolls their eyes at me again. "If you'd stop talking for a moment, I can explain. No one is making you go back home or telling your mothers anything."

Relief floods through me and I open my mouth to tell them that I have every right to talk as much as I want when my home has been invaded by strangers, but they hold their hand up to stop me. "That is, no one needs to find out you're here *if* you help us."

Fuck.

.

4

✦ MEZLI ✦

I t takes the intruders explaining themselves slowly to me multiple times until my panicked brain can digest the information. "So let me get this straight. You want me to work with this human and act like some kind of spy to catch a potential criminal in the act of handing off illicit goods? Are you insane? No!"

"Princeps Frye, your cooperation with us for this endeavor is paramount. Lives may be at stake," the ankite sitting across from where I've sunk down to sit on the floor says calmly. Agent Tysea. They have pale green skin and kind, generic features that begin to sharpen to match some of mine as we speak. A classic tactic from the changeling-like species—appear more visually appealing to put others at ease. This one doesn't realize it does the opposite for me. I can't stand false appearances after growing up part of Nexxa Itat's nobility.

"Call me, Mezli," I bite back at them in annoyance.

"If that is not sufficient motivation, please bear in mind that you emigrated to Spire Station using a fabricated identification and have committed multiple violations of station laws during your time here. As agents of the Consortium, we have the right to inform interested parties on Nexxa Itat of your presence, as well as seek legal recourse for your crimes," adds Agent Asshole. I refuse to remember the name of the person who faked a date with me and then followed me home so they could harass me to do my civic duty.

Ugh, it's just my luck that my home invaders are Xi Consortium agents rather than run-of-the-mill mercs looking to extort a noble. Extortion would've been easier to deal with. I have enough connections that I could've found a way to pay them off. After seeing their badges to confirm they're legitimate Consortium agents, my fear of harm has subsided, but my anger at my discovery and their interference in my new life has tripled.

"Like I'm the only person who's ever used a fake ID! You'd have to prosecute a quarter of Spire if you're going to use that against me in court. As for law violations, name one! I've done nothing wrong. You're just trying to scare me," I say, scowling at Agent Asshole.

The fidgety human woman with freckled beige skin and a mane of black curls who says her name is Eden—no "agent" as a prefix—flushes and gives me a slight smile, the crooked upturn of her mouth surprisingly charming. "From what I overheard them saying...indecent exposure. Public lewdness. Multiple times."

Shit, I didn't think anyone had caught those things. My confidence that they've got nothing on me wobbles, but I keep it from showing on my face. Maybe there's still a way to get out of this nonsense. Though all that's running through my head right now is a loop of the look on my mothers' faces when they find out their precious daughter has turned up and has a bunch of station violations to her name.

Agent Tysea's enormous eyes lock onto mine solemnly. "Princeps Frye, we only wish to make it clear to you how necessary your aid is. You will not be in any danger, and it should only take a few days of your time if things go smoothly. A week if any complications arise."

"You said that people might die. How the fuck is that safe for me?! Is this human supposed to be my bodyguard? She doesn't exactly look equipped to protect herself, let alone me."

Agent Tysea flinches slightly at my shrill retort, and the human looks ill after I speak. "No offense," I add in a gentler tone to Eden. Poor girl, I bet they roped her into this just like they're trying to do to me.

Agent Asshole shakes their head at me as if I'm a petulant child. I can't believe I found this dick attractive enough to go on a date with. "If we can't prevent the exchange of the black market schematics, yes, people may die. That doesn't mean you or Dr. Mori will be in any danger."

I huff out an exasperated sigh and throw my upper hands up. "Okay fine, whatever. I still don't see why, of all the people you could pick to play pretend for you, you chose me and a random human."

Agent Tysea clears their throat slightly. "Dr. Mori was selected because of her professional background. You, Princeps Frye, are a member of the third noble house of Nexxa Itat. Your social standing, whether you choose to avail yourself of it or not, is what we need. The suspected smuggler of illegal schematics is a member of nexxit nobility."

I blink slowly at them as a wry smile twists my lips. "If you want some polished socialite to charm this person, you've come to the wrong place. Look at me." My lower arms gesture down at my body while the upper ones reach out as if showing off my humble apartment.

This earns me a sigh from Agent Asshole. "Agent Tysea is trying to be delicate so as not to offend you, Princeps Frye—"

"*Mezli*," I snarl at them. No matter how many times I correct these agents, they refuse to call me by anything but my abandoned title.

They narrow their eyes and the sharp jut of their chin conveys just how little they think of my request. "I don't need Mezli. I need Princeps Mezlitrasta val Frye. True mate to Phelix val Nafar."

Ice courses through my veins, and my skin prickles with dread. I haven't heard that name in four years. Since the night I left Nexxa Itat and never looked back.

That was another life. Phelix means nothing to me. No, less than nothing. He doesn't even exist for this version of me.

Still, I need to know what he has to do with this nonsense. Surely he can't be the one...

Agent Tysea picks up on my expression and misinterprets it, giving me a watery-eyed, apologetic look as if I have love for my true mate. "Yes, Lord Phelix val Nafar is the suspected smuggler."

Fuck.

For the first time tonight, I'm silent. The weight of their anticipation of my reaction to the revelation smothers me until I feel lightheaded.

Agent Asshole is the one who finally speaks. "I apologize for giving you this news. I can only imagine how upsetting it is to find that your mate is not who you thought he was." They sound genuinely regretful, which is surprising. It isn't until they reach out slowly to place a hand on my shoulder to comfort me that I realize my whole body is shaking.

I instinctively pull away and my head snaps to look at Agent Asshole, who yanks their hand back, realizing the inappropriateness of the touch. A low roiling sensation starts in my chest, bubbling up my throat until a hysterical laugh bursts from my lips.

Everyone in the room stares at me in confusion and alarm.

"Why didn't you just lead with that? Phelix val Nafar may technically be my mate, but I hold no affection for that insufferable, arrogant bastard. If he's doing what you think he is, I'm more than happy to help you in any way I can. What do you need me to do?"

The agents exchange a quick glance, then Agent Asshole looks back to me and nods, obviously relieved at my cooperation. "Lord Nafar is here on Spire, ostensibly to attend a medical conference this week. However, we suspect he is also here to smuggle highly dangerous and confidential medical schematics to a buyer on the station. Because he is a member of Nexxa Itat's second house, our operation must be as subtle as possible. If we were to attempt a direct interrogation or interception, it could turn into a political shitstorm because of his status as nexxit nobility."

"Why can't you creeps just follow him around the whole time? Or sneak into his hotel and steal his stuff so he can't hand off the schematics? You're obviously pretty good at it." I may be on board with helping take Phelix down, but I still don't understand why they need me.

Agent Asshole rolls their eyes at me.

"Fuck you, it's a valid question!"

They scoff. "Princeps Frye, we've carefully thought through this mission far more than you have in two seconds. Lord Nafar's personal security protocols keep us from tracking him, so we're unable to monitor his movements on the station. Stealing the files will not aid us in our overall purpose for intercepting the exchange, which is to identify those higher up in the network of black market smugglers. We hope to use this opportunity to gain a foothold to take the whole operation down. Lord Nafar is simply the easiest access point to do so."

Agent Tysea nods. "So, that is where you, Mezli, come in. You will 'accidentally' reconnect with Lord Nafar while attending the medical conference and use your...charms to get close to him, confirm that he has the data, and find out when the exchange will occur."

They look at me as if preparing for me to reconsider my decision to help. Part of me wants to hold the silence and let them squirm, but my mind is racing too much to keep my thoughts contained.

"As much as I agree that Phelix needs to be taken down a peg, this still doesn't make sense. He's a member of the second highest noble house in all of Nexxa Itat. Why would he risk doing a smuggling job?"

"Who knows why the rich do what they do? Maybe he's bored and wants a thrill. Sounds familiar, doesn't it?" replies Agent Asshole.

"Leaving home isn't the same thing as endangering lives and becoming a criminal!" I bite back at them.

Agent Tysea winces. "From what we know of the Nafar house's finances, he could be doing this for the payout," they say tentatively, like they're worried they'll offend my delicate sensibilities by discussing something as crass as monetary needs with a noble.

I stifle a laugh. With any other nexxit noble, it *would* be distasteful. But I'm sitting here on my cheap synthetic rug in a handmade dress and worn heels. "What makes you think he'll want to see me? When we met, he wasn't enthusiastic about our situation."

That's an understatement. When we had our first meeting after our parents' discovered our mate bond through a mate finder, it was disastrous. He called me a dumb slut when he thought I wasn't listening and looked at me as if I were the last person in the galaxy he'd want to be with. Plus, I may have puked on his mother's floor. Just remembering that night makes me nauseated.

"Our records on Lord Nafar indicate that he has taken no lovers or even gone on a date since he learned you were his mate. Prior to meeting you, he sought companionship. I doubt he will risk losing a second chance with you, if it were presented to him in the right light," says Agent Tysea.

He hasn't been with *anyone*? That's kind of sad... Wait, I'm not seriously feeling bad for that prick, am I?

"Fine, I guess that makes sense. But then, why is she here?" I gesture over at Eden, who's been a mostly silent observer the entire time they've been here.

I expect one of the agents to reply, but she speaks, frowning back at me. "*She* has a name. I'd think you of all people would put in the effort to use mine since you seem so particular about what the agents call you."

I wince slightly at how rude I've been to her. I doubt she wants to be a part of this either. "Sorry, why is Eden here?"

Agent Tysea glances at Eden and I catch a flash of disappointment as they look at her. "We originally hoped that Dr. Mori would be able to connect with Lord Nafar at the conference, as a professional peer, and gain his trust that way. However, she...oversold some of her qualifications and we're not confident that she'll be able to take on the mission on her own. She kindly agreed to serve as your partner since you still need access to the conference." I don't miss the way Eden's eyes narrow when Tysea says the words "kindly agreed".

"You'll be posing as a pharmaceutical rep. Their work involves networking more than medical knowledge, so Lord Nafar won't expect more than a cursory understanding of the field," adds Agent Asshole.

This poor human lied on her resume and now she's stuck as my assistant for an entire week? I shoot Eden a sympathetic smile. "I'll definitely need your help. I work in marketing, not biotech or health. Though I know my way around bodies pretty well," I add with a wink at Eden.

A blush creeps onto her face at my words, and I'm momentarily dazed by how enticing she looks with a wash of color on her cheeks. I wonder what else I could do to get her to blush like that.

Maybe there are more perks to this mission than sticking it to my mate. Hopefully, having this pretty human around will make the week more bearable. Because as excited as I am in theory to get revenge on my mate for how he treated me, the thought of spending time with Phelix makes me feel ill.

It pisses me off that he still has a hold on me even after all this time. I hate that the past, pathetic version of me still exists enough to feel the pain of his rejection. That anger and the petty lure of getting to screw Phelix over is enough to push me past the alarm bells going off in my head warning me that this is a bad idea. Besides, I don't want people to die if he actually is here to sell the data.

Goddess, what did I do to deserve such a terrible person as my mate?

My comm's muffled ping chirps out from Agent Asshole's pocket and they fish it out, canceling the alert and punching in something I can't see. They reach toward me to hand the comm back, but grip my hand over it when I go to take it. "You can't tell anyone what you're doing. No one. Not your friends or your parents or your neighbor's flesstra. Not even station security. Do you understand?"

"Tell no one that I'm temporarily a badass secret agent and pretending to seduce my mate. Got it," I say, eager for them to stop touching me and go away so I can process everything and maybe go throw up a little.

They nod and release my hand and the comm. Checking it, I see I have a series of increasingly frustrated messages from Paul asking me where I am. Shit, the embassy opening! He's going to kill me, I'm so late.

As if reading my mind, Agent Asshole speaks again. "Cancel any plans you have this week. What you're wearing is a bit formal for the conference opening event, but it should suffice."

My comm clatters to the floor as my shock makes me lose my grip on it. "Wait, I'm starting this tonight?!"

5

✦PHELIX✦

"Is a bioscan truly necessary? They already scanned me when I arrived on the station!" The harried-looking aespian standing in front of me flutters his translucent wings in agitation. He frowns at the stony shikzeth security guard, who barely suppresses an agitated grimace in return. This buffoon complained non-stop about the wait for the past quarter hour, as if it was a personal affront to him, when it's standard protocol for an event like this.

I give the aespian my best patronizing glare, eager to get him out of the way so I won't be late to the welcoming event. "As a medical professional, I'd think you'd understand the need for multiple bioscans. Unless you want viral contaminants circulating uncontrolled."

His antennae vibrate, and his sickly green carapace takes on a grayish tone. Both signs of embarrassment in aespians. Good. He should feel chastised for his ridiculous behavior. "I–I–of course I know the uses for bioscanning–"

"If that's the case, kindly let this person do their job and quit wasting my time," I say, cutting off whatever excuses he was about to make. The seladin in line behind me snorts in amusement and the guard gives me an appreciative glance. The aespian is finally quiet and when his scan is done, he scurries away as quickly as his spindly legs will carry him.

Once my bioscan is complete, the guard waves me through into the bustling lobby of the convention hall. The amount of people gathered here is impressive. My stomach tenses ever so slightly at the thought that the finest medical minds from across the galaxy are here. This is my chance to make connections, and I can't squander it. I run through my mental list of people to keep an eye out for, and with each one, my heart rate speeds up.

I'm getting ahead of myself. I need to slow down and take it one step at a time before my nerves get the better of me. I inhale deeply, scanning the crowd and then exhale with a soft sigh. Every challenge can be tackled when broken down into smaller steps. I'll check in, get a lay of the conference hall, and *then* track down the people I want to impress.

A genial ankite at check-in barely contains their shock when I give my name. They keep their composure even when my polite smile falters when I see what's written on my badge. *Lord Phelix val Nafar.* As if what I was born into bears more weight than my decades of medical study.

Don't let it upset you. It's not a sign that things won't go well. Just let it go...

"There's a mistake with my badge," I say, my tone embarrassingly sharp as I slide it back to the ankite, who now looks distinctly more nervous. "It should say Dr. Phelix val Nafar. My title has no relevance to this week's events."

The ankite's pale orange skin looks moist from perspiration and their features shift slightly, mimicking the size of my eyes and my prominent nose in an unnecessary display of appeasement. "Apologies, Lord—I mean, Doctor Nafar. I will rectify that immediately." They race off to fabricate a new badge and I don't miss the tittering between the other check-in workers. Great. I should have just left it be. Now I'm the entitled noble everyone expects me to be.

Corrected name badge acquired, I smile at the ankite and thank them for their help to try to cover for my rudeness, but it doesn't seem to dull the worry in their eyes. With a sigh, I make my way toward the ballroom where tonight's welcoming party is being held. The dull roar of conversation guides my approach, and my pulse quickens again at the thought of just how many important people are at this event.

I veer off my course and into a hygiene room. Thankfully, no one else is inside the well-lit, clean bank of hygiene stalls to see my panicked expression. Locking the door behind me so no one else can come in, I stare into a floor-length mirror and inhale slowly through my nose, willing myself to calm down.

Goddess, I'm not getting nervous about being around a crowd, am I? How strange. I can entertain a host of socialites; it's absurd that the mere idea of small talk with my professional peers is setting me on edge. Nevertheless, here I am, hands shaking and neck sweating like I'm about to jump off a cliff. I frown at my reflection and tug at the stifling, too-tight fabric of my jacket. Would it look too sloppy to unbutton it? My fingers decide for me, undoing the fasteners. Despite the confines of my jacket no longer being an issue, my breath still feels labored and harsh.

My eyes close, attempting to shut out this unpleasant sense of impending disaster. Unthinking, I rearrange the datapads in my satchel. My breath slows slightly with the repetitive motion, allowing me to attempt rearranging my thoughts as well. I shift my self-criticisms to make room for the memories of my sister, Quila, on the day I graduated from medical school. She was so proud of me, claiming I was the smartest nexxit in the galaxy. Along with the most stubborn. Another gentler breath washes over me. My mother's harsh words are replaced by thoughts of the first delivery I assisted with and the look of pure joy and wonder on the mother's face as I handed over her newborn.

My breathing begins to even out. I can do this. I belong here, not because of my family name, but because I've earned it through work and dedication. If anyone chooses not to see this, well...

Honestly, I'm not sure what I'll do if confronted directly by the criticisms of my peers, but I've been training my whole life to weather the judgment of others. That's a standard part of life as a nexxit noble. The only difference is that I want these people to like me.

A rattling at the door stirs me from my thoughts. I re-fasten my jacket and check my datapads one more time, before exiting. The door swings open just as I go to open it, and a beige someone stumbles in with it, nearly crashing into me. The human catches themself against my chest and lets out a squeak of surprise.

Wait, a *human*?

I blink to clear my senses but yes, that is undoubtedly a human. They look back at me, equally startled, a flush rising on their rounded ears and their thick eyebrows raising as they take a step back.

Fascinating. They're oddly pleasing to look at, and their fresh, sun-kissed scent makes certain parts of me far more alert than they have any right to be. What is wrong with me?

My pulse quickens for an entirely different reason than nerves as I scan over their face, then down to their body. I try to pretend that it's scientific curiosity that has me ogling the human before me, but I know the truth. I've been dying to see one up close since a professional encounter with one I had about a year ago. She contacted me looking for advice, I helped her, and then we just... kept talking. The thoughts that I developed from our long comm chains ended up being far less professional than the initial subject matter. So much so that I had to cut things off before I let myself develop more than a simple attraction. I swore that I'd never open myself to that kind of heartache again, and something about her made it far too tempting to break that rule.

"Ahh, sorry about that! Didn't realize the door opened inward. Please forgive me..." the human's small eyes dart down to look at my name badge. Their pupils dilate for a second. "Forgive me, Dr. Nafar," they continue with a small grimace.

I look down at their badge, but it's twisted so I can't read their name. My eyes catch on their ample breasts for a moment too long and I tear them back to the human's face with a self-chastising frown. "No apologies necessary. It was rude of me to lock the door."

"Oh no, it's alright!" they squeak back at me with a violent head shake, their bouncy black curls bobbing with the motion. Are all humans so unrestrained in their expressions? It seems inconvenient. Though I can see the appeal...their pretty face and soft body are quite attractive.

"Eden, did you fall in the hygiene unit?" a husky, alluring voice calls out teasingly from the doorway. My skin prickles and a shiver runs down my spine. There's something so familiar about that voice, but I can't quite place it.

"No! Just almost knocked someone over. I'll be out in a moment," the human shouts back.

"Oooo, a cute someone? Do you need me to give you some privacy?"

"What?! No!" The human practically flinches after they speak and they give me a worried look. "Sorry, I don't mean to be rude! You're very handsome. I'm just not in here to…"

My amused snort comes out unbidden. I can't recall the last time someone called me handsome. "Again, no apologies necessary, doctor…?"

"Mori!" They flip their badge around allowing me to read *Dr. Eden Mori, she/her* written on it in Universal. "Though most people call me Eden." She gives me a beaming smile that leaves me feeling dazzled for a beat too long and I miss her extended hand.

Wait, *Eden*? I didn't register it when her friend called her name but… no. There's no possible way this is the same Eden Mori I exchanged medical advice with. The same Eden Mori I grew far too attached to. It must be a common name among humans. Otherwise, she'd remember my name, too. Unless she doesn't because those messages weren't memorable to her. Goddess, what a depressing thought.

She sobers her expression and pulls her hand back. "Whoops, sorry! I forgot that only humans shake hands," she mutters with a sheepish push of her curls behind her ear, before letting her arm drop to her side.

I reach out to grab her hand with my two right ones, startling her. "I don't mind following human customs for some things, Dr. Mori." My palms tingles with a thrilling warmth as our skin touches. She feels so good. It's almost like touching her is awakening a part of me I've kept asleep most of my life. *Please remember me,* I silently beg through the connection of our touch.

She pulls her hand back after a moment, and it takes all my social training to not show any sadness in my expression when she doesn't say anything. Goddess, of course she doesn't remember me. I'm pathetic.

"Excuse me, I should go." I nod and head toward the exit before I can make more of a fool of myself.

"Did you say handsome?" the stimulating voice from before asks from the hall, clearer and more entrancing the closer I get. "Maybe I'll take a shot at—oh, fuck me."

Oh, fuck me is right. The shocking sight of the most beautiful nexxit I've ever seen hits me like a punch to the gut. Now I know why her voice sounded so familiar.

"*Mezli?*" I manage to choke out her name, even though it feels like all the air's been sucked out of the room. My *mate* is standing here in the door to the hygiene room, wearing a dress that looks like it's been painted onto her deep pink skin. Her slim, elegant neck is bare and the intoxicating smell of *jasrin* blooms and her own heady scent wafts from her.

I realize in horror that the traitorous appendages in my pants are emerging from my slit, hard and desperate from the combined scents of these *xalas*. Even though I very much *don't* want Mezli. How could I want the woman who has so little respect for matehood that she couldn't keep herself from fucking around the night before she met me? The woman that *ran away* to avoid being mated.

Mezli drags her dark gaze up and down me pointedly, mouth twisting into a grin when I surreptitiously shift my satchel in front of my groin. "Well, look who it is. Who would have guessed the mighty *Lord* Nafar would be here, of all places? Let me guess, you're here looking for cutting-edge skin rejuvenation technology to keep your mother from looking her age. Only the best for members of the second house of Nexxa Itat."

My brain flounders helplessly, attempting to reconcile the biting words of the *xala* before me with the dim one I met four years ago. This can't be the same person. That *xala* vacantly stared at me across the dining table and couldn't string more than a few words together. Did I accidentally fall asleep in my hotel room? Because only my sleeping mind would be cruel enough to present me with a version of my mate that is so...intriguing.

But no, she's real and she's standing right before me, waiting for an answer while I stare at her, dumbfounded. I quickly set my expression to a haughty coolness. "Nothing of the sort. Mother has no need for such things. No doubt she's already sold her soul to some foul demon to not appear older than her children."

My wry retort wrests a peal of laughter from Mezli's sinful lips. "Probably the same one my mothers bargained with to hide away the shame of their daughter running off to join the peasants on Spire."

So she's been on Spire this whole time? If I'd known...I wouldn't have done anything. I'm not in the habit of chasing after *xalas* that clearly don't want me.

I shrug, attempting to look bored by the conversation. "I think they were circulating a rumor that you'd joined a techless cloister on Nexxa Strai, but that was a few years ago. I haven't kept in touch with them, or really paid much attention."

"You didn't think about me?" she asks with an exaggerated pout, crossing her lower arms under her chest to push the swell of her perky breasts higher. No doubt trying to entice me, though I have no idea why. I wish that it didn't work so well. "I thought about you..." she adds, her voice low, like she's telling me a secret.

I tear my eyes away to stop myself from ogling her assets. Goddess, preserve me, I almost believe her. I'm so hard, my cocks are threatening to rip through my trousers.

I dig deep into my social training to keep my cold demeanor, even when my body is screaming at me to grab her and show her just how much I've thought about her. "Noted."

"Are you here for business or *pleasure?*" she says, reaching out a hand to toy idly with the collar of my jacket. I simultaneously want to slap it away and beg her to pull me closer. My analytical mind can tell she's fucking with me for some reason, but my body doesn't care.

"I'm here to present some of my research and attend the conference's events. So unless you find listening to me speak on obstetric innovations and ethics erotic, it's for business," I say in as much of a monotone as possible.

"You'd be surprised what I'm into, Phelix," Mezli practically purrs. "Speaking of which—Eden, you almost done in here?" She yells over my shoulder into the hygiene room and the warmth of her breath caresses my cheek. I almost stagger at the wave of arousal that crashes over me. Dammit, I have to get out of here before I do something I'll regret. I'm not sure if I want to yell at her for acting like nothing bad happened between us or bend her over the sink and fuck her, but either would be a terrible decision.

"Almost! Can you help me with my fastener? It's stuck and I can't reach the damned thing," Eden replies from the room behind me. Right, I'm still lurking in the hygiene room, stuck between the human I had an unhealthy attachment to and my mate who abandoned me.

"Duty calls." Mezli slips past me in the doorway, her body brushing against my chest. I suppress a groan and the desire to pull her back against me. I shake my head to try to clear my senses, but everything is still lust-fogged.

"I won't keep you from your pressing business." I take a step out into the hallway and then pause, looking back over my shoulder. "Will I see you around the conference?" Dammit, what am I doing?

"Oh, you'll be seeing *much* more of me," Mezli replies in a low drawl. Then, as if nothing had passed between us at all, she heads inside and calls out to Eden. "You sure you don't want to just leave the jumpsuit down?"

Is Eden her lover? Are they going to have sex once I leave? Anger coils in my chest as I storm away, the memory of another evening four years ago coming back to haunt me.

I was wrong. She hasn't changed at all. Mezli's still the *xala* who will fuck someone else, even when her mate is nearby.

6

✦MEZLI✦

As soon as Phelix disappears into the stream of convention goers, I dart toward a half-dressed Eden. My mind barely registers the smooth expanse of her exposed back and the hint of her black panties as she blinks at me over her shoulder with a sheepish look.

"Sorry, that sounded like it was going well. But I really am stuck." Eden worries her plump lower lip between her teeth.

I nod and hold a hand up to her in acknowledgement before racing into one of the hygiene stalls to violently heave up the remains of my dinner. My mind flashes to the image of losing my meal all over the Nafar's pristine marble floor as the lady of the house gaped at me in horror. Apparently, the mere sight of Phelix is enough to trigger that reaction again. Fuck, this isn't good. How am I supposed to seduce him when being around him makes me anxious enough to puke?

"Mezli, are you alright?!" Eden's voice is tight with concern on the other side of the stall door.

"Never better," I mumble, more to myself than to her, wiping off my mouth and shakily standing again. Plastering a smile back on my face, I open the stall door and head past her to wash my mouth and hands in the gleaming metal sink. She trails after me and in the mirror I can see her mouth is open like a *drest* gasping for air. Fina always looks like that after I've said something completely scandalous, and thinking about my best friend makes my grin a little more genuine. No offense to Eden, but I wish Fina were the one here with me. I learned after she moved here that one of Fina's hugs is the quickest way for me to calm down. I wonder if a hug from Eden would have the same effect...she looks even softer than Fina, so I bet it'd be nice.

Once my mouth no longer tastes horrendous, I dry off and turn to address the nervous human waiting for some kind of explanation. "That went well, don't you think?" I say cheerily, rolling my shoulders back and relaxing my posture to one of trained ease. Eden gawks at me, her mouth opening and closing as if she's trying to think of a good reply to my nonchalance after being sick.

"Oh right! Let me get that fastener for you." I step behind her and quickly zip up the back of her pale green jumpsuit. My fingers accidentally brush against her freckled, silky skin when I get to the nape of her neck and she shivers slightly, the fine hairs on her neck standing up. If she's so reactive to a small, innocent touch like that, I wonder how she'd react if I touched her elsewhere...

Shit, focus! You're not here to seduce the woman working with you. Being around Phelix must've set off some mating hormone reaction in me, because now I'm absurdly turned on. Horny and nauseous, what a delightful combination.

"Thank you. Are you sure you're feeling okay? Maybe I should examine you. Your color looks a bit gray, which I'm pretty sure isn't good for a nexxit."

"I'm perfectly fine. Though, you can examine me as much as you want, Dr. Mori," I reply far too flirtatiously, clasping both sets of arms behind my back to press my chest out. Her thick, expressive eyebrows dart up and now she's the one who's changing colors slightly, a rosy tinge painting her cheeks. It could just be the flood of bonding signals still coursing through my system after being around my mate, but damn, she's sexy, in a naive, eager kind of way. I'd definitely let her play doctor with me. Shit, what were we talking about?

"Now's probably not the best time," she says with a chuckle. I catch her eyes darting away from the neckline of my dress, and she flushes even darker. How adorable.

"True, a public hygiene room probably isn't the best place for that. I'd much rather have somewhere private where you can take your time and be thorough in your examinations." I can't resist giving her a wink, and her sputtering, breathy reaction makes it totally worth it. "As far as—" I lower my voice and look around dramatically before leaning in to whisper, "the mission goes..." Eden shivers again and now I'm distracted with the thoughts of running my tongue along her neck.

Goddess, I've got to get myself under control. I take a step back, trying to ignore the way Phelix's lingering musk mingled with Eden's delicate scent fogs my mind. "That went about as well as it could have. Surprisingly well, to be honest. Guess he's desperate after four years of self-imposed celibacy. Did you hear how he wanted to know if he'd see me again?"

The laugh that bubbles out of me is tinged with dark pleasure, relishing how much I'd surprised him. I've worked hard to shed the skin of the meek, miserable girl I was at our disastrous first meeting. That girl is dead—replaced by a powerful *xala* who'll never make herself smaller for the bullshit of nexxit aristocracy ever again. Let him choke on the shock of how much of a *xala* I am, if he finds it objectionable. He tried to seem unimpressed, but the tent in his pants indicated otherwise.

"Were you able to see any of the contents of his bag when you bumped into him?" I add, before I let my mind delve too deep into the fantasy of stepping on Phelix's broad chest and grinding the sharp point of my heel in until he begs for mercy.

"Not really. There were a handful of datapads, but I couldn't tell if any of them were what we're looking for. I'm not exactly a tech expert," Eden says with a shrug. "From a glance, they looked like the kind coded to a genetic lock. We won't be able to open them and look for the files without his biosignature."

"Damn. Hopefully, our 'friends' will have some ideas about that. We have a while until we're due to meet with them, though. So, what do you say? Should we bother the mighty Lord Nafar more or ditch the conference's undoubtedly dull welcome party and go grab a drink at the bar instead?"

"Umm, probably best to leave him wanting more? If we push more tonight, he might get suspicious. We have the rest of the week to lure him in, so let's give him some time to think about you. I wish the agents had given us some kind of earpiece or monitoring device so we could just ask for help right away for the lock."

I'd had the same thought, but am glad they're not monitoring us. It creeps me out to think about Agent Asshole listening in. "I know, right? If they're going to wrangle us into their mess, they could at least give us some fun gadgets. Like a lipstick that can knock out someone with a kiss or...a vibrator that doubles as a listening device!"

"Wouldn't the vibrator's buzzing impede listening in on someone?" Eden asks with a giggle. The laughter lights up her whole face, momentarily stunning me with how pretty she is.

My own laughter echoes off the walls of the hygiene room. "Riiight. This is why you're the brains of this operation. I'd say I'm the beauty, but you have that covered too."

Eden looks away with a nervous smile on her lips and my mating hormone-addled brain finally clears enough for me to worry that I'm being inappropriate. "Sorry, Eden. I'm not usually this flirty. Well, no, that's a lie. I am. But I don't want to make you uncomfortable. So please tell me to quit it if I'm bothering you, and I promise I'll stop babbling about how pretty you are."

"N-no!" Eden looks back up at me, the flush traveling to her ears and neck, her hazel eyes sparkling with interest. "I don't mind. Though...I doubt you'd be saying these things if it weren't for the hormonal surge you experienced being around your mate for the first time in four years."

My eyes narrow, assessing her words. "Is that your professional opinion? Or do you seriously not think you're attractive? Because yes, I'm incredibly horny right now, but that doesn't affect who I think is hot. I'd much rather spend tonight getting to know you better than be around my terrible mate. Goddess, not that I mean I want to 'get to know you' right away. Unless you're interested... Shit, sorry! My hormones really *are* taking over. Let's start with a conversation." I head over to the sink and dab some cold water on my neck to try to cool off my overheated senses.

Eden places a hand lightly on my shoulder and my skin sizzles with pleasure where it makes contact with my bare skin. Her touch seeps into me, sending a wave of comfort that rivals a Fina hug, and I have to keep myself from leaning into it.

"Conversation and a drink would be perfect!" Eden says, patting me once before removing her hand. "I'm already feeling overwhelmed from being the only human here, so I won't complain about waiting longer to wade into the thick of the conference."

Her words shake me further out of my lust fog, reminding me of how awkward Fina and Paul felt being surrounded by aliens when they first came to Spire. Here I am, hitting on my spy partner and she's still trying to process being the only human at the convention. I thought I was in over my head getting conscripted into this mission, but Eden? She's probably already close to drowning. She needs someone to keep her afloat, not someone to fuck her.

"You know what might be even better? Let's go back to my place." I say gently, turning to smile reassuringly at Eden.

Her eyebrows raise so high they look like they'll merge with her hairline. "Not to fuck or anything!" I clarify with an urgent wave of my upper hands. "To let you decompress. My best friend, Fina, is human and I remember how hard it was for her when she first came to Spire. The last thing you need is some pervy aliens gawking at the 'exotic human' while you're trying to relax. And I swear I can contain my pervy side, even though it may not seem like it at the moment."

She relaxes and gives me another brilliant smile. "That sounds perfect. Thank you, Mezli."

"Of course!" I go in for a hug, but realize we're not at that level of friendship and touching her will probably set off my horniness again, so I lean in to whisper theatrically instead. "Anything for my new sexy spy partner." I pull back and gesture toward the hygiene room door. "Now let's get out of here before people start to gossip about the hot human doctor and the cute nexxit who spent all night in the hygiene room."

Eden giggles again and we finally exit the small space. I can't resist winking at an attractive seladin who raises an intrigued brow at me as we leave together. On any other night, I'd be heading over to chat them up, but I've got a mission to plan and a spy partner to comfort.

7

✦EDEN✦

"**S**o how the heck did you end up getting roped into this whole mess, anyway?" Mezli hands me a mug of hot, spiced tea and sinks down onto the chair across from where I'm bundled up in a blanket on her worn but comfy couch. Apparently, nexxit like to keep things much cooler than humans. A few minutes of shivering lead to Mezli wrapping me up in a blanket and rubbing her lower hands along my arms in a playful manner that I found far too exciting.

Sitting here cocooned in a blanket that holds her soft floral scent only heightens the way I feel around her. I almost asked her to warm me up in a different way, but there's no way I'm bold enough to do that. Sure, she flirts a lot and seemed interested back at the conference hall, but that was the mating hormones talking. I'm not about to throw myself at my spy partner and make the rest of my week awkward.

God, even just thinking about the fact that I'm on a spy mission with an alien makes my head spin. Thinking about the past six hours makes me even dizzier. It's a wonder that I'm even able to stay upright, and haven't collapsed into an overwhelmed heap on Mezli's couch. According to my parents, I'm great at being flexible and adapting to new situations, but they think I'm good at everything. I've never had to adapt so much, so fast. This is a *lot*, even for me.

So if I'm using a crush on the pretty alien who is my only lifeline in this bizarre turn of events to distract myself from freaking out, who cares? Her skin is my favorite shade of dark pink and her black eyes draw me in with a promise of mischief and fun that seems to always sparkle in them. When I touched her, I felt the strangest zing of energy that made my heart beat a little too fast and my core clench with arousal. Maybe it's just some weird alien thing, but it felt special.

I'd say I'd never felt anything like it before, but when Phelix shook my hand, I got the same tingles. Ugh, I'm reading way too much into things as always. I'm just a touch-starved virgin, and it didn't mean anything. How could it? He and Mezli are mates. Of course the two hottest aliens I've met are fated to be with each other.

It felt like the stars were aligning in a twisted way when the agents told me their target was Dr. Nafar. I tried to convince myself that it wasn't the same one I'd corresponded with about a year ago. A member of nexxit nobility wouldn't take the time to help out some backwater medic looking for advice on jury-rigging outdated medical equipment to assist with higher risk pregnancies. But when I saw Phelix, something inside me knew it was him—the nexxit doctor I laid awake at night thinking about, imagining him inviting me to Nexxa Itat after seeing how brilliant I am and falling madly in love with me once I arrived.

He didn't recognize my name, though. Just looked at my tits a bit too long, then acted like he couldn't get away from me fast enough. Yet another example of my ridiculous romantic imagination getting the better of me.

I focus on the soothing aroma wafting from the tea and close my eyes for a moment to clear away those depressing thoughts. No point dwelling on some guy who is apparently a real piece of shit and a potential criminal. I'd never have imagined that the doctor who seemed so passionate about helping patients would willfully endanger lives. Goes to show how good I am at reading people.

I take a sip, wincing as I burn my tongue, and glance over at Mezli to find her waiting for me to say something. Right, she asked me a question. "I've wanted to attend the medical conference on Spire for years, but never had the funds. I would've leapt at any chance to get off of Europa 3, but this trip is a once-in-a-lifetime opportunity. Or at least it was supposed to be. I saw a posting about the Xi Consortium sponsoring a human to attend the conference this year to 'facilitate ongoing relations between the Consortium and the human Coalition'. Turns out there was more to the deal than advertised." My mouth twists into a rueful smile. "I was thrilled when they accepted my application. A whole week with nothing to do but learn from the best medical minds in the galaxy and explore all the delights Spire has to offer! It was finally my chance to get lai–uh, my chance to get some life experience."

Mezli's mouth quirks but she doesn't comment on my almost confession. "Then Agent Tysea showed up at the docks when I arrived and told me I had to help them in exchange for them paying for my trip. It seemed like a simple decision. I'd get to attend the conference and help stop dangerous medical tech from falling into the wrong hands. But the agents took one look at me and realized there was no way I'd be able to handle this on my own."

I don't mention the conflict I felt when I heard Phelix was the one they suspected. I don't know if I can trust Mezli to not tell the agents about my connection to Phelix, and they'd certainly send me home if they found out.

"That definitely sounds like Agent Asshole," Mezli says with a scowl.

I snort at the rude nickname, but tense, looking around the room. "What if they're monitoring us?" I whisper. I don't think they bugged us but who the heck knows with alien tech?

Mezli chuckles and waves a rude hand gesture in the air. "If you perverts are watching us, kindly fuck off. Don't let that jerk make you feel bad. It's absurd they thought you'd be okay on your own. No one new to Spire would be, let alone someone not even from a Consortium species."

I sigh, relieved that she gets it. There's an excited flutter in my chest at how supportive she is. "You're right. I felt embarrassed at first, but after tonight I'm so glad I'm not alone in this. That I have you as a partner." My eyes linger on where her soft lips meet the rim of her mug, and an image of her mouth on my neck, alternating between sharp nips and caresses of her tongue fills my mind. Another mouth joins hers, sliding a path up my inner thigh as I imagine Phelix kneeling between my legs. I burn my tongue again as I take a sip of my tea to push my dirty thoughts aside.

"You're thinking awfully hard over there, Eden. Hopefully, that's because of me and not the shitty situation you were put into. Because I'm glad you're my partner too," Mezli says, giving me a wink.

"Oh, sorry!" My face flames, and I duck my head, pretending to take a sip of my tea while I compose myself. "Just uh, wondering how you're doing. Having to see your estranged mate must be really tough."

She sets her mug down and crosses her upper arms with a slight frown. "I was terrified to see Phelix again. When we first met, things went about as spectacularly bad as they could have. That disastrous night ended up being the push I needed to leave that life behind and come to Spire."

My eyes widen. "Really? I can't imagine someone meeting you and being anything less than charmed."

The smallest hint of a flush rises on Mezli's cheeks, but she laughs it off. "I wasn't the same person back then. I spent years hiding myself, trying to be the perfect daughter and not do anything unbefitting the Princeps of House Frye. But when my mom went behind my back and located my mate, things quickly fell apart. The night before I met Phelix, I snuck out and got wasted and tried to hook up with a stranger. I was just so fucking terrified of my inexperience and of the thought of being bound to someone without even knowing who I was. The next day I was horribly hungover and the meds I took to counteract it made me feel like I was floating above everything. So yeah, it didn't go well." She laughs again, but there's less humor in her eyes than before.

"Oh god, that sounds awful. I'd never considered how scary having a mate might be. Humans have nothing like that so it always sounded incredibly romantic."

That's an understatement. I've spent countless nights fantasizing about my perfect match finding me and sweeping me away from my dreary life on a passionate adventure filled with love and lust. I guess imagination is better than reality on that front. "That must've been terrifying, and then to be forced to relive those memories now? I'm so sorry."

I unwrap myself from the blanket cocoon to reach out a hand and place it on top of hers. Sparks of warmth and excitement ripple up from my palm when our skin connects, and Mezli's eyes dart to meet mine. We look at each other for a heartbeat, both confused by the impact of the contact. That's twice now that I've felt those strange sparks when I touched her. I desperately fight the foolish urge to read something into it.

Logically, I know it doesn't mean anything. In preparation for my trip to Spire, I went on a deep-dive into alien sexuality and stumbled upon info on nexxit mate bonds. There's a surprising amount of medical documentation on the phenomenon—along with educational videos I may have watched repeatedly. For research.

When nexxit are around their true mate, bonding hormones flood their systems, and they pump out mating pheromones to increase arousal. If I had to guess, my reaction is a residual effect from getting caught in the crossfire of all those mating signals. Too bad coming up with a logical hypothesis doesn't make my heart stop fluttering like a caged bird in my chest whenever Mezli touches me.

Mezli relaxes first, her eyes softening and the surprise sliding to a more flirtatious expression. "It's okay. It means I got to meet you. And hopefully I'll get to torture Phelix a bit before catching his nefarious dealings and becoming a galactic hero!"

I chuckle half-heartedly at the reminder of the accusations against Phelix. "Do you...do you really think that he's here to sell those schematics? I just don't know. Your history aside, everything I've heard about him—about his work makes me question things."

She shrugs and sighs, thankfully not catching my slip up. "Honestly? I have no clue. I barely know him. If he is who the agents think he is, then not knowing him is for the best. Even if he is my mate. I've done fine without him the past four years."

Thinking about the agents must summon them, because a moment later the door to Mezli's apartment chimes. Mezli answers, and when they enter, Agent Tysea looks at the sight of me snuggled up on Mezli's couch with curiosity, while Agent Ashlath stomps in and sits down in the chair Mezli was using. She rolls her eyes behind their back and takes a seat next to me, giving me a reassuring nudge. I do my best to refrain from showing the agents how much her proximity to me excites me, turning to give them my attention.

"Alright, let's make this quick. How did your first contact with the target go?" Agent Ashlath's flawless orange skin creases slightly as they narrow their eyes at us.

Mezli grins back at them, nudging me subtly again. "Ah, so you didn't bug us! Good to know you weren't listening in all night."

Agent Tysea blinks rapidly at us in surprise. "Of course not. It is unnecessary for us to monitor your activity directly. Debriefs like this will suffice."

"Don't make us regret that choice," Agent Ashlath adds with a scowl. "Be thankful I haven't chosen to monitor your comms and your apartment and hotel."

"Aww, and here I hoped that I'd get to put on a show for you," Mezli replies with a pout. I can't suppress my shocked snort of amusement and Tysea's mouth falls open, aghast.

Ashlath's scowl at Mezli deepens, who gives them a wink for good measure. "Enough. Tell us what happened," they bark out impatiently.

I speak up before Mezli can antagonize them any more. She may feel okay being flippant with Consortium agents, but I'm some nobody human from a colony most people haven't heard of, not a nexxit noble like her. "We made contact with, uh, the target. Mezli was incredible—there's no doubt that he'll want to see her again."

"Eden's right. We both nailed it. Phelix is salivating for a chance to spend more time with me, and our incredible Dr. Mori was able to get a good look at his datapads without him noticing."

"Can you tell us more about the datapads, doctor?" Agent Tysea asks.

"Oh, uh, of course." I swallow down a nervous lump in my throat that forms with their attention on me. Ever since they greeted me at the docks, I've felt foolish and incompetent around them. "So, uh, right... He carries a handful of datapads in his bag and all of them are the type that use a bio-lock. Sorry! But I'm s-sure you two have ways of getting past that sort of thing, right?"

Agent Tysea rubs the back of their neck and frowns at me like it's somehow my fault that the datapads require a biosignature. I barely bite back the urge to apologize to them again. "We can create a decryption key but it'll still take a sample of some of his biological material to bypass that kind of lock."

"What kind of biological material?" I ask, my voice a bit too high-pitched as my horny brain immediately goes to something inappropriate. You'd think I'm the one flooded with mating hormones. Mezli snorts, obviously having the same train of thought as me.

"Saliva, hair, skin cells...other fluids. Whatever you can get." Agent Ashlath turns their stern gaze squarely on Mezli. "Do you think you can handle that?" they ask, tone full of skepticism.

"Don't worry, I won't have trouble getting close enough to gather whatever you need, and more," Mezli says, raising a salacious eyebrow at me.

I choke back a laugh, and Agent Tysea gives me another critical look. They fish around in their briefcase, pulling out two small makeup compacts. Holding one up, Tysea shows a hidden latch that lifts up the shimmery cake of powder to reveal a storage compartment. "Use these for any material you gather. It will safely store it until you can hand it off to us."

Mezli elbows me in the side. "Ooo look! Finally, a sexy spy gadget. I was worried this whole thing would just be boring meetings."

I giggle, but stop when Agent Ashlath clears their throat loudly. "Lucky for you, this is our last in person meeting for now. Any future contact will be made via your comms. When you secure the biomaterial, put it in an envelope and leave it at the front desk of Dr. Mori's hotel for Garlsna Freix in room 4203. We'll deliver the decryption key to her room once it's ready."

I nod, committing the name and room number to memory.

"If we message you, it's imperative that you reply as quickly as possible. Lives may depend on your actions this week. Take this seriously," says Agent Tysea, looking directly at me.

My lips downturn into an involuntary frown. I know what's at stake and it's absurd that they're trusting two untrained people to do their jobs for them. But who am I to argue when they have the power to send me back home whenever my usefulness ends?

Both agents stand and Tysea gives Mezli a reassuring smile. "We're confident you'll be able to do this, Princeps Frye. Good luck and don't hesitate to contact us at any time, for any reason."

Mezli looks like she has a host of inappropriate replies on the tip of her tongue, but I speak first, despite the vote of confidence not being directed toward me. "Thank you, we will. Have a good evening!"

The agents head to the door, and Ashlath holds it open expectantly for me.

Right, I should go back to my hotel. I jump up from my spot on the couch, but get tangled as the blanket snags in the collar of my jumpsuit. Mezli's four nimble hands tug it free and goosebumps raise on my arm when she casually brushes against it with her fingertips in the process.

I quickly pull away as my face heats. "Thanks again for the tea! I'll message in the morning before I head to the convention."

"Perfect. Sweet dreams, doctor," Mezli replies in a purr.

Agent Tysea looks at my bare feet in distaste as I follow them to the door. Mezli thought removing my shoes when I got to her place was weird too, but living with my Japanese father for thirty years ingrained the habit in me. I slip my shoes back on at the door, scurry out the door before I can embarrass myself further in front of the agents. They don't speak to me during the short transit ride back to my hotel, but I doubt I'd have been able to pay attention if they had. All I can think about is how the hell I'm going to get through an entire week of this. Between the agents who could send me home at any moment and my attraction to my spy partner, I'm a mess. Add in our target being my penpal crush and I'm even more fucked.

8

✦PHELIX✦

The welcoming event for the conference turns out to be little more than a bunch of tipsy medics and scientists mingling awkwardly. It goes by in a haze—I vaguely recall introducing myself and exchanging pleasantries with many people, but no names or faces stick. All my attention is dedicated to suppressing the heat and anger coursing through my body after my brief encounter with Eden and Mezli. Everything I'm wearing feels too tight, and I have to keep adjusting my satchel to hide my unsettling, unflagging erections.

When even small talk becomes difficult, I decide to call it a night and head back to my hotel. The concierge immediately leaps to his feet as I enter the hotel lobby, scurrying over to see if "Lord Nafar" needs any assistance this evening. I shake my head and wave him off as politely as possible, but he visibly deflates at my dismissal. Pardon me for not wanting to get caught up in an interminable discussion of Spire's most exclusive nightlife when my blood feels like it's boiling.

As soon as I reach my suite, I lock the door behind me and lean against the cool metal with a groan. I'm burning up, and a hiss escapes my lips when I accidentally brush a palm across the hard bulges in my pants. Any thoughts of staking my claim as an influential figure at the conference are gone, along with worries about business I'll need to attend to before I leave the station. The only thing on my mind is them. Eden and Mezli.

Who gave Mezli the right to stumble back into my life, acting like I was a fond ex-lover instead of a jilted mate? Once again, she's accompanied by someone so alluring that I could never dream of competing. Someone who cared so little for our connection that she doesn't even remember me. They're both poison, wracking my system with desire and futile hope that I thought I'd inoculated myself against.

I kick off my shoes and tear off my stifling jacket as I stumble to the stairs, tossing them haphazardly to the floor. Something is definitely wrong with me—the nagging voice in my head that would tell me to put things away properly is utterly silent. Next, my pants and shirt come off and land on the plush bed. Once I'm fully undressed and my undergarments lie on the expensive mosaic tile of the hygiene room, I start up the shower, keeping the temperature ice cold. The frigid water pierces into my skin like tiny daggers, but I stay under the spray, waiting for it to cool off the rage and lust coursing through my veins.

After a few minutes pass, my cocks are still out and as hard as ever despite my teeth chattering from the cold. Dammit. Why can't I get myself under control?

I increase the water temperature. The downpour of blissfully warm water drags a moan from my lips and my eyes fall closed. My lower hands fist my lengths, pumping them roughly, and I almost cry out in relief and frustration.

I shouldn't be doing this. I *hate* that I'm doing this. I hate that a few minutes around my mate and my human crush have turned me into some kind of mindless beast, fucking my hands while thoughts of them come to me unbidden.

What would Mezli's hands feel like on me? Would she be gentle, taking her time to explore every inch of my cocks until I begged her for more? Or would she be as rough as I am right now, tugging harshly, brutally forcing my swift release? I thrust into my grasp, imagining that they're Mezli's nimble fingers instead of my own.

Fuck. How was I so wrong about Mezli before? She was sloppy and drunk when I first saw her, and dull and lifeless when we officially met. Losing her was painful, but tempered by the knowledge that she wasn't a good match for me. But the *xala* I encountered tonight is everything I'd hoped for in a mate—confident, teasing, and witty. I bet she's the kind of woman that would deny me my release, bringing me to the edge over and over while she watches in amusement. My cocks swell at the thought, but my stomach lurches at how upset I am that she's made me feel this way.

I scramble for another mental image that will wipe Mezli from my mind, desperate not to come from thoughts of the *xala* who abandoned me. That only makes matters worse, conjuring an image of Eden kneeling before me, her huge breasts bare and her mouth open in front of my cocks as she waits for my release as Mezli pumps me, lips twisted into a suggestive smile as she watches me and Eden. I'm a pervert, jerking off to thoughts of a human I've only just met in person, but Goddess, the image makes me harder than I've been in my entire life.

With a shocked cry that catches in my throat, I double over, barely holding myself up against the slick shower wall with my upper hands. Everything in my body feels like it is short-circuiting with pleasure as my cocks erupt, spilling hot jets of pearly pink cum onto my hands and the wall I'm braced against. It goes on for what feels like minutes until I'm wrung out, my lust and anger deflating to the dull sadness and pain that's always with me.

Wilting members in hand, I sigh as they finally return to my slit. I finish showering, making sure there's no remaining evidence of my shameful behavior. It's been a long time since base desire broke my willpower. I haven't touched myself since...since that night I messaged Eden, and then promptly severed contact with her.

There's an annoying stab of pain at how she didn't even remember me. I shouldn't care. She was a momentary weakness. That Eden appeared in my fantasy and drove me over the edge means nothing.

The lies I tell myself aren't the least bit convincing. She was far more than a weakness. Eden terrified me with how much I wanted her. From across the galaxy, she entranced me with her intelligence and kindness, making me go so far as to wonder if the mate finder was wrong. That Mezli couldn't be my true mate, because I'd never felt such an easy bond like I did with Eden. It was a pathetic crush, elevated by an even more pathetic desire to end my loneliness. As much as I hate myself for it, of course it hurts that it meant nothing to her.

Everything hurts tonight. That brief encounter with Mezli and

Eden left me battered. I must have done something to truly piss the Goddess off if she's throwing both the mate who abandoned me and the first person I'd ever felt a true spark of connection with in my path at the same time. I know I'm not the best person, but I'm *trying*. I suppose it's too little, too late.

What if she's brought them to you to give you another chance? a traitorous voice in my head whispers. *What if this is the Goddess' hand guiding you back to them?*

Impossible. I shove that weak part of me away like I did with the bullies who picked on me for being too large. The comparison is apt. Hope is a bully. Hope finds your greatest desires, leaving you weak and vulnerable.

Logic is what I need right now, my best defense against more torment. And logic dictates that a *xala* who's too selfish to commit to a mate hasn't come back into my life for any good reason. That Eden being here with her is nothing more than a frustrating coincidence. All of this nonsense is purely biological; a mating hormone spike raging through my system and clouding my judgment. Now that I've relieved some of the tension, I can see Mezli and Eden for what they truly are—a distraction.

Beautiful, tempting distractions...

I curse as my cocks start to slide out again. They're still hard as I put on my nightclothes, and even more insistent as I slip under the silky covers of my hotel bed.

Weak. Pathetic. I try to fight against the need building inside me, turning off the lights and shutting my eyes tight. But in darkness, I'm vulnerable to the hollow ache in my chest. In darkness, no one can see my shame and heartache as I take myself in hand once more. Building slowly this time, savoring the fantasy from earlier. Letting my mate's sweet wetness and heady scent envelop me as she straddles my face, riding it in pursuit of her own pleasure. Imagining the breathy gasps and laughter as she takes what she needs from me while coaxing Eden to sit astride me and take me inside her hot, slippery cunt.

It's too much. Too perfect. Tears well in my eyes as I come, and I frantically yank off my sleep shirt and bring it down to my cocks to catch my seed. I wipe myself clean, then press my face into a pillow, letting it absorb my tears. I cry until exhaustion finally sets in and I sink into the oblivion of sleep.

MEZLI TURNS *around at the bar, at once breathtaking in her beauty, and wild in her loose, intoxicated state. Instead of the anonymous nexxit female she was hanging over that night, it's Eden she's groping. Grabbing onto the human's hips and licking a hot stripe up the side of her neck before whispering something to her. I'm frozen, watching from across the room, my arousal and infatuation tinged with envy.*

They both turn and lock their eyes on me, and suddenly I'm standing right before the pair. Derisive laughter echoes around me as Mezli looks me up and down. "Look at this pathetic xalar. Slobbering all over the sight of us, desperate for our attention." *Shame roils in my gut as she laughs again, then turns to kiss Eden, moaning in pleasure as she does.*

I turn away, not wanting to watch anymore, but find Mother lurking on the other side of the room, frowning at me. "Shouldn't you wear something a bit looser? It would help hide some of..." *She waves at my stomach with her lower hands.*

I shut my eyes and inhale deeply, blocking her out. When they open, Mezli, as I saw her at our first official meeting, sits across the dining table from me, watching me with wide, vacant eyes. Trying to tune my presence out completely. I open my mouth to speak—to apologize for what-

ever about me is offensive, to make amends for judging her, to do anything to get her to stay. All four of my hands reach out across the table as she starts to vanish—

Sudden pain in my side jolts me out of my nightmare. I've fallen off the side of the bed, tangled in the slippery sheets, arms outstretched like they were right before I woke up. I groan and search my ribs with my hands for any serious injury, then gingerly push myself up off the floor.

It's not long until my alarm is set to go off, so I don't bother going back to bed. Even if I wanted to sleep more, I don't trust my sleeping mind not to torment me again, or worse, inflict more bodily harm.

Drained from a night of self-pity, jerking off, and terrible dreams, I decide to order breakfast up to my room. It took only one night for me to go back on my criticisms of the luxury I'm "enduring" here. Such a hypocrite.

The hotel attendant delivers my meal with relatively little bowing and scraping, so I tip generously in appreciation at their restraint. The artificial sunlight of the station streams in through enormous windows in the lower level of the suite, and I take a moment to bask in the feel of it on my skin, shaking off the remnants of my terrible night. Every new cycle is a chance to do better, and things never feel quite so bleak in the light of day.

Scanning the conference schedule, there aren't many panels that pique my interest. Later in the week is when they have the more renowned researchers speak. Still, I'll head over to the conference hall and have a look around at the vendors and exhibits. Better to stay as busy as possible to keep myself from worrying about the drop-off later in the week. My fingers itch with the need to sort through my satchel again and check for the millionth time that everything is still there.

On top of the stress of navigating social interactions with my professional peers and the delivery I need to make, thoughts of Mezli and Eden still rattle around in the back of my mind. It's annoying. I barely taste my food because I'm too busy trying to not think about those *xalas*.

My comm chirps as I'm clearing away the dishes and definitely *not* wondering if I'll see Mezli or Eden again at the conference today, and a notification pops up on the screen from my father.

With a gesture, the message expands, and my heart squeezes as I read, hearing Father's soft baritone in my mind.

> My dear Lix, hope your journey to Spire Station was safe and that the conference ends up being everything you've hoped for. Words cannot begin to express how proud I am of your choice to work for the betterment of the galaxy, not just the betterment of yourself. Though, speaking of your needs, I hope that you'll find some time in your busy schedule to relax and enjoy yourself. Don't be like your father and leave no time for fun. Trust me, you'll regret it by the time you're my age. Love you and am waiting to hear about what wild adventures you get up to on your trip. That's not a request— seriously, do something reckless or face my severe disappointment.

My face feels damp, and it takes me a moment to realize I was crying. Again. Is there something wrong with the air filtration system here that's causing my sudden lack of emotional control?

I wipe away my tears on a napkin, grimacing at my behavior. Father wants me to be reckless? I'm not sure I even know how. My one-track mind conjures an image of Eden spread across my bed's silken sheets, gasping as I thrust inside her while Mezli plays with her tits and demands I fuck Eden harder.

Goddess, stop thinking about them!

Seeking out the objects of my incessant fantasies certainly would be the most reckless thing I could think to do this week, barring violating station laws. But I have enough self-preservation to know that would only end in disaster.

Sorry, Father. I'm keeping things strictly professional this trip.

9

✦ EDEN ✦

When my alarm goes off, I groan, setting it to wake me again in another hour without even bothering to open my eyes. My bed feels extra cozy this morning, and the sunlight isn't hitting my face through the crack in my curtains like it normally does. Maybe I'll comm my first patient of the day and tell them I can't make it. A lazy morning in bed sounds nice after all the drama of yesterday.

Realization of where I am floods in and I sit up in the bed with a start. What happened last cycle was so surreal that my mind had almost convinced me it was a dream and I was still back on Europa 3. I kind of wish it had been.

But no, it's *real*. I stretch and haul myself out of bed, pressing a button so the shade on the window becomes transparent. The breathtaking expanse of Orion district bustles with early morning activity, and I can just make out the trees of the famous golden arboretum.

Holy shit. I'm on Spire.

It's not like I didn't already know that, but the reality hits me square in the chest. Overwhelming gratitude for this chance washes over me as I stare out the window. It's followed by a sense of determination.

I'm going to succeed on the mission. Sure, I'm in no way qualified to take it on, but when has that ever stopped me? I'm smart and capable, and with Mezli at my side, I feel strangely unstoppable.

I use that feeling to motivate myself to get ready for the day quickly, then send Mezli a message.

> Eden: Morning! Hope you slept better than I did. I'm going to head over to the conference if you want to meet there.

Mezli responds almost right away.

> Mezli: Nah, I couldn't sleep for shit. Stupid dreams about stupid Phelix. Ugh. Let's go find that loser so we can get this over with. Have any ideas for how to locate him?

> Eden: Yeah, I scanned the conference schedule and picked out a few panels that line up with his medical background, as well as some exhibits that might interest him.

I forward a highlighted schedule and convention map to Mezli's comm so we're on the same page.

> Eden: Maybe I go to the panels and you look at the exhibits? Whoever finds him first can let the other person know while we keep him occupied. Though I'm not sure how I'll be able to get him to stick around.

> Mezli: Just bat your eyelashes and ask him questions about his work. He's conceited enough that should keep him interested for at least a few hours. If that fails, flash him your tits.

I sputter at her message, glad she can't see how red I'm turning.

> Eden: I can't do that!

> Mezli: Why not? I know I wouldn't be able to look away if you did. Seems like a pretty good tactic.

> Eden: It's a medical conference! I can't go around exposing myself like that.

> Mezli: Fine, I guess I'll be the one exposing myself.

Another message appears before I can beg her not to do that.

> Mezli: Kidding. I don't need any more violations for public indecency on my record.

I wonder just how many violations she has...and what she did to get them. I'd ask her, but I need to focus on the mission. Thinking about Mezli naked is far too distracting.

> Eden: Okay, good.

> Eden: I'm heading over to the conference now. Good luck finding Phelix.

> Mezli: You too! Let's meet up for lunch and do some more strategizing if we don't see him before then. I don't know about you, but thinking makes me hungry.

I suddenly feel less motivated to find Phelix right away. Lunch with Mezli sounds fun.

> Eden: Alright. I'll comm you later.

With the first step of our plan in place, I head out of my hotel and make my way to the conference hall, excitement and anxiety thrumming through me as I wade through the sea of aliens on their morning commute. Yes, I'm surrounded by unfamiliar beings, sights, and smells. Yes, I'm nervous and scared of fucking this mission up. But I've also never felt more alive.

✦ PHELIX ✦

"GODDESS, I'M SO SORRY!" I hold out my hand to the seladin on the convention floor. The one I knocked over when I thought I saw a flash of beige skin the same shade as Eden's. My tea, thankfully lukewarm, spilled all over their crisp white suit as I crashed into them, making the situation even worse. So much for maintaining my professionalism and making a good impression on my peers.

I wince as they look up at me, their glowing eyes narrowed in frustration. They take my hand and I haul them back to their feet, glancing at their name badge to find out just how badly I just screwed up. *Ulena Breks A'Leth, she/her.* Not a name I recognize, thank the Goddess.

Once upright, the seladin towers over me by at least three hands. I brace myself for the onslaught of angry words about my carelessness, but it doesn't come. Instead, she frowns at her wet jacket, then strips it off unceremoniously, leaving herself with only a plain gray tube of fabric across her chest that blends into her charcoal skin.

After a shocked glance at her mostly bare torso, I tilt my chin up to look at her face. Others around us pause to stare blatantly at the now shirtless seladin with curiosity, distaste, or attraction.

"It's alright. I didn't particularly care for that jacket," she says with a shrug, finally speaking to me.

My top hands dart to the fastener of my shirt. "Here, take this. It's the least I can do for crashing into you like that."

Her lamplike eyes glow slightly brighter as she wordlessly watches me remove my shirt, but doesn't rebuff my offer when I pass it over.

"Thank you...Dr. Nafar." She looks down pointedly at my badge before saying my name. My shirt is far too wide and short to fit her properly, but she still manages to look elegant. That shade of green certainly goes with the subtle luminous markings that dot across her skin better than it does with my complexion.

"And here I thought giving someone the shirt off your back was just a silly human saying," a husky, teasing voice calls out to me from nearby. *Mezli.*

My exposed skin burns as she steps through the small crowd that had stopped to gawk at Dr. A'Leth. I can feel her eyes on me. No doubt judging my body and finding it just as distasteful as other nexxit do. I resist the ridiculous urge to wrap my arms over my stomach and chest. I don't care what she thinks of me. I tilt my chin up, bracing myself for a surge of arousal as she grows close enough for me to pick up her mating pheromones.

Show no weakness. She means nothing to you. Your body doesn't control you.

There's a flutter of desire as she grows nearer, but it's much more subdued than last night. Thank the Goddess.

"Mezli." I do my best not to let her see that her presence has any effect on me, but she grins playfully, and my cocks press against my seam as I recall my fantasies from last night.

Goddess, I'm fucked.

10

✦MEZLI✦

Luck must be on my side, because after only an hour of exploring the exhibit halls, I turn the corner past a booth filled with intricate-looking stasis pods, to find Phelix. And he's...shirtless? So much for Eden's insistence that we couldn't expose ourselves here.

The wide expanse of his back ripples as he hands his shirt over to a similarly topless seladin. Heat pools in my belly as I drink in the sight. Damn, he's *big*. Not some waif like most nexxit *xalar*. Broad muscular shoulders and arms, and a padded, thick waist and stomach that calls for me to sink my teeth into it.

Ugh, no! What am I thinking? I'm here to seduce him, but I don't want to be attracted to the jerk. Focus on the mission!

The seladin puts on his shirt, and I belatedly realize that I didn't even take the opportunity to get a free eyeful of a seladin babe. Phelix looks *that* good, damn him. I don't know what's going on with them, but I'm not about to let that seladin ruin my chances of getting Phelix's attention.

"And here I thought giving someone the shirt off your back was just a silly human saying," I call out as I approach. Phelix's spine straightens, and he whips around to look at me. Whatever amazing quip I had prepared as a follow-up vanishes at the sight of his bare chest.

"Mezli." My name escapes his lips in a startled rumble, sending a shiver down my spine. I don't immediately feel the same potent rush of bonding hormones that drove me wild last night, but arousal still snakes through my system from hearing his husky voice.

The seladin's luminous eyes land on me. "Your friend gave me his shirt because he spilled tea on mine," they say matter-of-factly.

"Ah, I thought he'd decided to strip to lure me to his side," I say, staring pointedly at the trail of dark hair leading from his belly button down into his pants. It's just a seduction tactic. I don't actually want to ogle him. Or follow that trail down with my mouth. Nope.

"I doubt that would work," he says in a dismissive huff. "More likely you sensed my embarrassment after crashing into this poor *xala* and came over to mock me."

I fight back the urge to scowl at his comment. What did I ever do to him that would make him think I'd do that? We barely spent an hour together four years ago. *He's* the one that said awful things about *me*.

"As I said previously, I'm fine. Thank you again for the shirt," the seladin says calmly, which keeps me from tearing into him. I give them a tight nod, forcing myself to calm down before I ruin the mission. I'm close enough now to see the name on her badge. *Wait a moment...Breks?*

"Before you go, is Breks a common seladin family name?"

"No." Her face is blank as she replies, but a look of understanding pops onto it a few moments later. "You know Maerlon."

"Yes! You must be his older sister. Maerlon and I work together at CiaXera and he's my best friend's partner. Wow, small galaxy!"

Phelix narrows his eyes at me. Shit, I'm supposed to be a pharmaceuticals rep.

"Well, rather, we worked together before I moved over to working in pharmaceuticals. Pay and benefits are a lot better than marketing," I say, laughing to cover my panic.

"Indeed. The galaxy is objectively quite large, but I get your meaning. Perhaps your friend spilling tea on me was not to draw you to him, but you to me." Ulena's small smirk is the only indication that she's not entirely serious.

"That must be it." I wink back at her. Phelix's face goes stony, any hint of warmth toward me evaporating at my casual flirtation. Fuck, I'm screwing this up so bad. My palms sweat as the same nausea I had after speaking with him last night builds. I wish Eden were here to flash her tits and distract him from the mess I'm making of things.

Ulena smiles, oblivious to my panic. "I'm having dinner with Maerlon and his partner tomorrow evening. If you don't have plans, join us." Damn, the one time I don't want a hot babe flirting with me!

Phelix is now actively looking away, as if anything else on the display floor is more interesting than us. I need to do something fast, before he leaves. Maybe I can use her invitation to my advantage.

I slide a hand onto his shoulder, and he flinches, looking back at me in shock. Heat flares inside me from the small point of contact, making it hard to focus enough to reply to Ulena. "Hmm, tomorrow night? I already have plans with Phelix and a colleague of mine. Would it be alright for them to come too?"

Phelix blinks at me in surprise and opens his mouth to say something, but stops when I give his shoulder a firm squeeze, letting my nails dig in slightly. A small hiss escapes his lips, and the sound hits me right between my legs. Fuck, I need to stop touching him.

"I don't see why that would be a problem. Maerlon's place is sufficiently large enough for that number of guests," Ulena replies, giving me and Phelix a nod.

Oops, I didn't realize I was inviting myself over to Maerlon's loft. I'll have to send him an apology in advance. Maybe book him and Fina a deluxe session at a simsuite. I wonder if I could convince Phelix to go to a pleasure sim with me...

Phelix's choked sound of alarm tears me out of that train of thought and I realize that my hand has slid down his back to rest on his ass. And damn, that is a nice, juicy ass. I quickly pull my hand away before I squeeze it.

Ulena clears her throat gently. "I need to go. Thank you for the shirt, Dr. Nafar. I will see you, Mezli, and her colleague next night cycle."

"See you then!" I call out cheerily as she heads off into the crowd, then plaster on a confident smile and turn to look at Phelix. His strange, beautiful green eyes bore into mine, simultaneously conveying frustration, confusion, and a hint of desire.

The look is so intense that I have to take a step back before I do something dumb like smack it off that awful, handsome face of his. Or kiss him.

"So, Lord Nafar, what are your plans for the rest of the day? Other than giving everyone a free show, of course," I say, clasping my hands behind my back to keep from touching him again.

He lets out a humorless laugh. "Nothing of consequence. As you said, I've already done my part to enhance the convention for the day with my physique." Phelix gestures to himself, a hint of deepening pink on his neck and cheeks as he speaks.

"If you'd like less ogling, I could give you my shirt. It probably wouldn't fit though."

His mouth downturns and the charming embarrassment he displayed a moment ago disappears. "I don't need you to tell me I'm large. I'm quite aware of my flawed figure."

Flawed figure? Sure, he's not thin, but nothing about the way he's built says flawed to me. He's probably just saying that to get me to fawn over him. Gross.

I can't stop myself from rolling my eyes. "Fishing for compliments isn't attractive, Phelix. You know you're handsome."

His eyes narrow. "Am I?"

"No. You're so ugly that it made me sick the first time we met." The words are meant to be teasing, but the color drains from his face and he stares at me in horror.

Ah shit, maybe he was serious about thinking he's not good-looking. I shake my head at him, letting some of my true self through the flirtatious veneer. "Goddess, you are the most attractive *xalar* I've ever met. And that's *despite* your personality."

Phelix lifts a brow at my hasty addendum. "So, it's my personality that made you vomit all over my mother's marble floors?"

"Yep!" I say with an emphatic nod. I'm veering off-course from my seduction mission, but I can't seem to stop now that I've let that facade drop.

He snorts in a mixture of disbelief and amusement. "Is there any way that I can convince you that I'm less nauseating of a person than your original assessment?"

"Probably not." The truthful reply comes out before I can stop it.

He raises a brow at me, doing his best to suppress a smile at my bluntness. Wait, is being honest with him actually working?

"Start by buying me some lunch. We can see how things go from there," I say, surprised by how part of me likes the idea of having a real conversation with Phelix.

He smiles at that. A full, genuine smile that lights up his whole face and gets rid of that constipated, "I'm a stuffy, arrogant, rich prick" look almost entirely. "Deal. You'll have to pick the place, though. I don't know much about Spire."

"And what makes you think I do?" I ask.

"You seem like a *xala* who knows her way around things," he replies, voice lower than usual.

I laugh, though it comes out a bit breathless. It's not the best line, but it works.

"Fine. We'll meet you at the convention entrance in an hour." I start running through my mental catalog of restaurants in this part of the district. Maybe I'll pick something run down just to see him squirm. "Oh and try to find a shirt by then," I add, raking my gaze up and down his bare torso.

Phelix nods, but as I turn to walk away, he speaks. "Wait, 'we'll'?"

"Yeah, Dr. Mori and I are a package deal since I already told her I'd take her to lunch. You don't mind treating both of us, do you?"

I suppress a laugh as surprise flashes across his face, before he schools his expression. "It would be my pleasure. She seems like a lovely *xala*."

A prickle of jealousy runs up the base of my spine. Is he attracted to Eden? And wait, why do I care? I'm attracted to her too.

A lurid image of the three of us entangled in my bed pops into my mind.

My lips spread into a grin. "Are you sure? Can you handle both of us?" I say, pitching my voice deeper.

He locks eyes with me and takes a step closer. "I can handle anything you want to give me, Mezli." We stand there, close enough to touch for what feels like ages before he backs off. "Now, if you'll excuse me—I need to go get dressed."

11

✦EDEN✦

A fter a morning of fruitlessly searching for Phelix in various panels, Mezli pings my comm as I'm exiting a discussion of recent developments in nanomedicine.

> Mezli: TARGET ACQUIRED. Rendezvous at location alpha in T-minus five minutes.

Location alpha? T-minus? I'm guessing she means the convention entrance. I wonder where she picked up all of that lingo. She sounds like she's from a vintage human spy movie. I decide to play into it, because if I'm forced to be a secret agent, I'm going to have a little fun with it.

Eden: Roger. Operation Honey Pot is a go.
Heading to the meeting point. Going silent until
then.

I grin down at my comm and make my way to the exit. A little flutter of excitement runs through me as I see Mezli waiting for me out on the walkway, casually leaning against a railing overlooking a lower section of the district. The pose gives me a lovely view of the curve of her hips and the long line of her slender neck, as well as the opportunity to continue with our game.

Creeping up as silently as possible, I slide in to stand next to her at the railing, keeping my gaze out over the district.

"The swallow flies at dawn," I say, remembering a code phrase from one of my dad's favorite spy films.

"And I swallow at dusk," Mezli replies, deadpan.

I snort at her innuendo and turn to see her grinning at me in delight. "Just at dusk?"

"A *xala* never tells. But I can say that all of this sexy spy talk is making me awfully thirsty." She licks her lips and gives me a flirty wink.

I do my best to smile back with equal bravado and not blush. No one's ever flirted with me, so being around Mezli is taking some getting used to. It seems like flirting casually is her default, so I try not to read anything into it. "R-right! So...lunch with Phelix? I take it you found him and used your charms to convince him to come?"

"Oh, it wouldn't take much for me to get him to come," she says with a shrug.

My face heats as I immediately imagine just how she'd go about making him come.

"Goddess, you're so adorable when you blush! I'll have to think of more things to keep a flush on your cheeks this week. But yes, I found him and invited him to lunch with us. I also got us an invitation to dinner at my friend's loft, courtesy of his sister. Who Phelix ran into—literally. Anyway, he took his shirt off, I insulted him, and he agreed to come to lunch."

I blink back at her, trying to make sense of what she said. I'm not sure where to start, so I settle on the part that seems the most problematic. "You insulted him and that made him want to have lunch?"

"Wild, right? I was trying to be all sexy, but he kept getting more and more closed off. I got so frustrated that I let my actual thoughts about him slip, and that was what got him to take the stick out of his ass for long enough to agree to lunch. He must have a degradation kink or something."

"Th-that's a thing?" I don't mean to ask that out loud, but Mezli laughs and pats me on the shoulder.

"Definitely! I went out with a vuloi who wanted me to spit in his face and crush his balls while I told him how weak he was. Didn't do much for me, but I'll try pretty much anything once," she says with a shrug.

I try not to gape at her, but I can't help it. I'm not sure if I'm turned on by the idea or repulsed. "W-wow, okay."

"Speaking of weird sexual needs..." Mezli rubs the back of her neck, and sighs. "You're a doctor. Do you know of any methods to help keep my libido in check? I never paid attention when my mothers discussed their mating bond because it was too gross to think about them fucking, and I had no interest in finding a mate. But I can't seem to keep my horniness under control and while I know I'm supposed to be seducing Phelix, it makes it difficult to think. Or sit down anywhere without leaving a puddle behind."

The flush on my face creeps down to my neck and chest at her mention of how wet she's getting. I'm too embarrassed to mention my diligent research into nexxit mating practices, so I pretend to consider her options for a moment. "Hmm. Most of my training was for human physiology, but I did take a few courses on reproductive xenobiology."

Mezli raises a brow at this. "Is that code for watching a lot of alien porn? Because if it is, then I'm an expert on 'reproductive xenobiology'." She does air quotes, a uniquely human mannerism that she must've picked up from her friend.

I sputter out a choked laugh. "No! I mean, I've seen some...but no! It was an actual medical study. From what I recall, the nexxit mate bonding hormones only subside after repeated copulation with their mate, but uh, other activities can help keep them in check."

"Other activities?"

"Yeah. Like intense exercise or, uh..." I look down at my hands to hide my embarrassment. "Or sexual release without your mate."

Mezli groans. "Ugh, I hate working out. Masturbation it is! Unless you want to give me a hand, *doctor*." She makes a lurid gesture with her fingers at me.

"W-what?" She can't be serious.

"There's that blush again. Gorgeous. Now come on, let's head to the restaurant so I can rub one out in the hygiene room before Phelix arrives."

As soon as we arrive at the bustling bistro set on a terrace overlooking a large retaining pond dotted with aquatic plants, Mezli makes a beeline for the hygiene room. "Be back in a bit!" she calls over her shoulder before disappearing inside.

She's not seriously going in there to...

A bead of sweat rolls down my neck as I wait under the artificial sunlight, despite the temperate breeze that sends ripples along the pond and rustles through the bistro's banners advertising the best *skrllpt* on Spire. Just thinking about Mezli doing *that* while I wait out here has me overheated.

"Dr. Mori?"

The low rumble of my name snaps me away from thoughts of just how Mezli uses her four hands to touch herself, and I look up to see Phelix approaching. He looks even more handsome than when I saw him last night. Every bit the picture of the perfect professional, with a tight-fitting dark green jacket that highlights his thick arms and torso, and crisp pressed pants that cling to his solid legs and draw my eyes toward his crotch.

He clears his throat and I tear my gaze away, face flaming. "Ah! Dr. Nafar. Good to see you again."

If he noticed me looking at his crotch, his inscrutable expression doesn't indicate any reaction. If I were a nexxit with a lifetime of experience reading their micro-expressions, then maybe I'd be able to sense how he feels around me.

He nods. "Indeed. Is Mezli joining us?"

"Yes, she's uh...she's taking care of something in the hygiene room." I resist the urge to swipe at the flustered sweat that's accumulated on my brow.

"I see." He stares back blankly. It's like talking to a wall. How is this the same nexxit I chatted for hours over comm with?

"So, um, how do you know Mezli?" I ask.

A flicker of tension crosses his face, and I mentally kick myself at my pathetic attempt at small talk. He quickly smooths it away and gives me a pearly smile, his teeth slightly sharper than a human's.

"We met through our parents a few years ago. It was a...memorable evening."

"Oh? How so?" Mezli told me it was a disaster, but I'm curious to know his side of the story. How did one evening ruin their chances at matehood?

Phelix snorts at my question, the brief amusement softening his stoic features and making him even more attractive. "She vomited all over my mother's floor. No doubt from being forced to endure my company. Hopefully, she's not in the hygiene room for a similar reason now."

"No! She's in there, um, freshening up a bit. Whatever happened before, she's excited to spend time with you now. As am I. Having the chance to talk to one of the leading experts in obstetrics tech is truly an honor."

Phelix's brow quirks almost imperceptibly. "You've heard of me? Or my work, I suppose?"

Well, that confirms he doesn't remember me at all. Damn. It's a good thing for the mission, but it still hurts to know our conversations meant nothing to him.

My infatuation with Phelix started when I ran into yet another issue with my clinic's secondhand medipod. It had been a splurge to invest in a medipod at all, but with the aging population of my patients on Europa 3, it felt necessary. The device was touted to have a huge array of functions—everything from cell rejuvenation to complex surgical procedures. But there was a reason why I got the medipod at such a steep discount—it was set on demo mode and more than half the functions required upgrade licenses to actually work.

When one of my patients became pregnant and I realized it would be a high-risk birth, I decided enough was enough. The functionality to deliver her baby as safely as possible was already programmed into the pod and the only thing stopping me from using it were the damn programming locks. So I decided to find a way to hack past them.

At the time I didn't know a thing about hacking that kind of device, so I reached out to people who might—under the false pretenses of asking for general medipod advice, of course. I didn't want the manufacturer coming to fine my broke ass for using their tech unlicensed. After a string of dead end conversations, I found an article written by a Dr. Phelix Nafar about optimizing medipod calibrations for successful obstetric procedures.

I wrote to him at my wits' end. I didn't even bother to conceal my intent to hack into the medipod. Whether it was because of my blatant honesty or my desperate plea to help me take care of my patient, Phelix replied. He refused to assist me in his reply to my unsecured message sent to his work comm, but an hour later used a secure channel to contact me and coached me through "calibrating" the medipod for the birth.

After that, we discussed other ways of bypassing the programming locks, which led to conversations about our shared disdain for gate-keeping lifesaving tech behind a paywall and the predatory practices of the medical tech industry. Which, in turn, led to more personal, though surface-level conversations about our daily lives and our hopes.

Talking to him felt so easy. He had a blunt humor and charm, and his vast knowledge and obvious intelligence were intoxicating. I had no clue what he looked like other than that he was a nexxit, and I refused to let myself give in to my stalker-ish desire to look him up. Plus, that would have spoiled my mental image of the nerdy but charming alien I'd built as I fantasized about what it would be like to have our conversations in person.

There was one night, when he'd messaged right as I was about to get in bed that made me hope my feelings weren't one-sided.

I realized after all this talk of bodies, I don't know a thing about yours, Dr. Mori. Though I must admit I've thought about it far too much.

The squeal of shocked glee I made was so loud it woke up my dad, who came rushing in from his bedroom down the hall to make sure I was okay. But that excitement was short-lived. By the time I looked back at my comm, the message was gone. Part of me wondered if I'd hallucinated or dreamt it, but I clung to hope that maybe he was just shy.

Now I know it must've been a figment of my overactive imagination, because he doesn't even recognize my name. I doubt I school my disappointed expression nearly as well as he can as I reply. "Oh yes, I've, um, I've read a number of your research articles." *Yes, I've spent way too many nights re-reading our correspondences and later touching myself thinking about the man behind the comms.*

"Ah. Well, I'm happy to discuss anything you'd like. Though I doubt Mezli will like me monopolizing our lunch conversation with medical talk. How do you know Mezli, by the way? Are you..." His jaw tenses as he trails off.

Oh crap, if he thinks Mezli's my lover, will that screw up our seduction plan? I assume he's monogamous because of the whole mate thing, but maybe that's wrong. I really should've asked Mezli more questions about what having a mate means.

"N-no! I mean, yes? What were you asking? We're colleagues! Or rather Mezli and I connected back when she helped me with some pharmaceutical, uh, issues I was running into back on my colony. We developed a friendship, so she offered to be my guide to Spire while I'm here. I've never been off Europa 3 before, so, uh, it would be a bit overwhelming without her." That last part is definitely true, even if the rest is crap, so I hope it helps sell the lie.

Phelix looks like he's going to ask me for specifics, but Mezli skips up to join us before he can. Thank god.

"Lord Nafar, thank you for gracing us with your presence!" Mezli says with an exaggerated bow, extending her upper hands to rest on his.

Phelix's jaw ticks at the mention of his title, but he bows in return and brings her hands up to his lips to press a chaste kiss to them. Though there's nothing chaste about the way his jade eyes bore into hers as he does. "Princeps Frye." A moment later, his nostrils flare and he swallows heavily as he releases her hands.

That answers the question of whether she actually was masturbating in the hygiene room or not. She gives him a wicked grin, as if daring him to say something, then turns to me with a sweeter smile. "Shall we eat?"

12

✦PHELIX✦

Mezli's scent lingers where her hands brushed my lips, and it takes all my willpower not to excuse myself to head to the hygiene room to take care of the ache in my groin like she apparently did while waiting for me to arrive. My cocks are already halfway out of my slit. I bring a surreptitious hand to my crotch when Mezli and Eden turn to walk into the restaurant, pressing as hard as I can to shove them back inside with a wince.

The pain is enough to pierce through my lust-fogged thoughts. What am I doing here? I told myself only a few hours ago that I wouldn't be this reckless, yet here I am, lust-addled by a fresh surge of mating hormones.

I can't blame my change of heart solely on base urges. When

Mezli was honest with me back in the conference hall, I saw a flicker of her true self, beyond whatever seductive persona she puts on. I liked that version of her enough to take a chance on lunch. If nothing else, maybe I can finally get some closure. Have an actual conversation with the *xala* who ran away after knowing me for less than an hour. Maybe an honest talk will make me bold enough to remind Eden of our correspondence. Work through both of my unhealthy emotional attachments in one sitting, so I can go about the rest of the week without obsessing over them.

Yes, it's worth the pain of confrontation and the ache in my cocks to get past the maddening hold these *xalas* have on me.

The bistro Mezli chose for lunch is a casual place that, with a quick glance at the holomenu floating near the entrance, features primarily shikzeth cuisine. Wonderful. Because what I need right now, while I'm already overheated, is scorchingly spicy food.

"This place looks...interesting."

Mezli scoffs. "Not up to the great Lord Nafar's standards? How shocking."

Frustration cuts through the haze of my arousal. "I didn't say that."

"You didn't have to. It's written across your pompous face."

Eden's eyes widen at Mezli's insult, then dart to me in concern, but I relish the sting of her words. I don't typically enjoy being insulted, but I'll take it any day over false niceties. Coming from the world of noble bullshit, Mezli's behavior is refreshingly *real*.

Besides, it'll take more than her saying something I know most people think about me to rile me up. Instead, I smile. "Shall we order? It's been ages since I've had some decent *skrllpt*."

"Hah! I'm surprised your refined tongue can handle *skrllpt*."

"You'd be surprised by just what my *refined* tongue can handle."

I hadn't meant for the words to be suggestive, but they come out thick and husky.

The disdain melts off of Mezli's face, and she licks her lips. Fuck, now I can't stop looking at her mouth. How am I supposed to have a conversation when all I want to do is slam my lips against hers?

The tension between us hangs in the air until Eden clears her throat. "Uh, what's *skrllpt*? Should I order it too?"

"No!" Mezli and I reply at the same time.

"Wow, okay no *skrllpt* for me," Eden says with a sheepish chuckle.

"It's very spicy. Like burn your tongue, cause you to have a coughing fit and cry level spicy for anyone who isn't a shikzeth. Definitely not for a human! But if Lord Nafar here wants to show off his masochistic tendencies, he's welcome."

"You're into pain?" Eden asks and then claps a hand over her mouth like she didn't mean to say that out loud. Mezli cackles as a bright pink blush stains the human's cheeks.

"Under the right circumstances, yes." I reply nonchalantly, though the image of Mezli flogging me as she gives me that devilish, satisfied smirk while Eden watches with rapt fascination fills my mind. My cocks twitch under the napkin on my lap. Shit, I need to find a different topic of conversation before I embarrass myself five minutes into our lunch.

Fortunately, our server appears at the table to save me. They're a tall, bulky shikzeth with curled horns and blazing red eyes that narrow when they sweep across Eden. We place our orders, with Mezli laser focused on me as I commit to ordering the *skrllpt*. She'll learn I don't back down from a challenge. Eden orders *frecha* cakes, the least spicy, most human-safe thing on the menu. Our server glares at her the entire time she speaks, though I can't understand why. It's not like she's asking them to bring her something not already on the menu.

Mezli's too busy raking her eyes over me when she thinks I'm not looking to notice the shikzeth's sour expression. I doubt she'd have let it pass without comment, otherwise. It takes a lot of willpower to not call the server out on their rudeness myself, but I was conditioned to not make a scene.

The way Mezli stares at me makes my skin feel too tight, a mixture of arousal and dismissive realism coursing through me. I know my appearance would never make me a nexxit's first choice for a bed partner. There's just too *much* of me. Too tall, too broad, too much body fat. When she looks at me with raw desire, I know it's only because of the mating bond. She'd never look twice at me otherwise.

When she finally looks away, she smiles brightly at Eden. "I hope you're excited for your first taste of something alien!"

Eden nods, her skin flushing under Mezli's radiant attention and suggestive phrasing. "I-I am!"

Mezli grins back at her like she'd love to give her a taste of something alien other than food. She may be forced to want me because of the mate bond, but I can see the raw interest and desire in her eyes as she looks at Eden. A look that Eden returns in her own shy way.

And why wouldn't she? Mezlitrasta val Frye is the most stunning nexxit *xala* I've ever had the pleasure to see in person. Which is no small feat, considering the number of Mother's parties filled with perfectly groomed and sculpted exemplars of nexxit beauty. But Mezli is on a whole other level.

Yet, sitting beside such beauty does nothing to dim Eden's own allure. Goddess, when I asked her that one lonely night what her body looked like, there was no way in the universe I could have imagined the human taking a seat across the table from me now. She's all softness, with her plush belly and spectacular breasts that take all of my willpower not to keep looking at. Inquisitive intelligence gleams in her eyes every time she speaks, a perfect compliment to the shrewd seductiveness that Mezli exudes.

They look perfect together. Perfect and in no need of a mediocre *xalar* like me.

The thought dampens my mood significantly. "What do you want from me?" I ask curtly, snapping their attention back to me.

Mezli glares at me and pointedly takes her time to sip her shimmering green cocktail, holding a hand up to Eden to let her know she'll answer me. "I'm not sure I know what you mean, Lord Nafar. Can't a girl ask her mate and her colleague to lunch?"

"I was under the impression that I disgusted you, *Princeps* Frye." My cocks twitch when I see her eyes flare with anger when I use her title as well. Dammit, goading her turns me on even when I'm upset. "So, what is it? You want to fuck me? I admit the mating hormones are quite potent. But you have a far more suitable candidate sitting beside you, and I'm not in the habit of sleeping with people that hate me for no good reason. Unless it's my family name you keep using like an insult that you object to. Which is more than a bit hypocritical don't you think, *Princeps*?

Mezli huffs out a humorless laugh. "You think *that's* why I don't like you? Fuck, you're more of an egotistical prick than I thought."

What is that supposed to mean? Suddenly, her biting honesty isn't as appealing. Some of my anger and pain bleeds through the cracks of calm veneer. "Then what, pray tell, did I do to you that made you run away from your Goddess-given true mate after a handful of hours in their company? Is it my appearance? Because I'm also not in the habit of seeking pity sex from *xalas* far out of my league."

She scowls. "What? No! I already told you, you're frustratingly attractive. So solid and... No, dammit, I'm not going to inflate your ego even more!"

"Then why? Why did you leave?" I know I've raised my voice far more than is proper for a public setting, but my boiling blood at her maddening behavior keeps me from caring. Fuck staying under control. After four years, I want to know *why*.

"Because you made it obvious I didn't measure up to your lofty expectations!"

What in the Goddess' name is she talking about? I barely said two words to her during that dinner.

Eden's eyes are as wide as saucers as they bounce back and forth between us, and that's what draws me back to my senses. Dammit, this isn't going at all like I'd hoped. I clear my throat and break my staredown with Mezli. "Apologies for my behavior, Dr. Mori."

"Why are you apologizing to *her*?! I'm the one you're being an ass to! I invited you here to try to see if we could start over. But if you're going to act like just as much of an asshole as you did when we first met, then forget it." Mezli throws her purse over her shoulder and pushes her chair back with a loud metallic scrape to stand.

My hand darts out to grab her wrist without thinking. She glares down at where our skin touches, but I can see even this small contact is making her burn for me as much as I am for her. Anger wars with lust in her eyes and I use her hesitation to my advantage.

"I'm sorry, Mezli."

Her eyes widen at my apology. I honestly can't believe I'm apologizing, either. Then again, I can't believe most of my behavior since I encountered her and Eden last night. "Please stay. I—I'd very

much like a chance to try again if I haven't already made too much
of a mess of things."

I didn't realize how much I wanted that chance until I said the
words aloud. It'd be much easier to let her storm out and go back to
shutting myself off from the world. I'm probably making a huge
mistake by asking her to stay, but she said she wanted to try to start
over. It'd be an even bigger mistake to squander that chance.

She slides her chair back in with a dramatic sigh, pulling her
hand away. I let her go despite everything inside me urging me to
hold on. "Fine. But only because the food is here and I can't resist
seeing you suffer for your bravado."

Our server approaches and slides a steaming plate of *skrllpt* in
front of me, then sets down Mezli's noodle dish. They slam down
Eden's *frecha* cakes, almost knocking her glass of water over, and
both Mezli and I turn to scowl in their direction.

"Sorry," they grumble, directing their apologetic nod to the wall
behind Eden rather than making eye contact.

"What the hell is their problem?" Mezli mutters as they leave.
"Do you want me to make a complaint against them? Because I will!
I love calling out assholes." Her gaze lingers on me as she says that
last part, a silent challenge glittering in her dark eyes.

"No, it's fine! I think we've had enough drama for one lunch."
Eden smiles tensely at both of us and my stomach sinks with guilt
about my inappropriate behavior.

"Again, I'm sorry to both of you for my rudeness. Hopefully,
seeing me eat this plate of *skrllpt* will be a good enough penance."

Eden giggles and takes a bite of her *frecha* cakes. "Seems fair.
Oh, wow, these are good!" She takes another bite and lets out a
little moan of pleasure that has both myself and Mezli focusing in
on her mouth. "What? They are!" she says self-consciously.

"Go on," Mezli says, turning to level a challenging look at me. "Unless you want me to think of other options for your penance."

Fuck me, now I do. I could show her just how good I am at appeasing her. I scoop up a large amount of the mashed, deceptively innocuous-looking substance on my plate. Not breaking eye contact with her, I place the spoon in my mouth and swallow, then lick my lips. An immediate sweat breaks out on my brow and it takes all of my willpower not to scramble to douse my throat with water.

"Good *xalar*," Mezli says with a smirk that makes my cocks throb and leak.

Eden coughs to break the tension, but it doesn't work this time.

"Is that enough to satisfy you?" I ask.

"Mmm, we're just getting started," Mezli purrs back.

Eden lets out a wheezing, choked sound that reminds me I shouldn't blatantly eye-fuck my mate in public. I struggle to tear my eyes away from Mezli, but a moment later, the sound of shattering glass breaks the fog of lust.

Eden has knocked her water glass to the ground, and is clutching at her throat, gasping and wheezing as her face turns a deep red.

"Oh, fuck!" Mezli cries out. "Eden, what's wrong?"

Fearful understanding floods my veins. I know what's wrong. She's going into anaphylactic shock.

13

✦ MEZLI ✦

"Oh Goddess, someone call a medic!" I scramble out of my chair to Eden's side, desperate to do something that will stop the panic in her wide eyes and the choked wheezing that gets worse by the second. Glass on the floor bites into my knees as I kneel beside her, but I couldn't care less about that right now.

In an instant, Phelix is at her other side, pushing away a gawking bystander with a growl to grab Eden's cheek and turn her face to look at him. He digs through his satchel with his right hands and attempts to focus her with the others. "Eden, I've got you. Squeeze my hand if you've used a cyrpaxiphrine injection before."

Eden shakes her head and manages to wheeze out, "N-no...is it...

l-like epinephrine?"

A flash of concern crosses Phelix's face, but he nods and pulls a syringe out of his bag. "Close enough. This will help." He rucks up her skirt to expose her thick thigh.

Flashbacks to the night when Fina had a bad reaction to an alien substance flood my mind. We thought she had an allergic reaction and used meds on her without knowing if it would be safe, and it ended in disaster.

"Wait! You can't just give her something without knowing for sure that it's human-safe!"

Phelix levels his steady gaze on me and some of the panic recedes. "I promise this won't harm her. There's a chance it won't help her as much as it would a nexxit, but it isn't dangerous. You have my word as a doctor."

I blink back panicked tears. Shit, why am I crying? "O-okay. But if you're wrong and you hurt her, I'm going to hurt you."

"Deal." He nods like it's reasonable for me to threaten him when he's trying to help, and that makes a small fluttery feeling rattle in my chest. Am I having some kind of allergic reaction too?

He uncaps the syringe and caresses Eden's cheek with an apologetic frown. "Sorry about this."

Despite his apology, she doesn't even wince when he injects her, but I start to feel clammy and lightheaded. I *hate* needles.

A tense couple of minutes pass while we wait to see if the injection helps. Phelix murmurs calm words of encouragement to Eden, continuing to stroke her cheek. Her breathing begins to even out, and the tight fists that Phelix holds his lower hands in ease.

The way he touches her is careful and almost reverent despite the situation. The fluttering inside me amps up. Definitely something I ate. I'm certainly not feeling *affection* toward Phelix right now, watching him touch my crush. Am I?

Oh goddess, I *am*. What the fuck?

I shake that horrifying thought away and smooth down Eden's skirt, giving her knee a gentle squeeze. "If you wanted us to stop flirting, you could've just asked."

Eden's laugh comes out a bit wheezy, but she grins back at me as she wipes the tears off of her face. "Good to know for n-next time. Sorry for making a scene. I didn't know I was allergic to any universal foods. Even did an allergy test before coming to Spire to make sure."

"Don't apologize! They must have mixed something up in the kitchen. I ought to go rip them a new asshole for endangering your life like that!" I'd already be back there yelling at them if the thought of leaving Eden's side right now didn't worry me so much. She's so sweet and *vulnerable*, and I have the strongest urge to protect her. Kinda like I do with Fina, and Paul to a lesser extent, but to the extreme. It's bizarre. I barely know Eden, yet I'd probably stab anyone who tried to come near her right now. Well, anyone but Phelix.

A dark look crosses Phelix's face that makes me wonder if he's feeling the same way. "You don't have any food allergies?"

"N-no," Eden says, looking startled by his sudden intensity.

He pats Eden's cheek one last time before standing and scanning the restaurant. His eyes narrow and without a word, he strides across the room to another table where our waiter is setting down their dishes.

He taps the shikzeth on the shoulder and when they turn around, his fist strikes their jaw before they can react. "Consider this your first and only warning. Harm a human again and you'll wish you'd never been born."

Eden gasps, along with a number of others in the restaurant. I gape at my mate like it's the first time I've seen him, and the fluttering in my chest turns into a needy pulse between my legs. Violence doesn't turn me on, but seeing him protect her sure does.

"What the *skreth* are you talking about?!" The shikzeth growls and moves to grab Phelix, but he steps out of the way before they can.

"I saw how you looked at her. You contaminated her food. Do you want to fight me and add assaulting a noble to the list of crimes that'll land you in a Consortium prison colony? I've already contacted station security—they should be here soon."

The shikzeth's nostrils flare and their eyes burn brighter, the only warning before they dart for the exit, knocking over a pair of aespians as they enter.

Mouth agape, I watch as Phelix straightens his jacket and strides back to the table with an air of total calm and control. *Holy shit.*

He offers a hand to Eden, who blinks at him rapidly before accepting his help to stand up.

"I don't know about you two, but I've lost my appetite. Allow me to accompany you somewhere less unpleasant?" Phelix says, like he's talking about the weather. "I'll need to observe you to make sure you recover fully. Unless you'd prefer to go to a hospital."

"Uh, sure. Of course, Dr. Nafar," Eden murmurs as she takes in the crowd still staring at us.

The host calls out apologies, which Phelix ignores as he leads us out of the restaurant. Eden and I trail behind him in stunned silence.

It's only when we're a block away that Phelix stops to speak again. "Sorry about all that." He looks sheepish and there's a slight flush to his cheeks. He clears his throat and puts his stoic mask back on. "Are you alright, Eden? How is your breathing?"

I wish he wouldn't do that "show no emotion" nonsense that nexxit nobility have made an art of. I was just starting to not completely hate him.

"I'm okay. I'll be shaky for a while, but my breathing is fine now. You were so gentle with your injection, I doubt I'll even have a bruise." Eden ducks her head like talking about his gentle touch embarrasses her. "Thank you so much, Dr. Nafar. You saved my life." She bites her lip, then steps closer to Phelix, her face turning the same shade of pink as his skin as she goes up on her toes to kiss his cheek.

His whole body tenses at the touch and his breath hitches. Bizarrely, mine does too. I should be jealous, but all I feel is warmth and arousal at Eden's gesture.

Phelix clears his throat as Eden steps back. "You would have done the same, doctor."

As captivated as I am by the exchange, my protective urge rises again. "Pardon me for interrupting this touching moment, but what about that shikzeth?! Where's station security? They tried to kill Eden!"

Phelix's lip quirks as he takes in my rage. "There's no proof they did anything wrong, as much as I'd like for them to pay for hurting Dr. Mori."

I frown at him. "What? What do you mean there's no proof? You said they contaminated her food!"

"Yeah, how did you know?" Eden asks, brow furrowing.

"I bluffed," he says with a shrug. "The way they were looking at her was enough for me to suspect them and from their behavior, it turns out I was correct."

Who is this *xalar*? That sounds like something I'd do. "You *bluffed*? My, my, that's awfully bold of you, Lord Nafar. What if you were wrong?"

"You'll learn that I'm not often wrong."

I scoff, opening my mouth to remind him he's a pompous ass who was wrong about me, but he continues. "At least not when it comes to matters that don't involve the heart."

"Ugh, stop making me like you!" I blurt, and the surprised way Phelix's face lights up at my words makes my stomach clench.

Eden laughs, though it still sounds a bit ragged. Immediately, I turn to her and rest a concerned hand on her arm, doing my best not to shiver at the strange thrill that thrums through me as I do. "Are you sure you're alright? Let's take you back to your hotel."

"B-both of you...with me at my hotel?" Eden swallows heavily.

I can't tell if the thought makes her excited or nervous. Is it bad that it turns me on to think it's a bit of both? I'm a sucker for the shy type—it makes it hotter when they finally come out of their shell and let go.

"Don't worry. I'll make sure Phelix doesn't do anything untoward," I say with a laugh.

He grumbles at the thought he'd be anything but respectful, but Eden's smile turns mischievous as she looks up at him through her glasses. "Ah, that's a shame."

Phelix sputters, whatever retort he had to my insinuation gone in the wake of Eden's unexpected flirtation. It's obvious he's not opposed to the idea and while I know that should upset me since he's my Goddess-damned mate, it sends another strange thrill through me.

Eden's smile flickers, interpreting his shock as distaste. "It's probably for the best. Don't want too much excitement in one day."

I don't like seeing her smile fade. "Just means we'll have to *get in touch* again while you're both here," I say, giving her a quick wink.

THE WALK back to Eden's hotel gives my mind enough time to clear after the shock of the attack. I'm not into Phelix. Those fluttery feelings were just adrenaline. I'm not absurdly turned on by the idea of Eden and Phelix together. That was just the byproduct of my mating hormones. Simple.

Your mating hormones would make you want to fight off a threat to your mate bond, not watch them fuck.

Shut up, brain! I'm just horny and confused because they're both so hot. I don't like Phelix, and I'm not going to go home and touch myself thinking about Eden and him together.

When we reach her hotel, Eden insists that she'll be okay to rest on her own. I don't argue, needing to get away from both of them to clear my head. Phelix doesn't seem happy about leaving her alone, only acquiescing after giving her his comm link and making her promise to message if she feels worse. It's sweet how worried he is.

Wait, I didn't just seriously think that he's *sweet,* did I? Now I know there's something wrong with me. He's a jerk! A jerk who's planning on selling dangerous medical data! All this drama and arousal is messing with my head. I need to focus on the mission.

When Eden parts ways with us in the hotel lobby, it's that thought—and absolutely nothing else—that has me closing the distance with Phelix. It's the mission that's on my mind, not genuine desire, when I grab his collar and tug him down into a kiss.

He lets out a muffled sound of surprise, but then he's kissing me back with all of my fervor and *more.* My tongue meets his as he opens his mouth to deepen the kiss, and all my traitorous mind can think about is how good that tongue would feel in my cunt.

The hotel concierge clears their throat and makes a disgusted noise. I pull back with a gasp, my chest heaving from disgust, not the sheer power of feeling his mouth on mine. Fuck, I want to kiss him again.

Tension hangs between us, so thick I could drown in it.

Right, I should say something. Something that isn't "that was the best kiss of my life and I'm so pissed I could scream, slap you, and then kiss you again". I force myself to smile. "Thank you, Phelix. For protecting Eden, not the kiss!"

Phelix inhales shakily and rubs at his scraped, no doubt bruised knuckles with a small smile. Goddess, he's sexy when he smiles. "Who knew that all I had to do to get two beautiful *xalas* to kiss me was punch someone."

I laugh despite myself. I want to do a hell of a lot more than kiss him. Fuck, I need to get out of here.

"I should go," I say abruptly. "See you at dinner tomorrow, Lord Nafar. I'll have Eden comm you the address."

I don't go right away, though. I kiss him again, hard and fast, swiping my tongue against his before pushing back and scurrying away before he can respond. I hear him call my name, but I don't turn to look. As soon as I'm out of his line of sight, I duck into a side hall and behind a potted plant, rummaging around in my purse until I find the makeup compact. I wipe my lips and spit into the hidden compartment. One of his short, dark hairs is on my sleeve, so I add that in for good measure.

There. I did it. I got what we needed, and he didn't suspect a thing.

The surge of excitement I thought I'd feel at getting one step closer to thwarting Phelix's plans doesn't come. Instead, my stomach aches as I wait for Phelix to leave, then drop the compact off at the hotel desk like the agents instructed. I feel lightheaded and nauseated as I make my way back to my apartment.

I know I did the right thing, but that kiss...

I scrub my face with my hands and groan. This is such a mess. I need to get my head on straight and stop letting horniness cloud my mind. Phelix might not be as awful as he was when I met him four years ago, but that doesn't absolve him of all his wrongdoings or clear him of suspicion.

The mission is what's important, not my ridiculous feelings. Once Eden's rested, and the agents use what I gave them to make the decryption key, we'll regroup and come up with a plan of action. Until then, I'll just, I don't know, make a list of all the reasons why I hate Phelix. Yeah, that'll help! That and masturbating to take the edge off. I'll get myself off while I think about the reasons I hate Phelix...

When I get back to my apartment, I'm so worked up I could cry when I slip my fingers between my legs. But then my comm chirps with a message from Paul.

Shit, Paul! I forgot to come up with an excuse for ditching our date last night. Honestly, I forgot about Paul in general. I'm a terrible friend.

I want to ignore it, but thinking about Paul makes me realize I should talk to him about the attack on Eden, since he works at the human embassy. It could've just been an isolated incident, but anti-human sentiment has been brewing among the more insular citizens of Spire. What happened to Eden could be a sign that things have escalated. I better comm Fina too, and warn her to be careful.

Anxiety roils in my gut, thinking about the potential danger for my human friends. Paul has the support of the embassy, Fina has Maerlon to protect her, but Eden...she's here all alone. I know what that's like. On top of that, she got attacked during this damn mission she didn't even sign up for. Fuck, she almost *died* because I was too wrapped up in feeling pissed and horny to notice the way the waiter was looking at her.

I didn't protect her. She's not safe here. I need to find a way to keep her safe.

14

✦EDEN✦

After a hot shower and changing into my favorite worn pajamas I brought for the trip to remind me of home, I flop onto my bed, savoring how the mattress cradles my body and immediately starts to relieve the tension in my back. I guess even mattress technology is more advanced in the Xi Consortium. A girl could get used to living here—if it wasn't for the fact that apparently some aliens would rather poison humans than have them on Spire.

If Phelix hadn't been there to intervene... I shudder at the thought. With how fast the substance they used to poison me took effect, I doubt I'd have made it to a medic in time. The only things anchoring me through my terror and panic were how gently his thumb caressed my cheek, sending sparks dancing across my skin, and Mezli by my other side, protecting me.

Now that I'm alone, it's a lot harder to feel safe. I checked the lock to my hotel room three times before I took my shower, afraid that some angry alien was going to burst in and finish the job. Logically, I know it was an isolated incident, and I was just the one unlucky enough to take the brunt of that shikzeth's ire against humans. That doesn't stop me from cocooning myself in a blanket to keep myself from trembling too hard.

Fuck, what am I supposed to do now? Tell the Consortium agents that I can't help them and rebook my passage home immediately? I'm obviously not the right person for the job. Not only am I compromised by my hidden past with Phelix and my burgeoning attraction to Mezli, but now I have anti-human fanatics to deal with. Agent Tysea was right. I'm not fit to be doing any kind of spy mission.

I'm finding it hard to reconcile the steadfast Phelix who saved me today with the idea he'd willingly endanger so many lives through selling illegal schematics. The right thing to do would be to leave and let Mezli handle things on her own. Go back home where I belong.

My body tenses even more at the thought, tears pricking at my eyes. It's taken me so long to leave Europa 3. Coming here was a once-in-a-lifetime opportunity. I'm scared after what happened today, but the idea of giving up and going home is even more terrifying. Could I live with myself if I ran home?

No.

I sit up and swipe away my tears.

I'm staying.

I didn't choose to be a part of this haphazard mission, and it's not my fault they chose the wrong person for the job. I'll get the info we need from Phelix—and hopefully prove he's not who they think he is. I won't let bad luck and one asshole alien ruin this trip for me. Though I sure as hell will be more careful about what I eat from now on. I'm staying, and I'm going to make every moment here count.

Excitement flutters in my stomach as determination sets in. This time on Spire is my chance to experience life like never before, and a huge part of that is sex. If I'm staying, I'm not going to sit around on my ass in this hotel room for the rest of the night. Now's as good a time as any to go out and find an alien to help get rid of my virginity.

As much as I wish that alien were Mezli or Phelix, I dismiss the thought. That would only make this messy mission even more complicated. It'd be better to take myself out of the romantic equation—there's nowhere for me to fit within their mate bond.

I'm digging around in my luggage to figure out what of the bland outfits I have will convince an alien to hook up with me when my comm chirps.

> Phelix: Eden, it's Phelix. I wanted to check in and see how you're feeling.

I smile to myself, knowing Phelix was worried enough to comm me.

> Eden: Thank you for checking on me, and for saving me at lunch today. I'm feeling much better! Don't think I'll be trying any new foods again soon, though.

> Phelix: I'm glad you're alright. Please continue to avoid strenuous activities for the rest of the cycle, just to be safe.

What a...professional reply. Ugh. He must not have felt the electric buzz present in his touch that I experienced despite struggling to breathe. I swear I can still feel it lingering on my cheek where he held my face.

As I stare at his reply, I realize that my comm recognized him as a previous contact. Oh god. This is so awkward. Should I mention it? He didn't say anything, but I can't think of a better excuse to bring up that we've spoken before. Maybe remind him that I'm the same human doctor he spent weeks talking to last year—and asked what her body looked like.

Dammit, I'm going to remind him. It's too weird not to say something.

> Eden: So, I don't know if you noticed, but my comm recognized yours.

> Eden: We talked over comms about a year ago. I totally understand why you didn't remember me. Why would you remember some backwater human medic looking for advice?

I feel sick as soon as I send the second message, wanting to toss my comm across the room to save myself from reading his reply.

> Phelix: Of course I remembered you. I didn't say anything because you seemed to not recognize me last night and I didn't want to make you uncomfortable.

A little squeak of surprise escapes me. He *does* remember me.

> Eden: Hah! I guess we both were being too polite for our own good. It's nice to talk to you again.

I type out "I missed you" and then quickly delete it. He's the one that severed our contact out of nowhere, so even though he does remember me, he obviously didn't want to keep in touch.

> Phelix: It is.

A minute passes and I think that's the end of the conversation. Dammit, I shouldn't have said anything. He was just checking in to be polite and I had to go and make things weird. I'm about to sink into embarrassed despair when he messages again.

> Phelix: If you find yourself in need of company this night cycle, I'm free to visit. Despite what Mezli said, I'm an honorable nexxit and won't succumb to any untoward urges.

I press my suddenly burning cheeks against the cool pillow and let out a muffled squeal into it. Just what untoward urges might he have? My core clenches at the thought. I know I shouldn't flirt with him, but I type out a reply and send it anyway.

> Eden: I wouldn't mind a little untoward behavior, if you were the one doing it.

Another long minute passes with no reply. Fuck. Clueless, horny Eden strikes again. I knew it was a bad idea. Of course he isn't interested. He has a freaking mate. A sexy, amazing, hilarious mate. Why would he want me?

I scramble to type out a reply before he's able to flat out reject me.

> Eden: Sorry, now I'm the one being inappropriate! Forget I said that. Goodnight, Dr. Nafar.

> Phelix: Don't apologize. I appreciate a xala that speaks her mind.

> Eden: If that's the case, I understand now why you're Mezli's mate.

There. I've acknowledged that he has a mate and we can move on from this awkward conversation. He takes far too long to reply, leaving me feeling like I'm going to die from embarrassment.

> Phelix: I suppose you're right. Though, Mezli and I don't have any relationship to speak of, as you saw at lunch. We're both free to pursue other options. Not that I have. Yet.

Holy shit. Is he flirting back? What should I do? I reply, digging the hole deeper for myself.

> Eden: Yet?

> Phelix: Mezli would murder me if I laid a hand on you. At least not before she got the chance to.

> Eden: What? She doesn't see me like that. We're just colleagues.

> Phelix: Ah. Of course.

> Eden: We are!

> Phelix: As you say. I should let you get more rest. Perhaps if you have a chance to discuss the parameters of your "working relationship" with Mezli and find that you're open to other collaborations, you'll let me know.

I stare at my comm, waiting to see if he'll send another

message, but that's it. Unused to flirting, and worried I'm misinterpreting the situation, I let the non-horny part of my brain come back on board and send back the safest answer I can think of.

> Eden: I will.

This time I really do throw my comm away from me, face-planting back down into the pillow. What is wrong with me? God, I hope I didn't screw up the mission with my inept attempt at making a pass at Phelix.

I don't have long to stew in my panicked arousal before an incoming message alert chirps from across the room. I scramble up off the bed and over to where my comm has landed on the floor, heart racing as I anticipate a reply from Phelix. But it's not him. It's a vid comm request from my parents.

I accept the request immediately, and a surge of homesickness hits me like a ton of bricks as I see the familiar faces of my parents sitting at their rustic kitchen table. Dad's eyes crinkle as he smiles, deepening the wrinkles he's developed over many years of beaming at me and Mom with that same loving look. Mom, on the other hand, bursts into tears the second she sees me, her pale nose red like she's already been crying.

"Hey Dad! Hey Mom—oh no, is everything okay? Did someone die?!" It's not an unlikely scenario with the elderly population back home. I fretted the whole trip here that by going away, I was leaving the community without a full-time medic.

Dad pats my mom's hand and shakes his head. "Don't worry, Edi-chan. No one died. She's just missing you. We both are. But now that we can see your sweet face, I'm sure her tears will dry up."

Mom nods, grabbing a tea towel beside her to wipe away her tears. "S-sorry, sweetie! How are you? I've missed you so much and you haven't commed since you got to the station and I was worried that something happened and oh, I'm just so relieved to see you!"

Dad squeezes her hand in support. It's clear she's been worried sick. I feel like the worst daughter in the world for forgetting to check in when I arrived. Between the agents recruiting me and the drama at lunch today, it slipped my mind.

"I'm so sorry I worried you! I got swept up in things and, uh, wanted to get settled at the hotel and the conference. I'll call every day I'm here from now on!"

"No, no, don't do that. You're living your dreams. I'm so proud of you, and I know how long you've wanted to go off planet. Don't worry about your silly mom, I'll manage my nerves."

"It's not silly to be worried about her on her first trip away from home," Dad says reassuringly.

In all my excitement for taking this trip, I never considered how much of a shock my leaving would be to my parents. We all took my presence with them on Europa 3 as a given. Never once did I imagine I'd actually get the chance to travel. Dreamed about it constantly, yes. But it felt like wishing to be a fairytale princess.

"I miss you both so much. I'll be home before you know it." Tears well behind my eyes, both from being away from my parents and from the thought of going back to my mundane life on Europa 3.

Dad must see the mixture of emotions behind my glassy eyes, because he frowns slightly. "You know..." He exchanges a glance with my mom and she nods. "If you need to extend your trip, we can help you with that. We have some credits saved up."

"What? No! That's for your anniversary vacation. I couldn't take that!" They've been planning a trip to a luxury vacation moon for their 50th anniversary for years. It's one of Mom's favorite topics of conversation. Though she's often morbid about it, saying it'll be their final off-world adventure before they pass on. They're older, but with medical advancements extending human lifespans, they've got at least another twenty to fifty years left before they die. With me around to check in constantly on their health, I'd like to hope it'll be closer to fifty.

With me around. My gut clenches at the familiar thought.

I love my parents. They're my favorite people in the entire universe, and I'd do anything for them. But I'm a thirty-year-old virgin who's never left the safety of home. In fifty years, I'll be eighty. Over half my life will have passed me by. Can I really go back to seeing the same handful of people day after day, caring for the sparse population of Europa 3 and watching my elderly patients eventually pass on despite my best efforts? I'll never find love—at least not unless a single retiree ends up on the backwater farming planet.

My parents' warm smiles spread their tender affection to me even through the barrier of technology, but it's unable to rid me of the guilt clenching inside me.

Mom pats Dad's hand. "We've talked about it already. Your dad found a closer vacation planet that's half the cost to visit, so we wouldn't have to cancel our trip entirely."

"But you've wanted to go there for years and—"

Dad holds up a hand, cutting me off. "Edi-chan, the gold sand beaches of Frellsia would be wonderful to visit, but you know what they can never compare to? *You.* You're our miracle. We've spent far too long keeping you close because you're the greatest joy we could ever hope to experience. But the rest of the galaxy needs a chance to experience you, too."

"Dad..." Tears stream down my face at his unexpected words, and looking at Mom I see she's also crying. My dad is a reserved, contemplative man. He doesn't usually express affection so strongly, though I know he loves me.

Hearing the depth of his love and emotion, it takes me a minute to respond. Their offer is overwhelmingly generous. Another week on Spire would give me time to enjoy my trip after the mission with Mezli is over. Though, the thought of exploring the station on my own doesn't sound as appealing as it originally did now that I've met her and Phelix.

But I can't take it. I'd never get over the guilt of ruining their trip for an extra week of selfish sightseeing. I shake my head. "I... It's too much, I—"

A loud chime from the door to my hotel room interrupts me, and I startle, looking back over my shoulder at the door in confusion.

"Just consider it, sweetie," Mom says, wiping away more tears. "We'll let you go so you can get that. Don't worry about your old parents, and have some fun for us, okay?"

"I... I will." I don't want to end the call, but the chime sounds again. "I love you both so much."

"We love you, too," Mom replies, and Dad nods in agreement.

I end the comm and hurriedly swipe away the tears and snot from blubbering a moment ago, then head to open the door. It chimes a third time right before I reach it, followed by loud thuds against the metal.

"Open up! Station security!"

Fuck me, as if this day could get any worse. What the hell is going on now? I open the door, mind racing with possible scenarios for why station security is here, but they all fall away when I see who's standing in the corridor.

"Hah, you should've seen your face!" Mezli grins at me, her black eyes sparkling with delight.

I frown at her. "Mezli? What's going on? Did something happen?"

She places her upper hands on my shoulders. "Breathe, babe." Her smile fades as she takes in my reddened face and wet eyes. "Oh shit, did something happen to you?"

"No, just my parents—"

"Ugh, say no more." She pulls me into a tight hug, her lower arms wrapping around my waist while her upper ones clutch my upper back. "My mothers are a nightmare. Well, it's probably more accurate to say that I'm their nightmare child that didn't fit their perfect plan for the next scion of House Frye. But I get how awful parents can be."

I melt into her touch, forgetting for a moment what we were talking about as little jolts of excitement dance across my skin at her nearness. "Thanks," I sigh. "Uh, my parents are wonderful. They didn't do anything to make me cry—I just miss them more than I realized."

"Oh! If you're not dealing with parental drama, do you want me to stop hugging you?"

"No!" I say far too eagerly, and she chuckles.

"Mmm, good." She nestles in even closer, and suddenly it's far too hard to breathe normally. Not with her pressed up against me and her unique scent filling my nostrils. I can't quite place what it reminds me of, but a sense of rightness washes over me.

"Damn, you're even nicer to hug than Fina," she murmurs against my shoulder.

I push down a shiver of pleasure as her breath dances across my skin. "That's your human friend, right?" I ask.

"Yep! She's fun to hug because of her squishy boobs, but your tits are even better. So full and soft."

"What?!" I squeak and pull away, my face flaming.

"Whoops, sorry, I probably shouldn't have said that out loud. I forgot how shy you humans can be."

"I'm not shy!" I protest, but I know I'm turning a deeper pink than her skin. "That's just not something people normally say to a..." I'm not sure how to finish that statement. I want to say friend, but we've only known each other for a few cycles.

"To what?" Mezli cocks a brow at me. "To someone they find attractive? Again, humans are far too prudish for their own good. Why can't I tell a beautiful woman that she's got amazing tits and I love feeling them against me?"

I sputter, unsure how to respond to her telling me I'm beautiful and that I've got a great rack.

She reaches up and twists one of my curls around her finger. "Hmm, I think you liked how it felt, too." Her finger releases my hair and I stop breathing as she slides it down the side of my neck, down to my collarbone, and then traces the neckline of my top until her hand is hovering above the swell of my breasts.

Is this really happening? My nipples harden as I silently beg her to take things further.

She breaks eye contact, her gaze falling to her hand, and I catch her small, sharp inhale.

Please touch me. God, I want you to touch me.

But then she steps away and pushes her long silken hair over one shoulder with a casual smile, like she didn't just have me panting for her at the slightest touch. The sting of embarrassment deflates my arousal. Between my failed flirting with Phelix and reading too much into Mezli's casual flirting, I feel like I'm back on Artem's doorstep the night he rejected me. When am I going to stop being such a clueless, inexperienced loser?

15

✦ MEZLI ✦

Poor sweet Eden looks like I kicked her pet flesstra. I shouldn't have flirted with her. As soon as I felt her body against mine, all I wanted to do is feel our bare skin pressed together. If she's so responsive from such a light touch, I can only imagine what she'd be like in bed. But for one of the rare moments in my life, sense returned to me before I took things too far. I'm not here to get Eden naked. No, I'm here to keep her safe.

Goddess, when did I get so mature and rational? It's very annoying. Fina's bad influence, I'm sure.

"So, uh, why are you here?" Eden asks, though she can't quite meet my eyes.

I give her an easy smile, pushing aside further thoughts of her gorgeous breasts. "Oh, that! Right, so I think you should go home."

Her mouth drops open. "What? Why?!"

I attempt to shrug casually, but it's hard to keep a conversation like this lighthearted when something inside me keeps screaming that Eden's in danger and I need to protect her. "You're not safe here. I stopped by the human embassy to speak with a friend. He didn't particularly want to talk with me since I was a no-show for our date, but I managed to make him listen—I'm very persuasive like that. Anyway, all of that is to say that there have been a handful of hate crimes across Spire since the official opening of the human embassy. Nothing fatal...at least not yet."

From what Paul told me, this is an escalation from the previous vandalism and threats a few of the ambassadorial staff members have faced since their arrival. They've brought the crimes to station security and the Consortium council, but the attack on Eden is a sign that things are escalating.

I can't stop myself from reaching out to grab her shoulders, worry clogging my throat. "Eden, lunch today was terrifying. You could have *died*. And knowing it's not an isolated incident, I can't stand by and let you risk your safety again. I'll tell the agents that I'm doing this mission on my own."

Her shocked look turns to an indignant one. "No. No way! I'm not going to let a few hateful aliens ruin my one chance at experiencing Spire. This stupid mission already messed up my plans, but I still have time to—"

"To what?" I interrupt, her rising frustrations kicking up my own temper. "To get yourself killed?"

"No! To *live*! To finally feel like I'm fucking alive, and experience something outside my mundane existence back home. I've spent my whole life waiting for this. This is my chance. I'm not letting you or anyone else talk me out of staying."

Her words hit me like a punch to the stomach, knocking away any arguments I was preparing. What she's said is so damn familiar it makes me remember the *xala* I shoved deep down inside me—the one I honestly thought I'd killed years ago. She was just as desperate for a chance to live outside the expectations pressed upon her. Eden says her parents love her, but so do my mothers. That doesn't change the boxes they trap us in.

"Sorry, I shouldn't have yelled." Eden frowns apologetically, mistaking my reaction for being upset at her tone.

"Why are you apologizing when you've done nothing wrong? Goddess, you humans are cute, but so strange sometimes." Fina apologizes for no reason too, but Eden seems to feel the need to apologize for everything. It's an annoying habit unique to humans, especially women.

Eden winces. "Sorry."

I shake my head at her apology for apologizing. "Eden. You're allowed to say what you think. Despite what seems to be conditioned into you, you're allowed to exist without apology. So stop."

She smiles ruefully. "I've tried! But it's easier said than done."

"Well, you have me now, and I'm going to call you on your nonsense."

She chuckles at my threat, small indents forming in her soft cheeks as the smile spreads across her face. "Thank you, Mezli. I've never met anyone quite like you...and I mean that in a good way!"

I preen a little at her compliment. "It's true. I'm one of a kind. But getting back to our original conversation, I'm the one who needs to apologize."

"You don't have to—"

"Yes, I do. I shouldn't have told you what to do. Goddess, I'm the biggest hypocrite in the galaxy, telling you to go back to safety."

Shame and memories from my first year on Spire flash through my mind. I wasn't safe then either. I was a young, dumb *xala* who'd never left home. It's a miracle I didn't end up robbed of all my credits during my first cycle on the station. No, that happened a couple of weeks into things.

"You're just trying to look out for me. It's very sweet. You're sweet." Eden's cheeks grow pink as she speaks, her melodic voice going soft. I've been so distracted by her pretty appearance that I didn't notice how alluring her voice is. It tingles down my spine, then spreads, pooling warm arousal in my core.

I resist the urge to flirt with her again, though I desperately want to. I'd thought my horniness was a byproduct of being around her at the same time as Phelix, but I haven't seen him in hours. This is just...Eden. Sweet, adorable, sexy Eden.

I clear my throat in an attempt to push that revelation aside. "Anyway! Now that it's settled that you're staying, what plans do you have for the rest of your time on Spire? Other than helping me seduce Phelix and stopping the exchange of dangerous schematics —all that boring spy stuff."

"Oh, mostly sightseeing..."

"Okay, comm me when you want to go out and I'll join you," I say, already thinking of all the places I could show her.

Her brows raise in alarm. "You don't have to do that!"

I frown at her, crossing my arms. "Yes, I do. There's no way I'm letting you wander around Spire alone. I'm not tattling about what happened to you to the agents, but in exchange, you're stuck with me as your shadow." I don't tell her that letting her out of my sight terrifies me after what happened earlier.

"But, uh..."

"But what? I know all the best places to go. Oooo, have you done a pleasure sim before? Those are open most of the night cycle so we could do that tonight!"

Eden blanches and I realize belatedly that I'm not giving her room to say what she wants to do. A bad habit of mine, according to Fina and Paul.

"Or we don't have to do that! What would you like to do?"

There. Look at me being considerate. Though when she takes more than a few seconds to consider, I feel like I'm going to burst from all the ideas I want to spew forth. I call on my social conditioning I've ignored since running away to Spire, forcing my expression to be placid. I'm out of practice so I can't keep my lower right hand from tapping against my thigh. Another bad habit that drove my mothers crazy.

Eden finally speaks, and I sigh with relief that I made it through waiting without exploding. "You have to promise me you won't laugh."

My agitation from keeping my ideas inside evaporates as curiosity sets in. I keep my face calm, the picture of refinement and understanding. "No laughter. You can tell me anything, sweet Eden."

She looks away and a flush spreads across her neck and chest. Goddess, she has a very pretty neck... Wait, what were we talking about?

"Say something!"

I realize I'm staring at her neck and totally missed what she said. I panic and say the most generic, reassuring thing I can think of. "That's no big deal."

She scowls at me.

Whoops, wrong answer.

"I'm thirty years old and I've never had sex! Of course that's a

EMILY ANTOINETTE

big deal! It's huge and embarrassing and I was going to go out and find a brothel and finally get rid of my v-card with whatever sexy alien will take my credits."

Yikes. My eyebrows shoot up before I can rein my reaction in, but luckily she's not looking directly at me as she explains her predicament. "Okay. Before I address the overall, uh, problem... what's a v-card? Is that some kind of special credit tab for sex?"

"It's a way of saying I haven't lost my virginity," she says, shame creeping into her voice.

I frown, feeling like I'm missing something—my translation chip must be malfunctioning. "You haven't lost your innocence? You're not pure? What does purity have to do with fucking?"

Eden presses a palm to her forehead with a sigh. "God, that would take far too long to explain. But in humanity's history, some cultures and religions thought that once you had sex, you became impure. Well, premarital sex. And that mostly applied only to women. Now it just means someone who hasn't had sex."

I can't keep the horror off of my face. "Goddess, humans are bizarre."

"Yeah, it's fucked up. But that's not the point! I need to get laid and I can't have you following me around when I go to do it." Eden throws her hands up in exasperation.

"'Get laid', now that one I know," I say, snorting at the human expression. "And yes, I absolutely can go with you to a brothel." Not that I particularly like the idea of her fucking some random alien, but I like the thought of her going out alone even less.

"But you're going about this the wrong way. Why should you pay someone to sleep with you when you're a rarity here? Any number of horny aliens would be happy to fuck you." I should stop there, but my damn mouth keeps going. "Myself, for one. Phelix

130

would volunteer too. I saw the way he was looking at you at lunch, even before someone tried to poison you."

She sputters, and I scramble to reassure her. "I know, I know. We need to keep things professional. Those were just examples to illustrate my point."

"Y-yeah, we should be professional. Right."

"As your colleague and foremost expert on finding sexy aliens to bang on Spire, I must insist you let me help you. Yes, a brothel is a 'safe' option. But do you want your first time to be safe, Eden? I get the impression you want to experience something wild and new. Meeting a stranger at a club and having a night cycle of debauched sex—now that's something you should try." Just imagining what would've happened if I'd met Eden out at a club makes my pulse quicken.

From the dazed look on her face, I think Eden is having similar thoughts. "I guess you have a point..."

"It's what I did when I first got to Spire. I was also a 'virgin'—I still can't get over how ridiculous a concept that is—when I ran away from home. Actually, that's one of the reasons I left..." My mood sours at the memory.

"You ran away because you hadn't had sex yet?" Eden asks, her brow furrowing. "Was it because you were scared to sleep with Phelix?"

"Hah! No." I can't hold back my scoff at the thought, but that's present-day Mezli talking. Past Mezli...she was a different person. "Fine, I guess that's one way of putting it. I was a 'virgin' and the thought of only sleeping with one person for the rest of my life scared me. Nexxit mates rarely take on other partners once they've fully bonded. It wasn't anything to do with Phelix in particular—though he didn't help matters by being a total ass when we met."

As I speak, it hits me. I've spent the past four years blaming him for why things didn't work, casting him as the villain in my dramatic tale. But if I truly think about my decision to leave home, the seeds for that urge were planted long before we met. He was just the thing to push me over the edge.

In some ways, I should be grateful to Phelix. If he wasn't such a jerk that night, I might still be back on Nexxa Itat, dying inside as I attended the same mind-numbing noble parties, pretending to be the perfect Princeps of House Frye.

Eugh. I grimace at the thought.

Eden places a hand on my shoulder and gives me a sympathetic smile. "You don't have to talk about the past if it makes you uncomfortable. I can only imagine how difficult it must be to have your past thrown in your face, let alone having to seduce someone you never wanted to see again."

I shake my head and pat the hand resting on my shoulder. Just feeling her hand on me soothes the scared *xala* still lurking inside me. "It's not that. Phelix is...not as terrible as he could be. I just hate self-reflection and profound realizations. It's much more fun to not think about how screwed up my mind is."

"At least you're aware that you do that. Although, I guess that on its own is a form of self-reflection..." Eden giggles as I deepen my frown for dramatic effect.

"So are we doing this tonight, or what?" I ask, eager to get back to the earlier subject and away from unpleasant thoughts.

"T-tonight?!" Eden asks, looking adorably flustered.

"If you wait, you'll overthink it." I wrap an arm around her shoulder and push her toward the door. "Come on. We're going to my place to find you something to wear, and then we're getting you laid!"

16

✦PHELIX✦

I try in vain to pay attention as the wizened vuloi drones on about the practical applications of *dresmil* excretions, but my mind refuses to stay in the crowded conference hall. No, it's still firmly focused on earlier events of the day.

Mezli's scent of her release on her fingers as she greeted me at lunch.

Eden's thick thigh as I tugged her skirt up.

Mezli's tongue tangling with mine.

Eden's flirtations and confession about remembering me during our comm conversation.

I'm so unfocused that I'd leave the lecture, but the last thing I need is for my peers to see the erections tenting my pants and assume I'm turned on by talk of excretions. Goddess, I need to get myself under control. I came here to learn and network, not obsess over *xalas*. You'd think I was an adolescent first discovering his cocks.

My hand finds its way into my satchel, and I start the ritual of rearranging my datapads as surreptitiously as I can so I don't disturb the other lecture attendees. I need order. If I can sort my things, I can sort my mind. After I've touched each pad, turned them off and on, and arranged them, I start to settle back into my rational mind. I sigh with relief as my cocks soften and retract.

That's better. It's time to remember why I came to Spire, because my professional reputation isn't the only thing at stake. Maybe I can move up the meeting and get this nerve-wracking business settled. *And then you'll be free to have some fun…*

Dammit, don't think about them again.

I swipe into my comm and open the secure channel with my contact.

> We need to move the drop-off up. Things have come up.

They don't need to know those things are my cocks.

A few minutes pass before I get a reply.

> Figure out your "things" on your own. The meet time is non-negotiable.

> Don't screw this up. People are counting on you.

So much for that idea. I close the channel and resign myself to enduring the rest of the lecture. Maybe by the time it's over, I'll have come up with a plan for how to deal with the intolerable arousal that's plaguing me.

✦

I'm able to make it out of the lecture and back to my hotel without embarrassing myself, but as soon as the door to my hotel suite slides closed, my Goddess-forsaken cocks extrude so fast it's almost painful. After two very unsatisfactory masturbation sessions in the shower, I'm still on edge, but at least my cocks have gone back inside me.

It's getting later in the night cycle, the artificial sky dark and the neon lights of Sagittarius district pouring in through the floor to ceiling windows of my suite. As I watch the multitude of aliens weaving through the walkways below, enjoying the nightlife the district has on offer, an idea emerges.

I need to fuck someone. Preferably tonight. Relieve some of the pressure so I can stop thinking with my cocks. My emotions and body's demands are so tangled up that I don't trust my judgment anymore. I desperately want to believe that Mezli's serious about giving our mating another chance, but is that real or is it just the bonding hormones talking? And where does Eden fit into things? It shouldn't be possible to want another person as much as my mate, and yet I do.

So yes, I need to find someone to sleep with so I can purge some of the arousal in my system and have any chance of figuring out what to do.

It's simple—in theory. With millions of aliens residing on Spire, there has to be at least a few thousand willing to sleep with me. I'll start at a nearby nightclub, but if that fails, there's always a brothel. I only wish that I didn't feel ill at the thought of sleeping with a stranger.

I dress in the most flattering shirt I brought with me that's casual enough to wear to a bar. I dislike the lack of sleeves, but at least the black coloring obscures most of my body shape. The pants aren't much better—I purchased them in a moment of rebellion against mother's constant "helpful advice" to wear the flowing garments in style on Nexxa Itat. They cling to my hips and thighs and will make any extrusions obvious. I can only hope that it'll serve as flattery to anyone I'm trying to seduce, rather than a means to call station security on the pervert who can't keep his cocks inside his slit.

As I wind my way through the walkways crowded with aliens enjoying the night cycle, the threat of getting hard wanes as nerves set in. I've never done this before. I haven't had sex in over four years. Why did I think this was a good idea?

I locate a nightclub, but the line to get in is daunting. At least a dozen scantily clad aliens with pristine grooming chatter excitedly as they wait their turn to enter. Maybe I should pick a less popular location... somewhere that doesn't have as pretty a clientele base. I could bribe my way in—I certainly don't lack the credits. But that won't solve the disparity between my attractiveness and the rest of the partiers.

When I back away to remove myself from the line, a startled voice chirps behind me. "Watch it!"

I turn and see an aespian, their light pink carapace covered in holographic glitter that sparkles in the neon glow of the club sign. "Apologies," I murmur, averting my eyes as I start to step away.

Their hand darts out and grabs my arm, stopping me. "Where do you think you're going?" they warble out in a melodic duotone.

"I was just leaving to meet friends elsewhere. If you'll excuse me..." I attempt to pull away, but they dig their fingers in harder.

"You're not going anywhere yet."

Shit. The aespian's eyes narrow, and I brace myself for insults or worse, a claim that I injured them and a demanded bribe for their silence on the matter. I've heard of many hapless nobles getting caught in such a scheme. Now I feel like an ass for laughing at their carelessness.

A striking seladin wearing a neon green tunic to match their cybernetic eye watches us in amusement over the aespian's shoulder. "Don't mind Gillea. That's her way of flirting. She dated a vuloi for too long and forgot that it's not polite to just grab strangers if you're attracted to them."

My eyes drop to the hand on my arm, then move back to the aespian's face in disbelief. "It is?"

Her antenna twitch, then droop slightly as she releases my arm and her mouth stretches into her species' equivalent of a smile. "It is. Hope I didn't scare you off. I didn't want to lose my shot with such a...*robust* nexxit. I love big."

The seladin's natural eye narrows. "That's rude, even for you, Gil."

Her wings flutter in embarrassment. "I didn't—that's not! Ugh, nevermind," Gillea says with a grimace and scurries out of line in a huff.

I nod my thanks to the seladin, catching their cybernetic eye scanning me idly as they keep their glowing white eye on my face.

They give me a fanged, apologetic smile. "Sorry about her. She means well, but doesn't understand that most people don't like being blatantly told they're someone's fetish."

"It's fine. Just unexpected. I can't say I've ever been sought out for my looks," I say with a sigh. My best option for finding someone interested in me just stormed off, as belittling as sleeping with her would've been.

"Surely you're joking," the seladin says, putting a hand on their hip as they blatantly appraise me. "Handsome face, nice arms, pretty eyes, strong hands. I can see the appeal, even without a fetish."

I blink back at them in surprise. This seladin is roguishly good-looking, with a hint of danger in the way they hold themself. Tall and leanly muscled with a sharp jaw and elegant glowing markings that compliment their charcoal skin. No one I'd ever expect to look at me twice.

They're objectively very attractive, even if I don't feel the pull of arousal like I do with Eden or Mezli. "Is that so?" I ask, still wary that I'm misinterpreting their intent.

"Well, I do have my share of fetishes, but I can't tell if you're a good fit for them just by looking at you," they say with a devilish grin.

Goddess, they're flirting with me. A surge of nerves hits me at the thought that my plan to have casual sex tonight might actually work. I swallow them down and smile back at the seladin. "Buy me a drink and maybe you'll find out."

17

 EDEN

I'm skeptical when Mezli brings me back to her place to find something for me to wear. She's petite and has four arms, with small perky breasts, while I'm round and thick, with enormous tits that need an industrial-strength bra to keep them in check. But she digs out a box from the back of her closet and dumps it out on her bed, then backs away and gestures down at the pile.

Shockingly, they all look made for a human with a similar build to mine. Or at least close enough that the stretchy material would make them suitable.

"Did these belong to Fina?" I ask.

I'm surprised when she flushes a darker pink and her hand goes to the back of her neck. She looks almost bashful.

"No. I, uh, I made it for her. I took her to a club when she first got to Spire and she had to wear some of my clothes. I thought the barely there look was hot, but she was so embarrassed that I wanted her to have things that fit. So I made her some outfits. Too many outfits."

"You made these?!" I card through the pile of bodysuits, tops, dresses, and more. They all look professionally made. "They're incredible! You're really talented."

Mezli grins at my compliment. "Thanks! I got a little carried away and ended up with a surplus. There's only so many times I can pretend to bring her outfits from a 'local boutique' before she notices I shouldn't have the credits from my day job to afford so many gifts."

"I don't understand. You didn't tell her you made the clothes?"

Her flush deepens. "I didn't want to make her feel like even more of an outsider. When she moved here, she was one of the only humans living on Spire. There weren't any shops selling clothes tailored for humans, and I didn't want that to be another thing to add to her list of why she didn't belong here. Fina's brave, but I know how tough it was for her to acclimate. Even with a gorgeous, delightful guide like me. I wanted her to stay—no, I needed her to stay. I mean, I obviously was fine on my own, but it was getting a bit...lonely."

The emotion in Mezli's voice surprises me. She comes off so carefree, but as I spend more time with her, the deeper, more complicated parts of her peek through. They make me like her even more.

"She's lucky to have such a generous and thoughtful friend," I say, placing my hand on top of one of hers. The touch sets off sparks across my palm, but I do my best to ignore it. Now's not the time to get turned on. I quickly pull my hand back and pick up a shimmering mesh bodysuit to keep myself from touching her more to feel that jolt again.

"Nah, I'm the lucky one. Fina was the one person who kept me sane when I ran away to Spire. She believed in me so much that it made me believe in myself. That's why I did my best to return the favor when she moved here."

Even though I don't get the sense that there's ever been anything romantic between Mezli and Fina, an odd pang of jealousy hits me. It's absurd getting jealous that she made these for Fina and not for me, but it doesn't stop it from happening.

Maybe she notices the shift in my demeanor, because she grabs a dress and shoves it toward me. "Enough about Fina and sappy nonsense! Try this on."

For a panicked moment, I think she wants me to get undressed right in front of her, but she gestures to a small hygiene room across the hall from her bedroom. "I'll go freshen up while you decide what to wear."

She heads into the other room and I hear the shower turn on. Knowing that she's naked across the hall while I'm getting changed does nothing to cool my heated thoughts. I slip on a dress, the slinky fabric caressing my skin in a way that makes me shiver. It's pretty, but isn't the best color for my complexion. I try on a few more things, but each one doesn't feel quite right. They're gorgeous, but obviously made with a different woman in mind.

I'm in the middle of tugging on a short, dark purple dress when the door to the bedroom swings open. I scramble to cover my ass and turn to see—oh *wow*. I stop caring about whether or not this dress fits right when I see what Mezli's wearing. Or rather, not wearing.

She has on a skintight white bodysuit that looks painted on. The cut of the legs shows off her wide hips, and a cutout at the midriff reveals her toned stomach. I realize now that we may be similar heights, but she's built like my polar opposite. It's an observation that she must be making too, and for a split-second I worry she'll think I look bad in this skimpy dress that dips so low in the bust that there's at least four inches of my cleavage on display.

"Fuck, you're so hot," Mezli says, dropping the brush in her hands absentmindedly as she assesses my outfit.

Just like that, the worry is gone. Which is good because the last thing I need tonight, when I'm going out to find someone to sleep with, is to be worried about my body shape. I'm fat and I've never cared beyond the annoyance of my gigantic tits. Why should I start caring now?

"Thanks, so are you!" I try to say it casually, like I would to a friend I was trying to hype up. It's hard to look away from her. Now that her sleek black hair is down from its usual ponytail, she's even more breathtaking.

She's still staring at me with her mouth agape, so I bend down and grab the brush for her to avoid staring back. She lets out a strangled squeak as I do.

Standing back up, I give her a questioning look. "Everything okay?"

"Yep! Your tits almost fell out, that's all."

Oh god. I shove the brush at her, and my other hand flies up to cover my chest.

She shakes her head at me adamantly. "Nope, I can already tell what you're thinking, but you're not getting changed. You look *perfect*. Abundant boobs ready to burst out of your dress at any moment is exactly the look you need if you want someone to sleep with you."

"A-are you sure? Do you at least have a jacket or something I can use to cover up with on the way to the club?"

"Hmm..." Mezli scans the pile on the bed, then snatches something that's definitely not a jacket. "Here you go!" She hands over a mesh top that's cut to only cover my arms and neck. "Better?"

Sensing I'm not going to win this argument, I slip it on. "I guess. Let's go before I back out of doing this."

.+

I SHOULD'VE BACKED out of doing this.

Mezli chatters the whole way to the nightclub, giving me so many seduction tips for aliens that my head is spinning by the time we get there.

Be direct and grab on to a vuloi to make my interest clear.

Compliment aespians on their antenna and talk a lot so they hear my pretty voice.

Mimic the movements and posture of ankites.

Get close to a shikzeth so they can scent me, but don't touch them until they give me permission.

Show off my neck to nexxit—that one explains why both Phelix and Mezli stare at my neck as much as a vampire would.

"Sorry, I don't have any tips for humans yet! My sample size was only two until a few days ago and one of them is my best friend so we didn't fuck. I was going to fuck Paul the night you got here, but alas...I'll have to wait to see if there's any fuss to be had about human men."

I let out a weak laugh. "I guess we're on even ground there. The only human man I tried to flirt with was 25 years my senior, and it did *not* go well."

Mezli waggles her eyebrows at me salaciously "Ooo, you like older men?"

"Hah, not really, but older people were the only option for me, and he was the first single person who moved to Europa 3 that wasn't old enough to be my grandfather."

I shouldn't use the past tense. I'm going back to Europa 3, and back to my lack of romantic prospects. Tonight is my shot and I'm going to make it count, but it'll be a blip on the unchanging horizon that is my life.

"Only old people live on Europa 3? That sounds unfeasible. What about technicians or spaceport workers? Eligible offspring visiting their parents?"

"There are all of those things, but they don't live on the planet. The farm bots and tech are mostly self-sufficient and things are so spread out that I rarely encountered anyone from off-world. I guess I could've hung out at the spaceport, but it was only staffed when residents had a scheduled transport."

"So it's *that* level of rural." Mezli's eyes widen.

"Yeah. It's beautiful and I understand why people retire there. Each homestead is almost completely self-sufficient. The only thing they need around on a regular basis is a doctor. Me."

"Shit, that's way too much pressure on one person! Aren't you afraid someone will get sick while you're away?"

My stomach sinks as she cuts to the heart of one of my many fears about leaving Europa 3. "There's a temporary medic covering things while I'm gone. Hiring them is draining the maintenance funds that everyone pays into, so it's not a permanent solution."

"Hold on." Mezli speaks so loudly that half the club line turns to look. "They're not paying their live-in medic as much as they're paying a *temporary* worker?"

My face grows hot at her indignant exclamation and the attention of people who've turned to see why she's shouting. "W-well, no. Most people don't want to live on Europa 3, so they have a hard time getting anyone to come at all. Hence the increased payment for the temp."

She frowns. "Do they at least subsidize your housing and living costs?"

"I live with my parents and pay for my own groceries so, uh, no. They don't." A pit is forming in my stomach the longer this conversation goes on. I'd never even considered that could be something I'm entitled to.

Mezli grabs my shoulders and brings her face so close to mine that I can feel her warm breath ghost across my cheek. "Eden. They're exploiting you. I don't care that your parents live there. That setup is ridiculous."

"It-it is?" She's so intense right now that the overwhelming urge to apologize for making her upset bubbles up and spills out of my mouth. "Sorry, I didn't realize..."

She sighs dramatically at my words, her hands squeezing my shoulders tighter, and pierces me with her dark gaze. "You need to start demanding more from life. Otherwise, people will keep exploiting you. You deserve better. Take what you need with no apologies."

Take what you need with no apologies. She says it with such conviction that I'm moving before I consciously realize it, smashing my lips to hers.

Reason resurfaces a second later and I pull away before I can let myself register or enjoy the contact, then immediately do what she just told me not to. "Sorry! I'm—"

She growls at me and grabs the back of my head, tugging me back into a kiss. She bends me to her will with her lips and tongue, taking control of my senses until all I can feel is her and the need for *more.*

When she's had her fill, and not a moment sooner, she pulls

back and lets go of my hair. An ankite in line behind us clears their throat to indicate that we're holding things up. Mezli uses her lower hands to make a rude gesture at them, and stands her ground, keeping her eyes on me.

"See how good no apologies feels?"

"Y-yeah..." I'm breathless and weak-kneed in the aftermath of that kiss.

"Good! Now let's get in there and find you someone to seduce." As if flipping off a switch, she shifts back to her casual, friendly demeanor. Like she didn't just alter the core of my being with one kiss.

18

✦MEZLI✦

The club I've chosen for tonight isn't one of my usual haunts, but I didn't want to worry about running into past dates and jilted lovers. I wore something less flashy than normal to keep the focus on Eden, but I doubt that'll be an issue, because she looks mouthwatering. There isn't an alien on Spire—at least one that's not actively anti-human—that wouldn't jump at the chance for a night with her.

Shit, *I* want a night with her. That kiss was unreal. Most of the alien races on Spire picked up the act of tangling tongues after contact with nexxit, so it doesn't come as naturally to them. Ankites aren't bad because they're excellent at mimicry, but if that's how all humans kiss, then even I've got some things to learn. It feels like I'm coursing with adrenaline and arousal, lit up by Eden's lips against mine.

Why the hell am I so adamant about staying "professional", when all I want to do is take her back home and find out what she tastes like everywhere? I'm not the kind of *xala* who cares about blurring lines or taking what I want. So why is it different with Eden? Something about this pretty human makes me feel...vulnerable. Like it would actually matter for once if I screwed things up with her. Which is absurd, since she's leaving in a handful of days.

Goddess, I should find someone to fuck tonight, too. I've been aching with unfulfilled need since I encountered Phelix and it just keeps building. If I don't find release with something other than my hands soon, I might combust. But how am I supposed to get laid when I'm not letting Eden go off anywhere without me trailing behind to keep her safe? She doesn't know that part yet, so it'll be a good chance to practice my sneaky spy skills before I need to use them with Phelix.

The fates must have an ironic sense of humor, because as soon as my mind goes to my mate, the crowded dance floor parts to reveal him over by the bar. There's a tall, thin seladin practically sitting in his lap, squeezing his thigh and letting out a low chuckle at something he just said.

What the *fuck*. Rage floods my vision. How dare they touch my mate! How dare he let someone touch him like that?

That's it, I'm done. I don't want to have anything to do with him —fuck the mission, fuck him.

"Ouch, Mezli, that's too hard!" Eden winces as I accidentally crush her hand I was holding to guide her toward the bar.

I release her, but can't take my eyes off Phelix as he leans in to whisper something to the seladin, who slides their hand further up his thigh. That trash looks like they want to jerk him off in the middle of the club. At least have the decency to go into a hygiene stall!

"What's wrong? What are you looking at—*oh*." Eden's gaze follows mine and I don't think I imagine the slight disappointment in her voice when she sees Phelix with someone else.

I'm storming over to him, ready to claw the seladin's glowing eyes out before my brain catches up with my anger.

What the hell am I doing? Why do I even care? He's not mine. It's just these damn hormones pumping through me, making me unhinged.

I stop abruptly, attempting to abort my attack before he notices me, and Eden crashes into my back, knocking me with enough force to push me forward and right into the flirting couple.

I slam into the seladin's chest, who makes a sound of surprise and grabs me around the waist. "Whoa there, darling. No need to fall into my lap if you want me to buy you a drink. You could just ask."

Their honeyed, flirtatious voice startles me, and when I look up into their face, I see a familiar cybernetic eye. "Hadrell?" I ask, pushing myself back up to my feet and smoothing down my hair.

"Mezli!" they say, sounding equally surprised.

Phelix's eyes dart between the two of us before narrowing in distaste as he looks at me. "You two know each other?"

"A little. We had a brief but memorable time together, but she's not the type to be tied down," Hadrell says, winking at me.

I honestly thought they'd be a little more pissed if I ever saw them again. I met the handsome seladin pirate out at a club with Fina and Maerlon. We hit it off, and I went back to their ship for what indeed was a very memorable time together. But I wasn't about to get tangled up with a space pirate who only was on Spire for a week or two, so I did what I do best—I ran away.

"She certainly isn't," Phelix says drolly.

"Ah, so you know Mezli, too!" Hadrell chuckles and reaches out to touch my arm playfully. Normally I'd bask in their attention, but it does nothing for me tonight. I still want to shove them away from Phelix, then yell at him for flirting with the hot seladin.

Phelix levels a stony glare at Hadrell, the ease they were sharing before I interrupted gone. "Obviously not as well as you do."

Why is he acting jealous? I'm the one that found him about to get a handjob at the bar.

Hadrell raises a dotted brow at the sudden mood shift. "Right. Well, it's been nice talking with you both, but I don't make a habit of getting in the middle of...whatever this is," they say, gesturing between me and Phelix. "If you'll excuse me, I think I see a delectable human over there who looks lonely."

"She's with me!" I say, panicking at their interest in her. Hadrell would be a perfect candidate to help Eden out tonight. They're charming, respectful, and amazing in bed. But I find myself frowning and wanting to go over and clutch at Eden to show she's mine. She's *not* mine. I need to find a way to get rid of that unhelpful impulse before I ruin her night.

"With you, or *with* you?" Hadrell asks, but then shakes their head at my frown. "Nevermind. Too messy."

They slide a few credits to the bartender and put a hand on Phelix's shoulder. "Good luck," they say with a knowing smirk, then head off into the club.

"Who was that?" Eden asks, stepping up to join me. "Hello, Dr. Nafar," she adds with a shy smile.

"Just an old acquaintance," I say, hooking an arm around her waist. The tension in my chest eases having her near. Damn, how the hell am I going to find her someone to hookup with tonight

SPACE FOR MORE

when even Hadrell, someone I trust not to hurt her, made me feel possessive?

"Nice to see you again, Dr. Mori," Phelix says, his eyes dipping to the deep line of her cleavage before darting back up as he swallows heavily.

My stomach clenches watching him check out Eden, but unlike with Hadrell, it's with strange arousal instead of anger.

"Sorry for ruining your night," Eden says, ducking her head with a flush as she notices Phelix's interest.

"Don't be. You didn't," he says, sounding almost relieved.

That's not the reaction I was expecting to us breaking up his flirting with the attractive seladin. "You weren't into Hadrell?"

"Not really." He doesn't expand on the answer, but his frown does the talking for him.

"So why were you letting them feel you up? You're that desperate?" I ask, a bit too much bite to my tone betraying my jealousy.

He flinches at the jab, and rather than feeling glee at the way my insult landed, there's a stab of regret. Finding weaknesses and exploiting them is a sport amongst the noble houses of Nexxa Itat. It's why we're trained to read micro-expressions and suppress our own. If he reacted, it's because it's a very painful topic for him. And there's a stupid, soft part of me that doesn't want to cause him that kind of pain. Annoyance and regret, yes. Self-hatred, not so much.

"I'm *joking*, Phelix."

He doesn't react. Shit, I really struck a nerve.

I should grab some drinks and leave him to wallow, but it's bothering me seeing him hurt. It's also bothering me that he was trying to sleep with Hadrell when he didn't really want to. He must be struggling with the same bonding hormones I am. The only difference is I have Eden in tow and can't go off to fuck a stranger to try to deal with them.

"Are you enjoying your time on Spire?" Eden asks in an obvious attempt to make the conversation less awkward.

His stiff posture eases slightly. "It's been alright. Better now that you're here."

Eden's flush deepens and she giggles.

I should be pissed that Phelix is flirting with someone while I'm literally standing right next to him, but it sends a thrill of excitement through me. These bonding hormones are so fucking weird.

An idea forms as I take in their mutual interest, paired with my lack of jealousy. I know how I can help Eden get laid *and* carry out the next step of our mission.

"Can you excuse us for a minute, Lord Nafar? I need to ask Eden a private question."

He nods and stands, grabbing his drink off the bar. "Of course. Have a pleasant evening."

"You're leaving?" Eden asks, sounding more than a little disappointed.

Oh yes, this is the perfect plan. I'm brilliant.

"He's not." I push him back down onto the barstool. "Be a good *xalar* and sit still while I go chat with our lovely human friend. If you listen, I'll even let you buy us a drink." I wink and turn away, tugging Eden behind me.

Once we're far enough away to not be overheard, I pull her close. Phelix's eyes track every movement, darkening at what might appear to be an intimate moment between us. I can't tell which one of us his jealous hunger is directed at, but it excites me far more than it should.

"What's up?" Eden asks, crossing her arms under her chest and drawing my eyes down to her amazing tits. "Is being around Phelix making things too weird? Because I was thinking...tonight might be the perfect chance for you to seduce him. He can't stop staring at you, and I could be wrong, but I think he was out looking for someone to take back to his hotel. Why else would he have been chatting up that seladin he wasn't really even into? Or out at a nightclub for that matter?"

I nod. "I thought the same thing, Agent Mori. Operation Honey Pot is a go tonight, but with one minor adjustment." I glance back at Phelix, then lower my voice and lean in to whisper conspiratorially.

Eden giggles at my spy lingo. "What's that, Agent Frye?"

"I'm not the one seducing the target. You are."

19

✦PHELIX✦

A slender ankite wearing an elaborate and uncomfortable-looking waist cincher steps up to take my drink order as I watch Mezli pull Eden closer. Jealousy and arousal slam into me at the sight of the enticing pair pressed close together, the air between them charged with desire.

It reminds me of the night four years ago, when I sat across a bar watching the most beautiful *xala* I'd ever seen seducing their companion. I sip my drink, trying to push the memories away with the burn of harsh aespian liquor, but they stubbornly remain.

The low rumble of conversation floods my senses as I attempt to focus on my companions for the evening. My coworkers insisted on taking me out tonight to celebrate my mating. It's pathetic that I have no actual friends to celebrate this momentous occasion with. At the very least, my siblings should be the ones dragging me out the night before the big meeting, but they're too busy. So I'm stuck making small talk with coworkers I barely know. I don't mean to be ungrateful for their kindness, but it's embarrassing.

I suppose being out in a loud, crowded bar is better than sitting at home with my thoughts. Can't spiral into despair while you have to put on a pleasant face for others. One of mother's many lessons she drilled into me since adolescence, though she's far more of an expert at feigning cheer in the face of despair and displeasure.

I wear my smile like a mask as I listen to Ghrest spout advice for my first meeting with my mate. The slightly graying xalar *has been mated for four decades, so I suppose he'd know. His words slip off my mind as I sip my drink slowly. Drinking too much is a bad idea. That's when it gets hard to keep up my facade. When thoughts of her come unbidden.*

Goddess, how did I get here?

I didn't want to find my mate. I'd already met a wonderful xala. *But Ristan was an alien and a "lower status"* seladin *at that, so Mother would've done anything to end our relationship. After months of jabs from the queen of subtle cruelty, Ristan finally had enough and ended our engagement.*

I didn't even have time to mourn the relationship before Mother revealed she'd found my mate, knowing it'd be the easiest way to force me into an "acceptable" relationship. What nexxit *can turn away a Goddess-given gift of a true mate?*

So here I am, spending my last night before meeting my mate in a futile attempt to forget what I've lost.

"And that's why you should create an excuse to speak alone with your mate as soon as possible!" My coworkers all laugh at the story Ghrest was telling, and I pretend to laugh along with them, despite the pit in my stomach.

"Anyone else need drinks?" I offer, gesturing over toward the bar and the mostly empty glasses at our table. *Mine is still mostly full, but after their kindness, buying my companions another round is the courteous thing to do. They all nod and give me their orders with thanks. I try to keep the distaste off my face when I approach the crowded, slightly sticky bar and place the drink orders. It's dark, loud, and has the faint odor of cheap* jefl'ka *and desperation. Not a place I'd ever voluntarily choose to visit, but from the din and press of bodies, it's obvious that plenty of others see an appeal.*

Someone stumbles into me as I'm grabbing the drinks, and half the liquid inside the glasses sloshes over the rim and onto the bar.

"Oops!"

I turn around, ready to give whatever drunken imbecile that knocked into me my most withering glare, and freeze.

Goddess. The nexxit before me is shorter than me by at least two hands, with a slinky black dress that clings everywhere. I can see her nipples outlined through the fabric. Not that I'm looking intentionally, it just...damn, she's stunning. She has the most sinful expression on her face, cheeks flushed as she gives me a lopsided smirk before turning back to her companion—a lithe nexxit with wavy dark hair and a skintight black jumpsuit cut down to her navel. The xala *in the jumpsuit orders them another round of drinks and when they arrive, the tipsy beauty unceremoniously downs both of them.*

"Baby, slow down. We've got all night," the xala *in the jumpsuit purrs, leaning in to nip at the other* xala's *slender neck.*

My eyes stay glued on the pair, though I know I shouldn't stare. There's nothing out of the ordinary about xala *couples—the Goddess herself was mated to the Divine Mother. There's just something about the one in the dress that makes my blood feel heated in a way I've never experienced. Not even with Ristan. She has the most wicked expression on her face, her cheeks flushed from the drink and her arousal obvious as she drapes herself over her companion and licks a stripe up her neck, letting out a hum of pleasure.*

I tear my gaze away. I've got to get myself under control. Only perverts stare at xalas *like I am right now. As I walk back to my coworkers, the pair heads to the hygiene room and a wild part of me wants to follow. Instead, I down the rest of my drink, then make excuses to my coworkers about wanting to be fresh for tomorrow evening. I'm not in my right mind if I'm lusting after a* xala *who wouldn't even be interested in me.*

The same hum of pleasure I heard that night tugs me out of the past, and just like that night, my cocks threaten to extrude when I hear it. Mezli and Eden have returned. I take a deep breath and turn to look at my tormentors.

It's unfair how lovely Mezli is. Her white bodysuit clings to the curve of her hips, which are more generous than the night I first saw her. Her cascade of jet black hair begs me to sweep it to the side and taste the long, elegant line of her neck and let her intoxicating mating pheromones claim me. She makes it far too easy to forget that she's the one who ran from our mating. I want to fall to my knees and beg for her forgiveness for whatever I did to chase her away. I want to do everything I can to prove I'm worthy of basking in her radiance, though I knew from the moment I saw her how undeserving I am. She knew it, too—otherwise, why would she have literally gotten sick after being in my presence and then fled to the other side of the system?

And Eden? Unlike the night I first saw my mate, I can't ignore the *xala* at her side. She's as compelling as Mezli, her soft, luscious body far too tempting in her tight purple dress. Her eyes sparkle with bright curiosity behind her glasses, and a depraved part of me wants to see her look at me like that as I cover them in my spend. It feels wrong to desire Eden with the same fire I have for my

Goddess-chosen mate, but I can't control it. The complimentary beauty of them together, appearances so different yet perfectly matched, makes it hard for me to think straight.

"Mmm, hope we didn't keep you waiting too long," Mezli says. She pulls out the stool next to mine and gestures for Eden to sit, sliding between them to grab one of the drinks I ordered. She takes a long sip of the iridescent cocktail, draining more than half the glass with ease.

I hold the other drink out to Eden, but she shakes her head. "I, uh, I'm already feeling a bit wobbly, so alcohol probably isn't a great idea right now."

Of course. I'm such an idiot. Here I am wrapped up in my lustful thoughts and forgetting she went through anaphylactic shock earlier. I can't keep the flash of worry from crossing my face, but fortunately, humans seem to be much less judgmental of outward displays of emotion than my nexxit peers.

"You shouldn't be here," I say sternly, as fear for her safety slithers up my spine.

Eden blanches. "I can go. I'm sorry for bothering you." Her words earn her a glare from Mezli, but she huffs back at her. "What? I'm allowed to apologize when it's obvious I'm bothering someone!"

"I don't think our dear Lord Nafar is bothered by your presence, sweet Eden," Mezli purrs in a voice that's better suited for the bedroom than this crowded bar.

If I were smart, I'd tell Eden she's right. I can't handle being near her, or Mezli for that matter. I should get up, go back to my hotel room, and shut myself in there until my meeting later this week. Being around these *xalas* is dangerous. It has me letting my guard down, and hoping for things I can't possibly have. Better to be rude and be done with them so I can go back to the safety of solitude.

I *should* say that, but what comes out of my mouth is a soft chuckle. "You're far from a bother, Dr. Mori." My fingers twitch, wanting to reach out and caress her cheek like I did earlier. "I only worry about your health. You shouldn't be out after what happened earlier. It could be dangerous."

"Yeah, yeah, I told her the same thing, but she gave me a *very* compelling reason why I couldn't keep her locked up at her hotel when she's not at the conference. Why don't you tell him why we're out?" Mezli gives Eden a wicked smile, nudging her with an elbow.

Eden's eyes grow as wide as an aespians, and her flush deepens. "Oh god, you can't be serious!"

"You're going to have to tell him at some point tonight," Mezli replies with a shrug.

Their strange discussion feels like I'm the brunt of some unknown joke. "Tell me what?" I bristle internally, but keep my tone low and even. If they're going to mock me, I don't want to give them the satisfaction of seeing it land like Mezli's earlier insult did.

Mezli looks expectantly at Eden, who opens and closes her mouth a few times, a hand coming up protectively to her chest like she's preparing to defend herself from my response to whatever she's going to say.

Mezli rolls her eyes. "Ugh, it's not that big of a deal, she's just never—"

"Fuck, fine! I'm a virgin," Eden blurts out in a high-pitched squeak.

There must be some alternate human meaning to the term that's getting lost in translation, but after a moment I put the pieces together. We spoke at length when I was assisting her with her medipod, and talk turned to her isolation and lack of life experience. By innocent and untouched, she means she's never had sex.

A flush rises on my cheek. Why are they telling me this?

"It means she's never fucked," Mezli adds crassly, mistaking my surprise as confusion.

"Ah." My voice stays calm, but inside I'm vibrating. "And this has relevance to me because...?" I take a swig from my drink to mask any reaction I might have to what she says next.

Mezli reaches out to toy with one of Eden's short curls, then slides her hand down to rest on her shoulder as the human's breathing speeds up. "Well, you see, our lovely Eden here was hoping to change that tonight. And you appeared to be searching for some companionship for the night cycle until I so rudely interrupted."

I almost choke on my drink, and it burns as I force it down. She can't possibly... Is Mezli seriously saying she wants *me* to sleep with Eden? "W-what?!" I stare at the two of them, slack-jawed as all the blood in my body rushes to my cocks.

Eden winces at my reaction. "I'm so sorry, Phelix! This was a ridiculous idea. It's just that you've been so kind to me since we met and I've been waiting so long to do this and it could be my only chance while I'm here... I would never have even presumed, but Mezli said it was okay and that you seemed interested in me. Just forget it!"

My stunned excitement vanishes, replaced by cold realism and anger. "You want me to fuck you because I'm nice, an easy option, and my mate doesn't want me?" I can't keep the bite out of my tone. I'd thought maybe Eden was different, but someone who's legitimately interested in me wouldn't ask for sex because I'm convenient.

"N-no! Not at all." Eden shakes her head emphatically, brow

furrowing. "I'm very attracted to you! When you sent me that message earlier, I couldn't stop imagining what it would be like. What being with you would be like."

"When he messaged you earlier?" Mezli's mouth downturns, but I detect more curiosity than jealousy in her tone. Why would she be jealous? From what Eden said, Mezli doesn't have any interest in me. This all is some amusing game for her, pushing us together like dolls.

I hate myself for even considering it. Only a fool would agree to such an arrangement. And yet, something inside my chest swells at Eden's confession. It's the fragile and pathetic urge to be wanted I've forced down for my entire life.

Goddess, no wonder I craved it—even this miniscule taste of genuine interest feels *amazing*. With my ex, Ristan, I always sensed that she was settling for me. Mutual respect and affection bonded us, but I wasn't her type physically. What would it feel like to fuck someone who genuinely finds me appealing? What would it be like to experience release from the touch of someone enthusiastic about my body? That's never happened, even when I'm alone.

Father's order to be reckless bubbles up in my mind, swirling together with my yearning and arousal.

Fuck it. I'm not going to refuse a gift like Eden. I'll deal with the consequences later.

"I'm honored that someone as beautiful and intelligent as you would choose me for this, Eden," I say, my voice husky with the strain of my desperate need now that I've surrendered to it.

She blinks back at me rapidly, obviously not expecting that answer. "Honored as in, 'thanks but I just see you as a peer' or as in 'it would be my honor to do this with you'?"

Mezli answers for me. "Oh, he wants to." Her eyes fall pointedly to the bulge in my far too tight pants with a grin, then return to my face, assessing me.

None of this makes sense. Even if this is just a game to her, her mating hormones should make her furious that I'm considering sex with someone other than her. So why does Mezli look so damn excited?

Mezli scoffs, like she can read my thoughts. "Ugh, but he's worried he shouldn't, because I'm his mate. You don't have to worry about that. I'm fine with it. I'll come too."

I let out a choked sound of surprise, that Eden echoes. "What?!"

"I'm not letting Eden go off alone with you, even if you seem trustworthy. So I'm going to come with you and make sure she's okay," Mezli says, placing a protective hand on Eden's shoulder.

"Absolutely not." I reply immediately. It doesn't stop the image of Mezli sitting in my suite's bedroom chair, her legs swung over the arms to splay herself wide as she watches me pound into Eden.

"Mezli..." Eden's pulse ticks in her neck, her breathing rapid and her pupils dilated. Oh Goddess, she's aroused by the idea too.

"Calm down," Mezli says with a breathy chuckle. She's not as unaffected by the thought as she pretends. She *likes* it. "I don't mean watch you fuck. I'll be in the other room to make sure nothing goes awry."

"Oh." Eden worries her lower lip between her teeth. "I mean, I wouldn't mind if you watched. Or joined us," she confesses, her cheeks turning bright red.

Mezli's eyes widen and dart between me and Eden, her breath coming rapidly and her nipples peaked against her tight bodysuit.

My head spins, but for the first time since running into my mate, I've found a way to gain some control. If I'm making myself vulnerable, so is she.

"Hmm, I don't know if she could handle both of us," I say, giving Mezli an assessing look.

Mezli's brows shoot up. "I-Is that a challenge, Lord Nafar?" she asks, her cocky demeanor faltering for a moment.

I smirk, finally feeling like I'm no longer at a disadvantage in our bizarre dynamic. "You know, I'm starting to like it when you call me that. You should use my title in the bedroom, too. Because by the end of the night, both of you will be begging me for my cocks as you worship me from your knees."

"Oh my god," Eden gasps, her breath hitching.

All three of us stand in silence as we wait to see if Mezli will take the bait. Will she tell me to fuck off and that I'll be the one begging for her? Or will she like the idea of being forced to heel? Fuck, does it even matter? Either scenario has my cocks swelling, eager at the prospect of being with these *xalas*.

A slow grin stretches across Mezli's face. "Alright. But you're not calling the shots tonight, *Phelix*."

I can't say I'm shocked at her objecting to me taking control. Though she surprises me with what she says next. "Eden will set the pace. She'll decide what she wants from us."

"I will?" Eden asks, breathless at the idea.

"Yes." Mezli and I say in unison, finally in total agreement.

It's the best scenario. Neither of us will have the upper hands.

"O-okay." Eden smiles up at us through her glasses, shy but eager. "I never thought my first time would involve two..." She trails off as her gaze falls to my groin.

Mezli lets out a peal of laughter. "Oh sweet Eden, get ready for the night of your life."

20

✦EDEN✦

I've had over a decade to imagine what my first time would be like. For a few years, I imagined that a traveling repair technician would see me from across a field as I was working up a sweat in the mid-day heat, and be so overcome that they had to claim me right there in the dirt of my family's farm. Then, the ill-begotten fantasies about Artem, the older man who would teach me about my body and all the ways to pleasure him with a gentle but firm hand. I even dreamed about what it would be like with the brilliant alien doctor when our comms a year ago grew more personal. But in all my fantasies, I never thought it would be with two people, let alone the two most attractive aliens I've ever seen.

Part of me thinks I must've had a bad reaction to the meds

Phelix gave me earlier, and this is just a fever dream. Though, my imagination wouldn't be this wild.

I chatter nervously the whole way from the club to Phelix's hotel, but as the door to his room slides open, I fall silent in awe. This isn't a hotel room, it's a penthouse.

"Only the best for the noble lord, eh?" Mezli asks, her tone laced with mockery. I guess she's seen places like this loads of times in the past. I can't imagine it was easy to give up a lifestyle where she'd get to stay in places like this. When she casually strides into the living area and sets a hip on the back of the sleek couch, letting the glow of the false fireplace wash over her rosy skin, she looks made for this level of luxury.

Me, on the other hand, I'm ridiculously out of place. The light fixtures alone look like they cost more than my parents' farm. I knew that Mezli and Phelix were nobility, but I didn't process what that truly meant until now. This place is the kind of fancy where I'm afraid to touch anything and sully it with my unrefined presence.

Phelix picks up on my trepidation, placing a hand on my lower back and guiding me further inside. "Can I get you something to help you feel more at ease, Eden?" His touch does the opposite of putting me at ease, and I inhale sharply as his palm slips down to rest just above the curve of my ass.

He quickly removes his hand and gives me a concerned look. "If you're not comfortable with this...with me touching you, it's okay. We don't have to do anything you're not ready for."

"No, god, I'm so ready!" I blurt, wishing he'd put all four of his hands on me.

He chuckles and steps closer, his thick, solid body on the cusp of pressing against mine but not actually touching me. Leaning down, he brings his mouth closer to my ear and I'm embarrassed by how loudly my breath hitches.

"Don't tell Mezli, but I'm nervous too," he whispers. "It's been a long time. Now there are two gorgeous *xalas* in my suite and I can only pray to the Goddess that I won't make a fool of myself before we even make it to the bedroom." His tone is teasing, but there's a genuine thread of vulnerability beneath it.

"Whatever happens, I appreciate you doing this. With me. With *us*." I gesture over to Mezli, who's moved to the kitchen, poking around and pointedly giving us space to talk.

"It's my absolute pleasure. I'll use all the skills I possess—even if they are a bit rusty—to make it your pleasure, too. I may need some of your expert advice on human anatomy. I know the basics, but trust you'll teach me the finer details of your body."

My core clenches at the way his voice deepens into a seductive rasp. I chuckle, pretending that I'm adept at flirting and not silently freaking out about how this is *finally* happening. "You're not an expert on human physiology, Dr. Nafar? I'm shocked."

"Oh, and you're any more versed in nexxit bodies, Dr. Mori?"

"I've studied nexxit anatomy. I know what you have going on in the most general sense." I wave my hand toward his crotch and his lip quirks. I don't admit that the study was because of my crush I developed on him last year.

My eyes dart over to Mezli, who's making herself at home in the suite's kitchen, pouring herself a full glass of wine. Shit, I still haven't told her that I know Phelix. I should've told her from the start, but I was scared she'd tell the agents and they'd send me packing.

I should call this off. The already blurry lines between our mission and my attraction to both of them are vanishing altogether. Mezli's hastily concocted plan for tonight was for me to get laid and for her to use the fresh decryption key the agents dropped off at my hotel room to hack into Phelix's datapads while he's distracted. It sounded perfect, at least until I lost my mind and asked her to join us. Now it's devolved into a threesome that doesn't help with the mission at all.

I want sex, and god, I want it with these two. But can I really prioritize getting laid over galactic security? My gut tells me that Phelix wouldn't do what the agents claim he's planning, but maybe that's just my attraction speaking. Do I really know anything about who he is after a few weeks of chatting about medical equipment and mild flirting?

Mezli raises two empty glasses toward us with a questioning look. "Drinks?"

I shake my head. Some alcohol would help me relax, but I need to clear my head. Which is growing increasingly harder with Phelix so close to me.

"Need to be drunk to stomach being with your mate?" Phelix asks coolly.

She scoffs and downs the glass of wine like it's water.

"That answers that question." Phelix steps away, and though his expression is placid, I can tell he's hurt.

I can't say I'm not a little hurt, either. Hurt and frustrated that she's getting drunk when she's supposed to be my partner on this godforsaken mission.

This was a mistake.

PHELIX

MEZLI ROLLS her eyes at me, setting the wine bottle down. "Relax. I'm not getting drunk." She pours another glass and refills her own, but not as much as before.

"Could've fooled me," I say, leveling her with a glare to disguise how much her need to be intoxicated hurts. I'm not sure why I expected anything different from the *xala* who got wasted and fucked a stranger the night before meeting her mate.

She lets out a humorless laugh. "Just playing into your concept of me. You know, being a drunken slut and all."

Eden gasps beside me, but I barely register it as realization sets in. I recall the despair-filled conversation I had with my sister when she commed to see how meeting my mate was going.

"I can't do this, Quila. Goddess, I can't."

"Calm down. Take a deep breath and think. Surely your mate isn't that bad. You've only just met her."

"No, I can't calm down! I gave up everything for this? She's barely said two words the whole evening. She can't keep up with a basic conversation!"

"Phelix. She's probably terrified and overwhelmed. Meeting your mate is life changing. Give her some time to adjust."

"That's not it! I saw her. I was out with work friends last night and saw her. She was shitfaced and crawling all over another xala. *The night before meeting her mate! I'm supposed to just accept that my mate is a dimwitted, drunken slut?"*

My indignant anger bleeds from me, leaving only shame and horror behind. "You... Oh Goddess, that's why you left. You heard..."

Mezli stares back at me, her expression frigid. "Yep."

My own stony guard slams down as my mind attempts to block out the pain of knowing for certain that *I* was the reason she ran away. Not my appearance or my family name or Mezli being selfish. My actions cost me my mate. Fuck.

I grit my teeth and brace myself for Mezli to run away again.

Eden shifts beside me, and I reluctantly turn to look at her, ready to see a similar disgust in her eyes. But all that's there is sadness and concern. She shocks me when she reaches out and places a hand on top of mine.

"Please don't do that," she whispers.

"Do what?" I ask, not understanding.

"Shut yourself off. Pretend like nothing is wrong. This is your chance to make things right," she says, squeezing my hand. Willing me to listen with her reassuring touch.

I freeze. Am I so obvious that this innocent human can read me with such ease?

"I... I can't," I whisper.

Eden rolls her eyes at me, surprising me with her reaction again. "Don't be absurd. If I can travel halfway across the galaxy and be brave enough to have an alien threesome, you can let your guard down for long enough to tell your damn mate that you're sorry."

Mezli scoffs. "You don't know much about nexxit nobility, do you? They don't apologize. That'd be admitting weakness. Lord Nafar would rather cut off his cocks than admit he fucked up."

Her assessment hits me like a slap to the face, stinging but bringing me to my senses. My feet carry me to the kitchen, and I tentatively reach out to touch Mezli's arm. "Mezli, I should never have—

She bats me away with a scowl. "Don't touch me!"

I pull my hand back and do the only other thing I can think of to show her just how wrong she is.

I fall to my knees at her feet.

"What are you doing? Get up!" Mezli squeaks in surprise as I look up at her in supplication.

"I know nothing I do will ever make what happened that night right. Goddess, I would never have said those things if I wasn't so upset, and I certainly would never have said them for you to hear." My voice trembles as I speak, and I beg her silently with my eyes to take me at my word.

Mezli stares down at me, mouth agape. Anger, surprise, pain, and confusion all flash across her face before she speaks. "Well, you did say them. And I heard them. Now get up off the floor and stop being so weird!"

I don't move. I won't move until she understands my sincerity. "No."

"What do you mean, 'no'?" Mezli shoves at my shoulders but I stay in place. "Get up! I don't need your pity. I told you, I don't care what you think of me. Yes, the stupid, weak *xala* I was four years ago was hurt by your careless words. I'm not her anymore. I'm so much more than you could've ever imagined."

A rueful smile forms on my lips. "You've always been a goddess, Mezli. From the moment I saw you, I knew. I was jealous of your lover and upset about losing my previous partner from my mother's machinations, so I said some abhorrent things in a moment of weakness to my sister. But it had nothing to do with finding you lacking. No, my own deficits were to blame. I know I'll never hope to deserve you."

"What do you mean from the moment you saw me?" Mezli's brow furrows as she glares down at me. "You looked at me like I was an abomination when we met! And what lover? You're not making any sense, Phelix."

"That wasn't the first night I saw you," I say with a sigh. "I was out at a bar with some colleagues to celebrate my impending mating, and you were there. You were there and hanging off of a *xala*, drunk and begging for her to fuck you. I didn't know it was you until I saw you the next day at the meeting ceremony. It felt like a slap in the face from the universe that my mate would be the most beautiful *xala* I'd ever laid eyes on, but so disinterested in our mating that she was out the night before with someone else."

Mezli blinks rapidly, her mouth opening and closing with unspoken replies as she processes my words. "Oh," she finally says, her dagger-like glare melting into a begrudging understanding.

When she doesn't continue, Eden lets out an exasperated sigh. "Ugh, you both are ridiculous! This only works if you let your guard down, too. Stop being a baby and tell him what you told me!"

Mezli scowls and crosses her upper arms over her chest. "Fine! She wasn't my lover. We didn't—I'd never been with anyone before. I was scared of committing to only being with one person for the rest of my life, so I got drunk and went out. Too drunk for anything to happen because I was so nervous. Are you happy now?" she asks, rolling her eyes at Eden.

Hearing her explanation makes me sag with relief. Unthinking, I reach out to touch her hips, needing to anchor myself to her. This time she doesn't push me away. Now that I've laid myself bare before her, I can't stop confessing. "I know I'll never deserve you," I murmur. "I know what I said is unforgivable. But will you at least allow me this one night to pay my penance?"

Tension fizzles in the air between us as she considers my offer.

"I think I'll give you two some privacy," Eden says softly.

Mezli and I break our staredown at the same time, heads whipping over to see Eden as she creeps toward the door.

"Where do you think you're going, sweet Eden?" Mezli asks in a husky voice.

Eden freezes. "S-sorry, just thought it'd be better if I headed out."

Mezli looks back down at me, and for once I can easily tell what she's thinking. She wants Eden to stay. I nod, wanting that too.

"Come here," I say in a deep command.

She obeys, walking over on shaky legs. When she's close enough, Mezli snags her around the waist and pulls her close. "Don't think you're getting out of this so easily."

I touch Eden's leg, sliding my hand up to toy with the hem of her dress. "Please don't go. Tonight is supposed to be about you. About giving you what you've yearned for. Do you still want that?"

"Yeah, who cares about our drama?" Mezli says, twining a finger through one of Eden's curls. "You're more important."

"A-are you sure?" Eden stammers. "This feels...weird. Wrong. Like I'm getting in the middle of your potential happiness."

Mezli and I exchange another glance, in unspoken accordance again. We're not going to let our drama get in the way of giving Eden what she deserves. I finally stand, moving to trap Eden between myself and my mate.

"I want you, Eden," I say, letting raw, honest arousal bleed into my voice.

"*We* want you, Eden," Mezli amends.

The pulse in Eden's neck quickens and a long moment passes as her eyes dart between me and Mezli. I'm about to step back and give her space when she murmurs, "Oh, fuck it," and slams her mouth against mine.

21

✦MEZLI✦

My mind is reeling from Phelix's apology and my own confession, but I push that into the corner reserved for shit I don't want to deal with. It's an overcrowded part of my mind that will probably explode at some point and cause a huge emotional mess, but for now, I'm able to shove it in.

Luckily, ignoring my feelings in favor of momentary pleasure is one of my greatest strengths. With Eden on offer tonight, how could I think of anything but her? I promised to help her out and while that didn't initially involve sex with me, I won't say no to the chance to be with her.

I'm not surprised that Phelix is able to put our conversation to the side, either. He's a smart *xalar*, and knows this may be his only chance to be with Eden, or with me, for that matter. I'm still not sure if I have it in me to forgive him. Even if I could, I doubt he'll want anything to do with me if he finds out I'm spying on him and thwarting his black market deals.

Eden melts into Phelix as he returns her kiss, and I slip behind her to join in on the fun. She gasps as I press my lips to her elegant neck and give her a gentle nip before soothing the sting with my tongue. She tastes like sunshine—like the feeling when the clouds part after a heavy storm. Pushing my body against her back, I bring my upper hands to tease her sides, fingertips grazing just the sides of her breasts. Phelix pulls her closer, wrapping a hand in her hair and snaking an arm around her waist. His hand accidentally connects with mine, and we both tense for a second. I don't have time to linger in the awkwardness, because he takes my hand and guides it to cup Eden's breast.

She pulls back from the kiss, and I wish I could see the expression on her face. "What do you want us to do, Eden?" I whisper in her ear.

"Th-that's nice..." She whimpers as Phelix directs our hands to toy with her nipple, the bud straining against the fabric of her dress.

"Just nice?" Phelix cocks a brow and we lock eyes over her shoulder. It would be so easy to turn tonight into a competition. Each of us seeing who could coax the most pleasure from Eden until she declared one of us the victor. But that wasn't what we all agreed to. Eden's comfort and enjoyment matters more than a petty contest.

"I, uh, I..." Eden's breathing comes faster like she's starting to get overwhelmed.

Phelix releases our hands and takes a step back at her hesitance. I move around so I'm standing next to him, allowing us both to see her face. She looks nervous, her skin flushed and her eyes wide, but there's more than that going on.

"Eden, it's okay if you don't want to do this," Phelix murmurs, stroking her arm in reassurance. He's so gentle and patient with her it creates a hairline fracture in the hard shell around my heart erected just for him.

She shakes her head adamantly. "No! I want this. It's just...I'm not sure how this is supposed to work with two people, let alone three."

"You don't know how sex works?" I ask, keeping my tone as non-judgemental as possible. If I'd known she was that naive, I wouldn't have suggested we switch roles for Operation Honey Pot.

She laughs weakly. "I know how sex works. At least I think I do—most of the same elements seem involved for both humans and nexxit. The thing is...I know you're trying to help make my first time as comfortable as possible by letting me call the shots, but I'm not even sure what shots to call. It's messing with my head."

I fight every instinct in me to offer a bunch of suggestions for what we could do. I don't want to overwhelm her.

Phelix nods. "Understandable. Why don't we try something as a warm up, then? You're not the only one that's a little nervous about doing this right." He shocks me when he winks at her, and when he notices my mouth fall open, he shrugs. "What? I have two incredible *xalas* in my suite. Of course I'm nervous."

Eden giggles. "You don't have to be nervous about me. You'll be the best I've had!"

We all laugh, and the tension in her body eases. A little voice inside me nags for me to share some form of vulnerability too, and though I try to tamp it down to maintain my carefree persona, it comes bubbling out. "You'll be the best I've had, too."

Phelix frowns slightly in disbelief. "Don't get your hopes up. It's been a while."

Ugh, he's going to make me say it. "No, I mean Eden will be the best human I've been with and you'll be the best nexxit."

Eden grins at the sentiment, but Phelix lets out a dismissive huff. "I don't require your flattery."

I cross my arms defensively. "It's true!"

"Wait..." Eden furrows her brow. "Oh! I think she's saying she's never been with a nexxit before." Her eyes widen. "Whoa, really?"

"Impossible." Phelix searches my face for any sign of deception, but he won't find any there. I've gotten freaky with plenty of aliens since moving to Spire, but being with a nexxit felt...wrong. I tried a few times, hoping it would clear away any cobwebs left still clinging to the hope of being with a true mate, but backed out each time before things went anywhere.

"Quit staring at me like that! It's not a big deal."

A slow smile spreads across Phelix's face that contains far too much canny recognition of my emotions. I want to smack it off his face, but I settle for changing the subject. "Okay, now that we've all shared, what was your idea, oh wise and noble Lord Nafar?"

"Right," Phelix says, turning back to Eden. "I don't know if humans enjoy massage, but I'm proficient at them. It might be a way to ease you into being touched in a way that's intimate but without a sexual goal in mind."

It's a decent plan, but I'm not sure where I fit in. I'm unable to hold back my frown, and Phelix catches it immediately. "Or you could do the massaging, Mezli. Whatever Eden feels most comfortable with."

Eden's cheeks have turned a lovely shade of pink at his suggestion, and she bites her lip as she considers. "Would it be too hard for you both to massage me at the same time?"

"Ooo, greedy girl," I tease. "I like it. I think we can get along enough to do that for you."

"I think we'll work together very well." Phelix's gaze is intent on me as he speaks, and now there's a flush rising on my cheeks. He extends a hand to both of us and I take it hesitantly, almost moaning at the contact when his fingers lace with mine. Goddess, it's surreal how that small of a touch makes me wet.

We head up a spiraling staircase to the lofted bedroom. As much as I'd love to poke at Phelix about the absurd luxury of his hotel room, I keep my mouth shut. I may have spent the last four years figuring out how to scrape together a living, but this used to be commonplace for me. A tiny part of me is jealous of the affluent life-style that I gave up. I don't like that part of me. Materialism and polished appearances were the bane of my existence when I was part of Nexxa Itat's noble society, and I hate that I haven't completely killed the part of myself that likes it.

Eden marvels at the bedroom, eyes scanning the enormous bed draped in expensive linens.

I nudge her with my elbow. "Bet you didn't imagine your first time in a place like this, did you?"

"Hah, not at all! I figured it'd be in a mediocre brothel or in my tiny hotel room. This is... Wow, thank you for doing this. This feels like a dream."

"I'm glad you find the suite to your liking. I'll endeavor to measure up to it," Phelix says solemnly.

Something about his words is painful and familiar. As nexxit nobility, the crushing pressure to be deemed worthy is our birthright. While I broke out of that cage, he's still trapped in it.

"You're enough, Phelix," Eden says gently, somehow knowing exactly the right words to soothe the constant criticism running through his mind.

His gaze softens, his guard slipping to leave him completely open and vulnerable. In this moment, he shows us both his true face, and Goddess, it's perfect. Perfect and painful because even with all the work I've done to change, I can't say for certain I've ever shown anyone who I truly am. I'm not sure *I* even know that true version of myself.

Fuck, there I go again, thinking way too hard instead of focusing on pleasure. "Take off her clothes, Phelix," I command, needing to get control of the situation. If I'm in control, then I can't be caught off guard by more of these damn uncomfortable emotions.

Phelix gives Eden a questioning look, wanting her consent, and she nods. He slips behind her and finds the fastener for her dress, slowly undoing it with a lower hand as he uses his upper hands to slide the straps of the dress off her shoulders. It falls to the floor, pooling at her feet, and she gasps as he traces the smooth expanse of her back with his fingertips, moving up and down until he settles on the clasp of her bra.

As much as my fingers itch to touch her as well, the show is spectacular. Eden's beige undergarments are simple, but who cares about what kind of underwear she has on when she looks so fucking *soft*. Her breasts strain against the cups of her bra, and it must take a feat of engineering to keep them pressed so high and tight against her torso. It looks uncomfortable. Does she wear a contraption like that every day?

"Help her get more comfortable. Take off her bra so I can see those gorgeous tits."

Phelix undoes the clasp, and when her bra comes off, her breasts spill out. If they aren't the prettiest sight I've ever seen, I don't know what is. Heavy teardrops tipped in pinkish-brown nipples, they look even more enticing now that they're free.

"Fuck, Eden." I move closer to get a better look at her. Her whole face and neck are flushed a rosy pink and I can tell despite her nerves, she enjoys how both Phelix and I are looking at her. He has the same expression of hunger and lust that I do as he brings one hand to cup her breast, testing the weight of it.

Her lips fall open, and she lets out a sound of protest when he takes his hand away.

"Couldn't resist," he murmurs, sliding his hands to the waistband of her panties.

"You both are really into boobs, aren't you?" Eden asks with a breathy giggle. "I guess that's a good thing. I was a little worried they'd be too big for aliens."

"They're *perfect*," I say, unable to stop looking at them. "They remind me of a painting of the Goddess my mothers had in our sitting room, all full, luscious curves. I used to stare at her during their interminable parties, and it was the only thing that kept me from bouncing off the walls."

"I remind you of your goddess?" Eden asks with a small smile.

"Well, you're missing a set of arms and your skin isn't pink, but yeah. Fuck yeah. You're a goddess, Eden," I say, utterly sincere.

Phelix slips her panties off as she takes in my words, letting his lower hands trace down the sides of her thighs as he sinks to the floor and helps her step out of them. "A goddess," he agrees. "Now it's time that you were worshiped like you deserve."

"O-oh. Alright. That sounds good." Eden's melodic voice sounds a bit dazed by our admiration of her body.

Seeing her fully naked makes the heat pooling in my core spread throughout my body. My thighs are slick with arousal and I ache with the need to touch and be touched. Her rounded stomach dips at the navel and flares again into a plush cushion above a thatch of dark curls that hide her pussy. I want to press her down to the bed and spread her thighs open to see all of her.

I know the basics of human anatomy. How could I not after the erotica Fina and I passed back and forth as part of our informal book club? I've seen a bunch of human pussies and cocks in vids, but I doubt they'll compare to the real thing.

"Lie down on the bed," I say, and Eden listens like a good girl, moving over to the bed and lying flat on her back.

Phelix and I exchange a tense look, uncertain about how to approach this. Who is going to massage where? Should we take off our clothes? Hating my hesitance, I break away from his gaze and strip naked, tossing my clothes in a pile near the stairs. I raise a brow at Phelix, and he shakes his head in amusement at my challenge, pulling his shirt off over his head.

"You're both so beautiful," Eden says, watching us with desire sparkling in her eyes.

I preen and strike a pose, but Phelix scoffs. He opens his mouth to argue, but I cut him off. I'm over his insistence that he's unattractive. "We are, aren't we? Though, I think our Phelix would look even prettier with his cocks on display, don't you?"

She nods shyly, her gaze falling to his crotch in anticipation and curiosity. "Please. I'd love to see all of you."

Phelix takes a deep inhale, no doubt steeling himself for our disappointment. But how could anyone be disappointed by him? His broad torso paired with his soft stomach and thick arms make me wonder what it would feel like to be held by him. To be pinned underneath his bulk as he held me down and fucked me like I've needed since I saw him again. Or to ride him and be in control of a *xalar* who could easily overpower me. Damn, it all sounds good.

It gets even better when he unceremoniously tugs off his pants and I finally see what he's working with. Goddess, Eden and I are in for a great time tonight.

22

✦EDEN✦

I t's hard to formulate any coherent thoughts when Mezli and Phelix get naked. Mezli is *so* pretty. She's what you'd imagine a nymph or a fairy from a fantasy story would look like— magical levels of pretty. Her deep pink skin is smooth and flawless, save for an adorable smattering of stretch marks across her hips and thighs that I want to kiss. I understand why my breasts are a novelty to them, but Mezli's are equally enticing in my eyes—small and perky, with deep pink nipples. But what turns me on the most is how comfortable and confident she looks in her body. She owns all of herself and knows how lovely she is. I shiver with anticipation thinking about some of that confidence focused on me.

Phelix, on the other hand, is *large*. Much bigger and more solid than any other nexxit I've seen. He has a powerful body, and his dusty pink skin paired with his soft stomach and thick thighs lend to his own kind of beauty, just as enticing as Mezli's. He's been so gentle and restrained with me, making me eager to see him unleash some of his strength on me. And when he takes off his pants...

"*Wow.* If I'd known what you're working with, I wouldn't have run away," Mezli says, eyeing Phelix's cocks shamelessly. Not that I have room to judge, because I'm doing the same.

Holy shit.

It's my first time seeing a penis in the flesh that's not attached to an elderly patient, and I have to stop myself from gasping aloud. I knew there'd be two of them, but are they supposed to both be that *big?* The front one is thick and slightly shorter than the back one, with a tapered head and ridges along the entire length. It's already leaking some kind of thin pearlescent precum and juts up proudly. The back one is longer, with a swollen bump at the base. There's no sign of testicles on him, unless they're internal... There's a seam spread around his cocks where they must've extruded from.

Even with all the alien porn I watched, this is a lot to take in.

Phelix's cheeks darken, but his cocks visibly throb at my stunned stare, the front one leaking even more of that shimmering slick liquid. "Don't worry! You don't have to take them at the same time. I can use either one, depending on what kind of experience you're looking for. The front one helps to relax and arouse my part-ner, while the back one—"

"The back one is for if you want to breed someone and make them come over and over in the process," Mezli finishes.

My skin heats at the idea of Phelix *breeding* me. That's not possi-ble, but it sounds so primal, and I shiver at the thought of taking it inside me and him filling me up as I come around him.

Phelix mistakes my reaction for distress, holding up his top hands in appeasement. "It's not only for that," he says with a glare at Mezli. "Yes, it allows insemination, but can be used just for pleasuring a partner. As a doctor, you know I can't 'breed' you as Mezli so crassly said, but if that thought makes you uncomfortable we don't have to—"

"I want to!" I interrupt in an embarrassingly high-pitched squeak. I clear my throat and try again. "I think I'd like that."

Mezli laughs harder, though it's fond rather than mocking. I grow even hotter when she grins at me and moves toward the bed. "Mmm, you want our Phelix to breed you? Or do you want him to put both cocks inside your pretty little pussy? I'm not sure they'll both fit, but maybe if he's good you'll let him use each one of his cocks on you? One to open you up and make you beg for more, and the other to push you over the edge while he fills you with his cum."

Phelix lets out a low groan and brings his lower hands to palm his cocks. "Would you like that, Eden?" he asks, voice thick with desire.

I can't believe he's so turned on at the thought of being with me. Inexperienced, unremarkable me. I feel lightheaded from how both of them are watching me and my answer comes out a little shaky. "Y-yes."

His gaze darkens with hunger. "Good. Turn over onto your stomach and let us take care of you. When you're fully relaxed and ready, I'll be happy to give you either of my cocks."

Mezli's eyes dart between us with unrestrained hunger, and I'm reluctant to look away from the sight of him leisurely stroking said cocks. I roll over and press my burning cheeks to a cool pillow, trying not to tense up with nerves as I wait for what comes next.

"Is there anywhere you don't like being touched?" Mezli asks, and the bed dips as she sits on it beside me. She strokes a hand down my bare back, and even that small touch lights me up, leaving a trail of goosebumps in its wake.

"I-I don't think so. Most of my body has never been touched by anyone but myself," I say, turning my head to the side so it's not muffled into the pillow.

"That's okay, sweet Eden," Mezli says, stroking my back again. "Just promise you'll tell us if you don't like something." I nod as best I can. I can't imagine anywhere on my body I don't want them to touch. Maybe my armpits? Even that might be nice, though. I'd rather they touch me everywhere. After all, tonight might be the only chance I'll get to experience it. I need to make it count.

Shit, now I'm making myself depressed. I let out a deep sigh and try to let those thoughts fade away. Mezli and Phelix take this as a signal to touch me, because suddenly there are four hands on me— two of Mezli's running along my right side and two of Phelix's along my left.

"*Oh,*" I sigh again, in pleasure this time, as they work in tandem. Everywhere their hands touch sends tingles of sensation scattering across my skin. They've barely started touching me, but my body already feels like it's going to overheat from arousal.

That heat flares even higher when Mezli shifts to straddle me, her legs on either side of my waist and her hot, wet center pressed up against my back. I almost choke at the sensation as she leans forward, dragging her breasts along my back, two hands sliding up the sides of my spine while the other two run along my arms.

I gasp, and she chuckles against me. "Feel good?"

"Y-yes!" I say, gasping when I feel Phelix's hands caress my legs, trailing down until he reaches my feet before coming back up and dipping in toward my inner thighs. His touch is firmer than Mezli's teasing strokes, and the juxtaposition makes my brain short-circuit.

Mezli brings her hands to my neck, kneading away the tension I didn't realize I was holding. "Mmm, you have such a pretty neck."

She's mentioned that before, and curiosity briefly overtakes my desire. "Why are necks a thing for nexxit? I mean, the words share similar sounds in my language, but I doubt that's the reason."

"It's one of the areas where our pheromones are the most concentrated," Phelix explains, thumbs digging into the backs of my thighs and causing my legs to fall apart slightly. "It's also an erogenous zone for nexxit."

Mezli leans forward again, draping herself over my back to press her lips to the back of my neck. "Is it an erogenous zone for humans, too?"

I whimper at the feel of her lips on my delicate skin, my clit pulsing with the desperate need to be touched.

She chuckles. "I'll take that as a 'yes'."

"Every part of me feels like an erogenous zone when either of you touch me. Maybe it's because I've never been touched before, but it's surreal to feel so much pleasure when you're not even touching me... there." It's silly for me to shy away from saying "pussy", but thinking it and saying it aloud are entirely different things.

"I feel it too, Eden," Mezli whispers, bringing a hand up to massage my scalp as she nips at my neck. "Don't you feel how wet I am against you? And you can't see it, but Phelix's cocks are leaking so much he's going to make a mess soon."

Phelix lets out a low groan. "Yes. I feel it, too."

I'm about to tell them to skip the rest of the massage and touch me where I need it the most, but Mezli sits back up and moves off of my back.

She makes a humming sound like she's thinking. "Do you have

any body oil? We should get Eden slick all over if we want to give her a good massage."

"No. I could call down to the desk..." Phelix says, sounding upset with himself that he didn't anticipate the unlikely scenario where he'd need massage oil.

He's so hard on himself, it makes my heart hurt a little for him. "You could, um...use some of your, some of the stuff coming from your top cock. It looked really slippery and if you said it helps with arousal and stretching, maybe it'll be good," I say, eager to reassure him. I'm glad I can't see either of their faces as I make the filthy suggestion of Phelix rubbing his cum all over my body.

"You're a genius, Eden," Mezli purrs, the fingertips stroking up and down my spine joined by a second hand. "What do you think, Phelix? Think you can give her some of your cum?"

"Only if you help," Phelix says in an unexpected challenge, and I roll onto my side to see Mezli's reaction.

She frowns at him, but there's heat simmering behind her glare. "You want me to stroke your cock before we take care of our pretty human, Lord Nafar? How selfish of you."

I sit up, worried things between them will take a turn for the worse and they'll call the whole night off. "I'll do it!"

"You don't have to, I was only—" Phelix starts, but I cut him off.

"I *want* to. I've wanted to do this for so long, and the thought of making you come turns me on. I don't want to just lie there. Please, let me. Just...uh, tell me if I do something wrong."

"So eager to learn, Dr. Mori. I'll help coach you through it," Mezli says with a wicked grin.

Phelix's eyes widen, encouraging my boldness. Fake it until you make it is my life's philosophy. Sure, that's what got me into the mess of this whole Operation Honey Pot nonsense, but it's also how I became a doctor. How I ended up halfway across the galaxy with two naked aliens, about to jerk one off so we can use his cum as massage oil.

I sit up and slip my glasses back on. If I'm going to do this, I want to be able to see every detail. Mezli beckons Phelix back over as I join her on the edge of the bed. He stands in front of us, his cocks stiff and bobbing as he waits with bated breath for me to touch him. It's intoxicating how aroused he is at the thought of my hands on him. I bet it'll be even more exciting when I watch him come.

23

✦PHELIX✦

Somehow we went from easing Eden into her first sexual experience to her jerking me off so we can cover her skin with my release. I should protest, but I'm not stupid enough to turn down her offer, and my cocks are certainly more than happy to let this happen. It won't take long for her to coax out my cum, even with her inexperience. I've been ready to explode since I saw Eden and Mezli naked. No, since they first offered this night together.

If I weren't so turned on, I'd find Eden's creative idea amusing. She always found unique solutions and offered colorful suggestions when we worked together to help optimize her medipod. For all my education at the finest institutes on Nexxa Itat, she has a mind that shines far brighter than my own. That she's here on Spire for the conference is no surprise.

With a slight smile, Eden reaches a hand out and touches the tip of my front cock, tracing the path of a bead of pre-cum as it slides down the length. Her touch is featherlight and nowhere near enough, but I don't want to get in the way of her examination. She gathers up the pale pink liquid I've already released and rubs it between her fingers, her mouth falling open as she analyzes it.

"It's so slick! Like lube, but, oh! It tingles!"

Mezli watches her with the same rapt fascination that I am, but her lips downturn when Eden brings her fingers up to her mouth. Her hand darts out to grab Eden's her wrist. "No! You don't know if it's toxic to humans."

Eden freezes, then shakes her head. "When I did my allergy test prior to my trip here, I, uh, tested for other things. We're compatible. It's not a problem for any of us to, um, ingest."

Smart. I wonder if she tested just for nexxit, or for all aliens?

Mezli releases Eden's wrist, who immediately slips the digit coated with my essence into her mouth. Her brow raises and Mezli tenses, despite Eden's assurances.

"Are you okay?" she asks nervously.

"Whoa. You taste so interesting. It's like a mix of strawberries and something herbal, like rosemary."

I don't know what either of those things taste like, but she doesn't seem repulsed by the flavor. I wonder if she'd take more of my release in her mouth? That'd defeat the purpose of why she's testing it in the first place, but the thought makes both my cocks twitch.

Eden giggles, and brings her hand back down to my length, circling it with her whole hand this time to give me a tentative stroke. "Sorry, didn't mean to lose focus," she says with a smile that makes my stomach tighten. I'm not going to last long.

"You're touching his dick. Don't apologize! You can take as long as you want." Mezli gives me a devilish look, showing me just how much she'd love for Eden to tease and torture me with her explorations. She allows her a few light strokes before her hand wraps around Eden's. "Give it more pressure. Slide your thumb along the underside of the head and tease the tip with each stroke."

I fight the urge to buck up into the tunnel of their combined hands as Eden follows her instructions. "Like this?" she asks, gazing breathlessly at Mezli.

"Just like that," I answer with a groan. Fuck, watching them look at each other while they pump my cock has me perilously close to the edge.

Mezli grins. "That's great. Let's get him nice and slick so it feels even better." Without preamble, she leans over and spits on my cock. Eden follows her lead, spitting onto me, their combined fluids making their hands glide over my cock with ease now.

"Fuck," I grunt, hot tension gathering in my groin.

"Mmm, he's close already. You're doing such a good job, Eden."

Eden flushes under her praise, and her hand working me speeds up with Mezli's guidance. The motion has her breasts swaying and I can't resist reaching down to grab them, pressing them up closer to my cocks so my lower length brushes against the sinfully soft flesh.

The pretty human's eyes flutter as I thumb her nipples, and Mezli takes that as her cue to release her hand over Eden's and bring it up to her cheek, turning her face away from my cocks.

They share a heated look before their mouths crash together. Eden must be a good multitasker, because she continues her perfect strokes even as Mezli deepens the kiss.

Fuck, it's too much. Between the tight grip of her hand, the brush of Eden's breasts against me, and the sight of these *xalas* lost in each other's kiss, I lose my battle to keep from coming so soon. "Shit, I'm going to come."

Eden pulls away from Mezli in time to watch me boil over, her eyes widening as a thick stream of my release shoots out and splatters across the bridge of her nose and onto the lenses of her glasses. She gasps and her mouth falls open, right as more pulses out of me, hitting her on her lips and chin. I bring a hand down, mortified at the mess I'm making of her even as waves of white-hot pleasure wash over me, but she just grins and angles my cock down so the final two pumps of my cum paint her breasts.

"Well, that's one way of getting your cum on her," Mezli says, raising a brow at me. The hint of amusement in her tone makes me shudder and my top cock releases more of my spend, sliding down the slick length.

"Apologies, Dr. Mori," I say with a groan. I don't know why I'm being so formal with her while she's covered in my release, but my brain isn't working properly anymore. It short-circuited as soon as I coated her face and chest.

She chuckles and releases my spent cock, reaching up to remove her glasses and swipe my spend off of the lenses. "Glad I put these back on. I didn't realize how...explosive of a reaction you'd have to me." She sees my concern and grins, gathering up more of my cum from her face. "I liked it," she adds, and I'll be damned, but my upper cock starts to swell back to life.

"Looks like he could give you more, if you don't think we have enough," Mezli says. There's an evil glint in Mezli's eyes that lets me know how much she'd like to force my release from me over and over. And fuck, if that doesn't make me swell even more. Maybe she'd be the one to wring it from me this time. But Eden is practically panting with need. That fantasy can wait.

"We have enough. Get on the bed, Eden. I can't wait any longer to touch you."

"O-oh, okay!" She's surprised at my forceful tone, but eagerly obeys. She lies on her back, treating me and Mezli to a perfect view of her soft body and her cum-covered tits.

I gather up some of my spend from her chest, and she squirms as my thumb brushes over her hard nipple. As much as I want to touch her perfect breasts more, I want to explore other parts of her. I slide down to the foot of the bed, spreading her thighs apart so I can rest between them.

Mezli follows my lead and moves to straddle Eden's waist, blocking my view of Eden's reactions to my touch, but placing her gorgeous backside right in front of me. I'm so tempted to grab onto her hips and dig my fingers into her flesh, staking claim to both my mate and my human obsession. I don't, though. I don't know if she'd welcome my touch. She needs to make the first move to show me I'm worthy of her.

I can at least prove my value to Eden tonight. Many times, hopefully. I massage her inner thighs, teasing with slips of my fingers toward the patch of curls between her legs but never touching her there.

She lets out small sighs and whimpers as Mezli and I massage her, and after a few minutes, she's wriggling under our touch, begging for more. Mezli must give it to her, because Eden moans and my mate chuckles at her reaction. "So needy. Look how hard these nipples are for me. Are you wet for us, Eden?"

"Y-yes, oh god, this feels so good. Everywhere you touch me is lighting me up and Phelix's release is making it even more intense. I need more. Please, I can't stand it."

Eden's legs fall open wider, treating me to a view of her pussy and, Goddess, she's soaked. Small, petal-like folds frame her entrance, begging me to spread them open and see her blossom as I sink my fingers inside her.

Mezli tilts forward and Eden keens. No doubt the *xala* is worshiping our human's breasts finally. I'd be jealous, but Eden's beautiful cunt is just as enticing.

"What do you want me to do?" I ask, needing to hear the words from her lips.

"Please touch my...p-pussy." Eden stumbles through the word like it's the first time she's said it aloud. "Put your fingers inside me, rub my clit, do anything. Just touch me!"

Permission granted, I use my lower hands to spread her wide, holding her thighs open so she can't hide from me. I trail my upper hands up her thighs and drag them ever closer until they brush against her soft curls. She gasps as I brush a hand down the center of her, spreading my remaining release across her pussy and mixing it with her own arousal, then returning to the top. I know from my "studies" that her clit is a small bump that needs to be stimulated for her to orgasm, not dissimilar to the ones that nexxit have. While a nexxit's pleasure spots are easily found, it takes me a moment of exploration until I find Eden's, resting under a hood above her entrance.

She bucks up against my touch as I press a thumb to it. "Ah!"

"Too much?" I ask, pulling back the pressure. Nexxit need firm pressure against their pleasure spots, but that doesn't seem to be the case for humans.

"It's v-very sensitive!" Eden gasps. "I usually rub around it."

Ah, so she needs me to tease the clit. I follow her instructions, slicking two fingers with her moisture and circling around the sensitive nub. She sighs in pleasure as I repeat the careful move- ment, gazing at her pussy with singular focus. I'm throbbing and ready to explode again at the thought of working this tiny pleasure spot and causing her to reach her peak.

She grows even wetter as Mezli and I lavish her breasts and cunt with attention, and she begins to move her hips, seeking out her release. Her pussy clenches as I tease around her opening with another hand, dipping in ever so slightly with a finger to test and see if she enjoys that.

"More," Eden says in a breathy whine, so I press my finger further inside her, marveling at how small her entrance is and how hot and tight and wet she is around me. Will I even be able to fit in here? She only shows signs of pleasure as I move my finger inside her, so I add another, testing her. She gasps and presses her hips up to meet the thrust of my fingers, stretching beautifully around them. Goddess, I can't wait to feel her stretch around one of my cocks.

Mezli's hips rock as she continues to play with Eden's breasts, leaning forward to lie over her and kiss her. The movement exposes her asshole and a sliver of her pussy, dripping with arousal. I want to bring my remaining hands up to play with her so badly it almost hurts. Feeling both of them come from my fingers would be heaven. I won't touch her without express permission, but it's killing me.

My suspicion that Mezli knows what she's doing to me is confirmed when she sits back up, turns over her shoulder, and has the audacity to wink at me. "Use your mouth on her, Phelix. She's ready to come," she orders.

Her command makes my cocks throb. "With pleasure," I say, replacing my fingers on Eden's clit with my tongue. Her taste matches her divine appearance—robust and intoxicating. "Fuck, she tastes good."

"I want to taste," Mezli says with a pout, and my foolish mind interprets that as an invitation to sit up and bring my mouth to hers, swiping my tongue against the seam of her lips to share some of Eden's nectar. I tense once I realize what I've done, waiting for her to push me away.

But Mezli doesn't resist at all, moaning as she opens her mouth and slides her tongue against mine to gather up the taste. "Mmm, she does taste good."

I don't linger on Mezli's lips, too eager to taste Eden again. She's practically writhing against us as Mezli returns to sucking and pinching her nipples and I renew my efforts between her thighs.

It only takes another minute before Eden inhales sharply. "Oh god, oh fuck, you're going to make me—"

She doesn't finish her warning as I suck her clit and she shatters, crying out as she comes. Feeling her pussy clamp against my fingers and having her arousal smeared across my face is almost enough to make me come, too.

When she descends from her peak, I ease off of her and release my grip on her thighs. Mezli gives her one more kiss and moves off of Eden to lie beside her, allowing me to see Eden flushed and breathless from pleasure. If I thought she was stunning before, it's nothing compared to seeing her glistening with the sheen of my cum all over her skin and my mate nestled in beside her, idly stroking her stomach as she whispers praise.

"How are you feeling, sweet Eden?" Mezli murmurs.

"Amazing...like I'm going to float away from my body," she replies dreamily.

"Don't float away completely yet," Mezli says with a fond chuckle. "We're just getting started with you."

They look so comfortable and right together that my chest squeezes with both affection and painful longing. I don't belong in this equation. Goddess, I want to, but look at how happy they make each other. Mezli might be my mate, but it is clear that her bond with Eden goes beyond hormones and primal urges. They *like* each other. They mesh so well. I'm a sharp edge that will tear into them and burst their happiness if I get too close.

I should give them some privacy. Claim an emergency and let them enjoy each other without me in the way. I push myself up to my feet and step back from the bed.

"Where the fuck do you think you're going, Phelix?" Mezli snaps, apparently not nearly as absorbed in Eden as I'd thought.

"I, there's, uh, something I need to attend to..." Goddess, I'm not usually this horrible at lying, but her withering stare and my heartache is messing with my head.

Mezli huffs dismissively at me. "The only thing you need to attend to is Eden. Get over here on the bed with us."

Eden gives me a warm smile, sitting up and reaching an arm toward me. "You don't have to do anything else if you don't want to, but I'd like you to. Come lie next to me. Please."

The sincerity of her words takes my breath away, and though I should know better, I'm lured in by the promise of her affection.

24

✦EDEN✦

This is the best and most surreal night of my life. I just came harder than I ever have on my own, with Phelix's tongue and fingers on my pussy and Mezli's mouth on my breasts. My whole body tingles with pleasure and anticipation for what comes next. I'm ready for anything—my entire being primed for these gorgeous aliens.

Phelix comes to lie beside me, the glint of sadness in his eyes shifting to hope when I ask him to stay. My chest aches for him. It's obvious how hard he tries to mask his emotions, and being with his mate like this must be strange and difficult for him. I wish I could tie them both to the bed and refuse to let them free until they work things out. Sure, that would end in my being the odd one out, but I want them to be happy. They deserve to be mated, and though they're blind to it, from the outside it's easy to see how they complete each other.

Besides, I'm only here for a few more nights before I go back home. It would be silly to factor myself into things. If my softness and inner romantic can help them come together, that will be almost as good as being with either of them myself. Almost.

I'll allow myself one night of pleasure with them. One amazing night that I can remember for the rest of my life—and use as masturbation fodder when I'm alone back on Europa 3.

With them sandwiching me in, stroking me and pressing kisses to my skin, I sink into the sensation and tune out my bittersweet musings. Despite my orgasm, I'm buzzing with anticipation and the need for more.

"So, how do we do this?" I ask. "Mezli hasn't had a chance to..."

The nexxit in question flaps a hand at me dismissively. "I'm fine."

"But what if I want to make you come?" I feel silly saying the words, but her delighted smile helps soothe the embarrassment.

"You truly are the most adorable person I've ever met," she says.

"Just adorable?"

"Adorable and fucking sexy. Alright, Eden. Make me come." She sits up, propping her back against the headboard, and spreads her legs in a challenge that has my heart racing. I maneuver myself between her legs, just as intrigued and excited by exploring her as I was with Phelix. Her pussy is a dark pink, almost purple shade, already so wet and enticing. With her legs spread wide, I can see she has a bifurcated entrance framed by a single set of wide labia, and around the perimeter are slightly raised, deep pink spots.

"Are you just going to stare at me, or are you going to do something?" Mezli teases, reaching down to stroke my cheek, her thumb trailing across my lower lip.

I stare between her spread legs in fascination. She's so beautiful. I also realize that in all my research I never paid attention to if nexxit have anuses or cloacas like some other aliens do. "You have an asshole!" I blurt.

Phelix snorts in surprise and my face heats.

God, why did I say that out loud? I don't know why it surprises me more than anything else. She also has a belly button and nipples, but I didn't question those similarities with humans. Though, now I am. How strange that we're so similar despite evolving on opposite ends of the galaxy.

"Uh yeah?" Mezli says, huffing out a small laugh. "You can play with that too if you want, but that seems a bit advanced for your first time. Maybe Phelix will let you finger his, if you're that into butt stuff." Mezli waggles her eyebrows at me, making me flush even more.

"No! I mean, if he wants me to I wouldn't mind...but no!" I'd honestly do anything these two asked of me if they said it would bring them pleasure.

Phelix seems perplexed by the idea, if his furrowed brow is any indication.

"Okay. Right." I bring a hand up and stroke it along her inner thigh, then skate it across her center. "You're so lovely," I say huskily, exploring her in awe. She's just as wet as I am, and the small, slightly raised bumps framing her entrance that make her squirm when my fingers pass over them. "Tell me what you like."

Mezli smiles down at me between her legs. "I like lots of things. Humans have clits, but nexxit have pleasure spots. If you press on them, it won't take long to get me off. Or, you could put your pretty mouth on me. I love having a tongue and fingers inside me."

EMILY ANTOINETTE

"I-I can do that. Or at least try my best," I say, eager to try, but realizing it would be a lot easier to accomplish that task with more than two hands.

"Your best is perfect," Phelix murmurs, watching the two of us with rapt attention.

Encouraged, I lower my mouth to Mezli's pussy and give her a tentative swipe with my tongue. Her tangy taste sends a shock of excitement through me, so I do it again, lapping at her entrance to gather as much of her arousal as I can.

"Oh fuck, okay!" Mezli gasps, obviously surprised that I dove into things head first. Literally.

She brings a hand down to assist me, her fingers splaying to the sides of my mouth to press into her pleasure spots. "Goddess, I'm going to come really fast. I'm so horny and you look so perfect between my thighs," she says with a hoarse chuckle.

"She does," Phelix says, his voice dripping with desire.

I need to get him involved somehow... Neither one of them is going to make the first move, but I know they both are aching to touch each other.

I pull back and Mezli whines. "No, don't stop!"

"Phelix, play with her tits," I say, trying to make my voice as commanding as possible.

They both freeze, but the longing in their eyes spurs me on. "Help me make her come," I order, more firmly this time.

Mezli shrugs, attempting to seem unfazed by this development. "Well, you heard her."

Phelix hesitates only a moment before he reaches up to fondle one of her breasts. She bites her lip to keep from moaning at his touch, but the look between them says it all.

They were made for each other.

I bury my head back between her legs, trying not to let the thought that I'll never have a match like that make me too sad. I'm not allowed to be sad when I'm finally tasting a pussy. I add a finger to her lower channel as I thrust my tongue into her upper one and Mezli cries out.

"Fuck, that's it. Dammit, I'm going to come!" She sounds angry that it happened so soon after Phelix started touching her, and he lets out a low rumble of pleasure.

"Come for us," he growls, and she listens, gasping as she breaks. A flood of wetness gushes from her, coating my face and chin as she clenches against my finger and curses as she rides out her orgasm. It's just as messy as making Phelix come, and I love it. I want them both to coat me in their combined essence—claiming me and showing me just how much I've pleased them.

I sit up to see a dazed Mezli and a smug Phelix, their dynamic switched for the first time tonight. It looks good on them.

"Was that okay?" I ask, all false innocence.

"Hah! You're ridiculous. It wasn't okay. It was *awesome*. You sure you've never done that before?" Mezli's approval makes my insides melt.

"No, but I've thought about it. A lot."

She laughs, the sound warming me even more. "I bet you have, dirty girl. What else have you thought a lot about?"

I glance over at Phelix, eyes dropping to his cocks, both fully erect and needy. Emboldened by getting the pair of them off, I say the thing I've been avoiding but so damn eager to try. "Feeling a cock inside me, fucking me hard."

"Think you can help her with that?" Mezli asks. "I would do it, but I left all my cocks back at my apartment."

It doesn't surprise me that she has multiple strap-ons. I bet she has one for each kind of alien cock out there. And probably ones that don't even exist in nature. I wonder if she'd use them on me. Or on Phelix... Damn, why does *that* idea make me so hot?

"It'd be my pleasure to fuck you, Eden. How do you want it?" Phelix asks, jarring me out of the fantasy of Mezli railing him with a giant alien dildo.

I pause to consider, and Mezli fills the dead air, looking apologetic for answering for me but unable to keep from blurting out her thoughts. "He could fuck you on your back while you gaze lovingly into his eyes. Or he could pound into you from behind. Oh, or you could ride his cocks. Or he could—"

"It might be best to start with you on top, so you can control how much you take. I don't want to hurt you," Phelix interjects.

The thought of sitting astride Phelix's thick body and using one of his cocks for my pleasure makes my pussy clench. "Okay. Y-yeah."

He smiles and lies on his back, his cocks pointing proudly to the ceiling. I move astride his waist and lean forward to kiss him to alleviate some of my nerves. He returns it with fervent, tender motions that make me dizzy. I lose myself in his kiss until Mezli clears her throat.

Shit, I shouldn't be kissing him like that. I pull back and give her a sheepish look. She grabs my chin and tips my head up, leaning over to kiss me. Her lips on mine feel just as good as Phelix's, though there's something possessive about her kiss that wasn't there in his. It feels like she wants Phelix to know I belong to her. Which is crazy, because I don't. I would love to belong to both of them, though that's not possible —even if the mate thing wasn't a factor, I'm leaving in a few days.

She nips my lower lip, her slightly sharp teeth just shy of piercing the skin, then pulls back and smacks my ass. "Go on, then. Ride him."

I try to maneuver his front cock to my entrance, since it's shorter and slightly less intimidating, but realize I'll be squashing his other dick at this angle. I don't want my first foray into penetration to end up with a trip to the hospital because I broke his dick. With a heavy swallow, I release the smaller cock and take the other in hand.

Mezli notices my hesitation and wraps her hand around mine, helping me to position it, grabbing his other cock unceremoniously to hold it out of the way.

Phelix gasps at the combination of our touch, and I feel his cock throb in my grip. The back cock is long and thick and just as textured as the front one, and even feeling the head pressed against my pussy is enough to send a shiver of excitement and nerves down my spine.

I attempt to sit down on his rigid cock, but the tip barely slips inside before my body stops it. "I'm sorry I'm so tight." I grimace, attempting to relax and push my way further down. I'm so wet and eager to have him inside me, and after years of using sex toys, I don't have a hymen to contend with anymore, so you'd think it'd slip right in. Apparently not. Heat prickles on my cheeks and neck, embarrassment creeping in.

"Don't fucking apologize," Phelix says, before Mezli can chastise me for my bad habit. "You're perfect." He reaches a lower hand up and strokes the cock pressed up against my belly, gathering up some of his pre-cum, then brings it down to where we're attempting to join. He spreads it across my labia, teasing the stretched entrance and the head of his cock.

A few moments later, gravity and his pre-cum work their magic, allowing him to slide in enough for the entire blunt head of his cock to nestle inside me. I gasp, and he smiles up at me.

"There we go," he says in a deep groan. "You've got this, Eden. That sweet cunt was made to take me."

Fuck me. My whole body erupts in goosebumps at his words. I know it's just dirty talk to help me relax, but god, thinking that I was made for him flips a switch in my brain. I press down onto him and he slips in the rest of the way, his impossibly thick cock somehow fitting inside me. The stretch burns for a moment and I suck in a sharp breath. It's not bad at all though, and the pinching quickly melts into a pleasant fullness as Mezli teases my nipples and kisses my breasts.

"Good girl, you're doing so well." Mezli nips at my neck, soothing the sting with her tongue. As good as it feels to have her caressing and kissing me, I want her to be more involved.

"I want you to sit on his face," I say, my voice shaking at the feeling of Phelix so deep inside me and the thought of watching her taking her pleasure from him.

Phelix groans as I tighten around him. "Fuck yes, please," he begs, his cock pulsing inside me.

Something shifts behind Mezli's eyes as we wait with bated breath to see what she'll do. Her teasing facade dissolves into hesitant yearning. She wants this as bad as the rest of us do.

I silently plead for her to be brave enough to let her guard down and truly experience this, reaching out to touch her hand. Phelix looks like he's fighting not to bring up his own defenses in the face of her hesitation, and I place my other hand on top of the one gripping my hip.

Warmth and an overwhelming sense of rightness washes over me as I connect with both of them. Mezli's eyelashes flutter and Phelix's eyes widen, and I know they're feeling the same thing.

Please. I know you want this.

Coming to a decision, Mezli shrugs, attempting to appear casual even though I can feel her hand trembling in mine. "If you insist."

As she moves astride Phelix's chest, I reach forward and raise up enough off of his cock to kiss her. I press all of my desire, excitement, and reckless hopes for the three of us into her lips. Showing her how amazing this moment is. Showing her how she can take what she wants, just like she urged me to earlier today. Showing her she's safe.

25

✦PHELIX✦

It's been torture since I first encountered Mezli and Eden at the conference, my cocks aching and swollen for them, and my mind a fog of lust and confusion. But that makes the blissful relief of sinking inside Eden's pussy and seeing Mezli's cunt inches from my face so much sweeter. My body sings with a sense of fulfillment I haven't experienced in years.

No, if I'm honest with myself, I've never felt like this before, even when I thought I was in love. I'm certainly not in love with either of these *xalas*, but a pathetic part of my heart is desperate to open to them. We've spent less than three full cycles together. Falling for either of them would be the epitome of foolishness.

Though...Father told me to take a risk. Fucking the two people you've become borderline obsessed with and letting down your guard certainly fulfills that request.

Goddess, get yourself together! I'm far too close to coming, and even worse, to letting my feelings get involved in what is meant to be a casual night of sex. I run a list of things I hate through my mind, attempting to anchor myself back down to reality and away from the edge of release.

Dinner parties with nosy nobles sharing "helpful" fashion advice for my body shape.

Scratchy blankets that give me hives.

Overripe yesle *fruit.*

Mezli and Eden moan as they kiss and Eden rocks back down onto my cock.

Overripe yesle *fruit as Mezli bites into it and the juice drips down her throat to the tips of her pert breasts...*

No. Shit. Focus!

Things only get worse when Mezli moves her hips back and positions her dripping pussy over my mouth. I hungrily tug her down the rest of the way, cocks pulsing as she gasps when my tongue makes contact with her slick cunt. Goddess, she's delicious. Nothing like overripe *yesle* fruit at all. She's sweet and heady, like the most decadent dessert—one I know I shouldn't indulge in, but that I can't resist. I'll happily endure the repercussions of gorging myself on her ambrosia, no matter how painful they'll be.

Mezli moans as I eagerly fuck her with my tongue, my upper arms wrapping around her thighs to hold her to me and press my fingers into two of her pleasure spots. The position makes it a little hard to breathe, but the way she bucks against me and gasps makes it more than worth a little asphyxiation. I would die the happiest

I've been in my life with the taste of her cunt on my lips and Eden's snug channel choking my cock as she slowly moves herself on top of me.

I let out a broken moan when a hand wraps around my upper cock, pressing it firm against Eden's curls and soft stomach. I can't tell if it's Eden or Mezli, but it doesn't matter. Nothing matters but the added stimulation and friction, and I can't help bucking up into it.

"O-oh fuck!" Eden cries out as my lower cock bottoms out inside her with my thrust. I can't reply with words, so I grab onto her thighs with my lower hands, pulling my hips back as much as I can and then pumping up into her as I pull her down onto me. Her cunt flutters around me as she cries again. I should let her set the pace, but fuck, I'm desperate for more.

"How does he feel? Is his cock good enough for you?" Mezli asks, her attempt at a cocky tone undermined by the shakiness of her voice as I push her toward the edge with my mouth and hands.

"It feels so good, god, Phelix, fuck me!"

Knowing Eden is just as crazed with the need for more spurs me on, and I thrust up into her welcoming cunt as hard as I can. The sloppy sounds of her wetness and my tongue working against Mezli's pussy have both of my cocks throbbing with the need to release.

This is agony. I've never been more aroused in my life and every cell in my body screams at me to release inside the warm, wet cunt I'm filling. Eden's pussy is unreal, Mezli's essence wraps around my mind, and fuck, all I want to do is breed these perfect *xalas* over and over.

I've never felt an urge like this before. To not just fuck, but to rut. It's a good thing that Eden can't get pregnant, because I can feel my seed gathering, my lower cock throbbing inside her and the knot at the base swelling as it begs me to lock our bodies together and make her come until we're both delirious from pleasure. And then to slide out of her and mount my mate and do it all over again —preferably with Eden lavishing my other cock with her tongue.

Gathering up all the willpower I've honed living under the constant scrutiny of my mother and my noble peers, I fight off my impending release as best I can. It's a losing battle, but I manage to hold out long enough for Mezli to climax, her release coating my mouth and chin as she curses, her cunt grinding into my face as her hips rock.

"Fuck, fuck, Goddess I'm coming!" Mezli gasps.

Hearing my mate come because of me is my undoing. My upper cock coats the hand holding me, dripping my cum down onto where Eden and I are joined. I groan as Eden bounces on top of me, chasing her own pleasure and all I can do is take it as both these *xalas* use me. My upper cock's release coats my lower one with Eden's frantic movements, and I let out a shocked moan when the bulge at the base pops inside her just as the first jet of my lower cock's seed boils out of me.

Mezli collapses forward and moves off of me, allowing me to take in a gasping breath as my knot swells inside Eden, my cum splashing inside her over and over.

"Shit!" I curse, stunned at the pleasure coursing through my body and the fact that my knot is inside Eden's small channel. It's never fit inside anyone before. It's only supposed to be able to fit inside my mate, but here I am locked inside a human that most definitely isn't mine.

I push myself up onto my elbows to take in the sight of where we're joined and Eden's shocked expression as I come and come and *come.*

"W-what's h-happening?" she asks, eyes blown wide as my cum

causes her own cascade of pleasure. "F-fuck!" Her orgasm hits hard, clamping her cunt down around my cock as she milks even more of my seed from me.

I attempt to push back the waves of pleasure enough to apologize for not warning her. I didn't think I'd need to. This shouldn't have happened. Panic about hurting her seeps into my bliss, but I can't get any words out, only managing a guttural groan as I feel Eden come again as she writhes on top of my cock.

Mezli lets out a derisive huff, and I tear my eyes away from Eden to see her glaring at me. "Looks like Lord Nafar got greedy. I'm going to go get a drink while you two are...stuck together."

"We're stuck?!" Eden squeaks, then collapses forward as her third orgasm hits.

"Yep." Mezli pats Eden's arm, and then shoots me another withering look. "Have fun."

"I didn't mean to! I didn't know it could happen! I'm sorry— ungh!" I say, groaning as more pleasure hits. Apologizing to my mate as I come is agony. She looks like she wants to tear my cocks off, and Eden can't stop whimpering from the overload of pleasure.

Mezli pushes herself off the bed, and I try to grab her wrist to beg her to stay, but she curses and pushes away. In a panic, I attempt to lift Eden off of me, but she doesn't budge. We're truly trapped together.

"Mezli, w-wait!" Eden says, sending her a pleading look.

Her expression softens, and she strokes Eden's arm. "I'm fine. I'll be back in a bit."

It's obvious to me that she's not fine, but Eden seems to accept it, nodding. Mezli snags a robe from the hygiene room, then stomps down the stairs to the lower part of the suite and out of sight.

Fuck, I've made a mess of this.

"E-Eden, I'm so sorry," I groan, another rolling release hitting me. "My cock will release us in a few minutes, but until then, it'll be...a lot."

The sweet, lovely human sits up, her eyelashes fluttering as pleasure hits her, but she smiles down at me. "I did ask for a memorable first time." She chuckles weakly and then moans.

Neither one of us can talk or think much as we wait for my knot to go down. She lays her plush body across my chest and I stroke her hair, reveling in the press of her breasts and stomach against my body as sensation washes over us. It's undercut with worry about Mezli's reaction, but damn, it still feels incredible. My heart splits open and pours out into Eden and it may sound crazy, but I get the sense hers does the same.

When my knot finally releases, both cocks sliding back into my slit, Eden inhales sharply at the rush of my cum flooding out of her overstretched pussy.

"Apologies," I murmur as she eases herself off of me and sits beside me on the bed with a slight wince. Seeing her in discomfort cuts through the heady fog of pleasure we just shared, and like a popped balloon, all my happiness bursts.

I sit up beside her and place a hand on her thigh. "Shit, Eden, are you alright?"

"I'm okay. More than okay. That was amazing. Best first time ever," she laughs weakly. "Just might need to, uh, rest for a while before doing it again."

My single-minded cocks threaten to swell and extrude again in record time at the thought of fucking Eden again, but worries about Mezli keep them contained. I smile at Eden, stroking her thigh in a way I hope conveys the affection I feel for her. "I'm glad it was alright. You were perfection."

Eden kisses my cheek, warming my heart even more. "I'm sorry Mezli got so upset. If I'd known that would happen, we could have stopped."

"You did nothing wrong." I shake my head adamantly. "I assumed it would be a non-issue since it's not normally possible..."

"Why not?" Eden asks, though I sense she already knows the answer.

"It's not something that can happen with most partners. As Mezli mentioned, it's for reproduction. With a mate." I sigh, placing my face in my hands, wishing I could scrub away the way Mezli looked at me when she realized what had happened. Did she think I somehow forced it just to spite her?

"Oh." Eden is silent for a long moment, leaving me to wallow in thoughts that I've hurt both of the *xalas* in my bed tonight. When she speaks again, her voice is soft and hesitant. "It's not possible with someone who's not your mate?"

I look up at her with a humorless smile. "No. Though, we obviously disproved that theory. Maybe it's a myth. Or maybe it has something to do with human anatomy."

"Oh," she says again. I give her space, not brave enough to expand on my answer.

A long silence stretches out between us before she speaks again.

"I thought maybe it was because there's something between us," she says softly.

My chest fills with bubbling elation at the thought of her feeling the same way I do about her.

"I can't help feeling like it's somehow my fault that you could knot me. That the whole 'only possible with mates' thing is more about the depth of the feelings someone has. As it was happening, it felt like..." Eden breaks eye contact, looking down at her hands. "It felt like my body knew that you matter to me and let you in."

Goddess, I felt it too.

"Eden," I say, cupping her chin and bringing her face so she meets my gaze. So she can see the sincerity of what I'm about to say. "There *is* something between us. I felt it a year ago and I feel it again now. I'm sorry I ended our connection before. I was scared and things were still...complicated with Mezli. And now, they're complicated for you, too."

Confused emotion roils in my gut when I mention my mate, but I continue. "I know you care for Mezli and I don't want to get in the way of that. Tonight was incredible. The best night of my life. I'm honored that you shared it with me. I won't be foolish enough to hope for more."

"Why is that foolish?" she asks, almost in a whisper.

My eyes widen. Surely, she's not saying she wants more with me. Goddess, please let that be what she's saying.

"Maybe I was meant to bring you and Mezli back together. Our bodies got carried away in the moment, but before that...you two fit so well together. If I could be the thread to mend the broken connection between you, it would be *my* honor." Eden's eyes shine with emotion.

My heart sinks with disappointment, her selflessness like cold water splashed in my face. Wanting Eden, asking her for more while I have a mate, would be beyond selfish.

I nod. "Perhaps you're right. Though, I'm not sure how to make amends with Mezli, even with your help. She's run away. Again."

"I'll talk to her. Don't give up. You two were meant to be." Eden smiles and pats my leg, but I don't miss how she swipes at the moisture in her eyes. "Sorry, I'm just a bit overwhelmed after my first time and all. Wow, sex is wild! Thanks again for doing that. Doing me!" She snort-giggles, and I'm almost taken in by her adorable ruse, but recognize the shield of levity she's putting up.

I wish she'd just tell me she wants Mezli for herself. She doesn't have to sacrifice her happiness for me. I wouldn't stand in her way. I'm entirely undeserving of either of them.

26

✧⊹MEZLI⊹✧

I'm not jealous. I'm not! Do I kind of want to stab Phelix in the seam right now? Sure, but there's nothing new about that. Did it make me feel like I was going to cry when he was able to knot Eden? No!

I'm not going to cry.

Why would I care that when I opened my heart up to the possibility of giving my mating with Phelix another chance, he proved that our supposedly divine connection isn't anything special? Is only being able to knot your mate made-up propaganda to make mate bonds seem more special? Is *everything* about having a mate a lie?

I grab a pillow from the sofa and use it to smother the sound as I yell into it.

They're still up there, stuck together and enjoying the euphoria of multiple orgasms. I can hear them whimper and sigh as they take their pleasure from each other. Pleasure that should be mine! I should be the one making adorable Eden come again and again. I should be the one locked on to my mate. I should...wow, I should calm the fuck down.

Easier said than done. These goddess-forsaken mating hormones are making me crazy. I don't want to be livid, but something inside me broke when I came on Phelix's face. Instead of calming me down, it made me even more feral for him. On top of that, wires in my mind must've gotten crossed because I'm just as possessive about Eden, even though I have no claim on her.

I take five deep breaths, using the pillow mashed against my face to help ground me in reality. I don't have time to give a shit about the pair upstairs. I need to focus on the plan. The decryption key was waiting outside Eden's door when I got to her room earlier. When we ran into Phelix, we agreed that I'd snoop around his place, find the datapads, and use it while she was occupying his attention. This is the perfect opportunity. He's literally stuck up there with her.

I let myself get distracted when Eden asked me to join them— thoughts of what it would be like to show her pleasure and to explore my connection with Phelix fogging my head. But now things are much clearer. I'm here to get the info the agents need and stick it to the pompous motherfucker currently trapped by the dick inside my human crush.

The need to scream rises again, so I toss the pillow back on the couch and set to work before I let it overwhelm me. I take a swig from the open wine bottle, not that it'll help calm me. After that disastrous night out before my mating and the worst hangover in my life, I've never been drunk again. As soon as I made enough credits from my job at CiaXera, I splurged on an implant that neutralizes toxins when they enter your system—including alcohol. Now I drink because it sets others at ease, thinking that my inhibitions are dulled. It excuses my expressiveness and openness, and helps me be the life of the party while I'm still in control of myself. Some might say that's manipulative of me, but I don't care. It lets me have fun without the risk of actually letting my guard down. Letting my guard down is when I get hurt. Dammit, I shouldn't have let them in.

Focus. None of that matters. I locate the satchel of datapads Phelix left in the hall closet and ease the door open, keeping an ear out for any movement from the bedroom. When I'm confident he's still very much caught up with Eden, I pull out the decryption key from my purse and click it in place on one of the datapads. The screen lights up and a stream of code flashes as the datapad unlocks and its contents are downloaded onto my comm using some high-tech link the agents set up. If I'd been skeptical of their methods before, I'm not now.

I go through each datapad as quickly as possible, listening as the gasps and sighs from above fade and shift to murmured conversation. A petty part of me is pissed they didn't immediately come seek me out as soon as they separated, but I'm sure Eden is just stalling him. She wouldn't think I'm actually upset by what happened. This plan was my idea, after all.

I'm on the last datapad when I hear movement above. I yank the decryption key out and hope we got enough for what the agents need, then shove the datapad back in the satchel and stick it back in the closet, closing the door just in time to see Eden coming down the stairs, followed by Phelix. Both looking thoroughly fucked.

A sharp stab of pain and longing strike my chest as they exchange a small smile.

It doesn't matter. You don't need them in your life. She's leaving in a few days and he's a potential criminal. She's just here to have fun, and he thinks you're a drunken slut. It doesn't matter.

"All finished?" I ask, putting on my best carefree grin as I saunter over to Eden and give her a once over. She's still flushed from the sex, but her eyes look a little puffy. Was she crying? Oh goddess, I left her up there, literally stuck with Lord Fuckwad, even though she trusted me to make sure her first time went well. I'm an ass. "You all good?" I add, with a frown as I reach out to take her hand.

The instant our skin touches, the seething anger inside me turns to white noise, and I forget why I was upset. Touching her is like a balm to my frayed senses. The way her smile brightens makes me hope I'm the same for her.

"I'm great." She takes Phelix's hand with her free one and squeezes it too. Rather than feel annoyed, my sense of calm and connection grows. "Thank you both for such a wonderful evening. Truly, I couldn't have asked for a more amazing first time."

The tenderness I feel toward her threatens to spill out of my mouth, but I tamp it down. "Sweet Eden, you don't have to thank us. Just promise me you'll think about me when you're rubbing one out back on Europa 3." I wink to punctuate my words. There, that's fun and casual Mezli. No one wants serious, besotted Mezli.

"It was my honor," Phelix says, his eyes locking on mine for a moment, making my heart leap into my throat.

It doesn't mean anything. It doesn't matter.

BY THE TIME I get Eden back to her hotel, we're both exhausted. She's quiet until we reach her door, but when I go to wave goodbye, she pulls me in and kisses me so sweetly I want to melt against her. Kissing Eden is like seeing the world in color for the first time. Everything is so much brighter and saturated with her around. I don't resist when she takes my hand and guides me into her room.

"I know you're upset, but please stay with me," she says, setting her purse down on a table and slipping her boots off.

"Ready for more already? You humans are insatiable."

She chuckles and shakes her head. "I just don't want to be alone. And I think you could use some snuggling."

"I'm fine. I'm not upset," I say, dropping my purse beside hers and sitting down on the edge of the bed to unzip my boots.

"You don't have to hide your feelings from me, Mez." Eden using Fina's nickname for me makes my cheerful facade soften. I don't really know Eden, but I believe her. She may be the only person other than Fina I've trusted when they tell me I can.

"Okay, fine." I sigh and kick off my boots, wiggling my sore toes in relief. "Seeing Phelix like that was...weird."

"I'm sorr—"

I raise a brow at Eden, and she stops herself from apologizing. "Good girl. I'm not upset with you at all. It was my idea. I just didn't anticipate how I'd react."

"I could tell it was weird. We shouldn't have done that. It wasn't fair to either you or Phelix."

"I think it was pretty fair to the dude getting to blow his load inside you again and again," I scoff, my bitter sadness rising.

"He cares about you, Mezli. He felt awful about how you reacted. I kept him upstairs to make sure you had time to get what we needed, otherwise he would've come down as soon as we...separated."

"Good for him. I don't care about him." I sound like a petulant child, but I can't stop the defensive reflex.

Eden sits down on the bed next to me and wraps her arm around my shoulder, pulling me into her. "Suuure you don't."

I flap a hand dismissively at her. "I don't!"

"It's okay to care, Mezli. It means you're human. Or nexxit. You know what I mean!"

"Caring only leads to getting hurt," I say, the cracks in my walls I've built over the past four years deepening.

She nudges me with her shoulder. "Don't be so melodramatic. You care about Fina, right? You'd have to after all the things you did to help her when she moved to Spire. You made her a fake clothing store, for fuck's sake."

"Of course I care about Fina," I grumble, knowing where she's going with this. Why does she have to be so smart and logical? It's annoying. And just what I need.

"Has caring for her only led to pain?"

"She can be a pain in the ass sometimes..."

Eden's warm laugh at my answer is light shining through the fissures in my facade. "Okay, fine! You're right."

"What happened between you and Phelix sucked. You both still feel the hurt of it. But are you the kind of person who lets pain keep her from living? No! You're the most confident, amazing person ever. If you want him, take him. He's yours. You just have to have the guts to let him in."

"Like you did?" I ask with an eyebrow wiggle and she scowls at me. "Kidding! I hear you. Mostly the part about being the most amazing person ever. But also, the part about taking what I want. Someone really cool must have told you that."

"The coolest. The prettiest too." Eden grins and waggles her eyebrows back at me. "With a pussy that tastes like heaven."

I bring a hand to my mouth in fake shock. "Eden! What happened to the shy human who'd never been laid? Don't tell me I turned you into a sex fiend."

Her smile widens. "Nah, I think I already was one. Just hadn't had the opportunity to explore it."

"Well...you're still here for a few more days..." I say, giving her a slow look up and down. Just sitting and laughing with her makes me crave her.

"Are you offering your services to me again?" She giggles, her face flushing.

"Absolutely." I'd give her whatever she asked for.

"I'll consider it. Not tonight, though. I'm so tired."

I kiss her shoulder, tasting a hint of Phelix's release on her skin. It should be an upsetting reminder, but it only makes me want her more. Want him more too, but I'll never admit that out loud. "Okay. I should send these files to the agents anyway before they shit their pants waiting to hear from us."

Eden perks up. "Oh! So you got the files?" She pauses, her brow furrowing. "Did you look at them?"

I shake my head. "I didn't have time. I can forward them to your comm if you want to. I doubt I'd even know what I'm looking at."

"Please." Eden's expression grows serious. "What if the schematics are in there? I don't—do you think he's going to do what they claim? The more time we spend with him, the less convinced I am he'd willingly endanger so many lives."

I answer honestly. "I don't know Phelix. Neither of us do. I was inclined to believe the worst of him, but now... I don't want it to be true, but we still need to do our job. Even if it hurts to know the truth."

Eden bites her lower lip, looking down for a moment. "I know him," she says, barely above a whisper.

Oh sweet, naive Eden. "Banging someone doesn't give you insight into their true thoughts. Though that'd be pretty nice if it did. Would've saved me a lot of hassle."

"No... I know him," she repeats, shaking her head. "I, uh, I reached out to him about a year ago because I needed help in his field of expertise. We talked for a while. I should've told you right away, but I didn't think it would impact the mission and I was worried the agents would send me home if they found out."

My gut clenches as I war with the instinct to get angry at her for keeping this a secret from me. I hate that she didn't trust me, but would I have done any differently in her shoes? It's silly to care that she didn't tell me she worked with him in the past. She told me now that she trusts me, and that's what matters.

"I... I wish you'd told me sooner." I say, patting myself on the back for how reasonable I'm being.

"I know. I'm sorry! You've been so good to me since the moment we met. I... I feel so safe when I'm with you."

Seeing her upset with herself, especially when tonight was supposed to be special for her, makes my frustration fade even more.

I pull her hand in and squeeze it. "You *are* safe with me. Part of keeping you safe is not letting you get blindsided if Phelix ends up being a criminal. He may have helped you in the past, but you never know what lies in someone's heart. Especially not a nexxit trained from birth to mask his emotions."

She sighs and squeezes my hand back. "Yeah. You're right." She looks so sad that I pull her in and press my lips to hers, trying to soothe her worries away. I'm used to people disappointing me, but I don't want to see her get hurt.

27

✦EDEN✦

Gentle fingertips stroking my side and thighs rouse me the next morning. Once again, it takes me a moment to realize I'm not back at home in my tiny bed in our farmhouse and that there's someone in the bed with me. Not just someone, an *alien*. My life has changed drastically since I came to Spire. It feels like it's been years instead of a handful of days. I want to drift back into sleep, enveloped by Mezli's warmth, but her touch is too stimulating.

"Morning," I whisper, testing to see if she's awake.

Mezli purrs and snuggles in closer to my back, her face burrowing into my shoulder. "Mmm, go back to sleep. It's too early."

A quick glance at my comm tells me it's already almost mid-day cycle. It also shows a number of missed incoming messages. Mezli snatches my wrist and brings my hand up to her lips. "Ignore that. Let's stay in bed all day."

Sparks dance across my skin where her lips touch, tingling down my body until heat pools between my legs. I try to shake it off and clear the sleep and arousal from my mind, but when Mezli's mouth travels to my neck, I moan softly.

"W-we should probably get up! I want to look at that data you gathered, and I'm sure the agents will want an update on our progress."

"I sent them the data before we fell asleep," she murmurs, the hand stroking my side teasing just beneath my breast.

A sinking sense of dread fills my gut. I wanted to look at the data before she sent it, and now it's too late. I would've been able to see if Phelix had the schematics and then decide...

Decide what? If it was on his datapad, would I have tried to tamper with the evidence? My head is a mess. After finding out he remembers me and cares for me, the thought of him being a criminal who'd willingly endanger lives across the galaxy makes me sick. That I'd even consider trying to protect my crush over galactic security makes me even sicker. Shit, Mezli did me a favor by taking that choice out of my hands.

Mezli nips at my neck. "You're thinking too hard, Eden. Whatever they find, we'll handle it. We make a great team."

I sigh, letting her smooth voice pull me back under her spell. "Yeah. You're right."

"I know." I can feel her playful smile against my skin. "Let me help take your mind off of things."

I shouldn't. I'm already too attached to her, but how can I say no? The memory of my cold, lonely bed back home is a powerful motivator. I'll allow myself to soak up her warmth and company and hope it sustains me for at least a little while when I return to my mundane life. That's the only logical choice to make when a gorgeous alien is in your bed, right?

"Okay," I whisper.

She kisses my neck again, inhaling against me with a soft groan. "You smell so good, Eden. I know humans don't have the same pheromone system as nexxit, but fuck, it sure seems like it. I get so wet with just a hint of your scent."

"Maybe far back in the history of the universe, the progenitors of human and nexxit life shared similarities. I mean, we're both mammals, so it would make sense why we're compatible... Oh!" I gasp as she snakes her hand down between my thighs and another palms my breast.

"Oh, we're compatible, Dr. Mori. I thought you would've already confirmed that hypothesis last night." Her fingers slide through my curls to dip into my wetness and then back up to circle my clit lightly.

"A good scientist doesn't base conclusions on a single test. We should—ah!" Mezli pinches my nipple as she continues to circle my clit and I buck against her touch. "We should conduct more tests."

"Of course. That's the only responsible course of action," Mezli says, the mock seriousness in her tone somehow making me wetter.

She spends the next ten minutes exploring me. Teasing me, testing out how I react to her touch and what makes me moan the loudest. Two fingers inside me, her thumb rubbing my clit, and hard pinches of my nipple as she whispers praise bring me dangerously close to tumbling over the edge. I attempt to roll over so I can touch her back, but she pins me against her body. "Not yet. I want to focus on every reaction as you come for me."

A few moments later, the sensation overtakes me and I come in long pulses that make my body feel like it's melting and being lovingly reshaped by her touch.

When she releases me and I roll over to face her, she has an enormous grin as she studies me with a contemplative head tilt. She brings her fingers coated in my arousal to her lips and licks them, her eyes sparkling. "Hmm, decent results."

I chuckle and move her hand, pressing my lips to hers. She lets out a pleased hum as my hands roam up her sides to cup her breasts. They're small, perky, and delectable, just like the rest of Mezli.

"Let's do one more test," I say once our lips part.

She laughs and kisses me again, her lips melding so perfectly with mine. "Just one?"

OUR EXPERIMENTS GO on until late afternoon, breaking to order some room service before Mezli shoves me back into bed. When I can't handle any more, she slaps my ass and hops in the shower.

Alone with my thoughts after being tangled up with Mezli, I check my comm. There's a message from my mom telling me to think about their offer, a huge data transfer from Mezli, and something from Phelix. My pulse races as I swipe open his message.

> Phelix: I hope you got some rest last night. Please let me know if there's anything I can do to help you recover from our vigorous activity. Or if you'd like to meet up today at the conference.

Shit, that message was from three hours ago.

I glance at the door to the hygiene room, chuckling as Mezli belts a horribly out of tune song, then message him back.

Eden: Sorry, I just got up!

I hesitate to tell him why, but figure honesty is the best policy.

Eden: Mezli stayed with me.

Eden: She hogs the bed.

I add that last part in an attempt to lighten the situation. A few tense minutes later, during which I beat myself up for sleeping with Mezli after telling Phelix I wanted to help them be together, he messages back.

Phelix: Unsurprising. Both the bed and the fact that she stayed. I'm glad you're alright. Hope the rest of your day with Mezli is pleasant.

He's upset, but too polite and self-sacrificing to say it. I need to salvage this or both the mission and his chance at a relationship with his mate will be ruined.

Eden: I was going to head in to the conference soon, if you're still free. Mezli's going to her friend's place to help set up for dinner tonight. You're still coming, right?

Phelix: I didn't know if the invitation still stood.

Eden: Of course it does! She wants to see you, Phelix. She cares about you. What's between me and Mezli is just for fun. Just a friend helping me have a good time before I go home.

It stings to type those words out and acknowledge that truth, and a heavy tear slides down my cheek. The shower turns off and I swipe it away quickly, taking a deep breath to calm myself before I turn into a blubbering mess.

> Phelix: Ah. In that case, shall we meet outside the conference hall in an hour?

> Eden: Sounds great!

I close out the chat and flop back down onto the bed as Mezli emerges, her long hair wrapped in a towel but otherwise completely nude. She does a salacious eyebrow wiggle when she sees me still on the bed. "I thought you were getting dressed."

"You're one to talk," I say, rolling my eyes.

"Just figured I'd see if I could tempt you one more time before I have to head out."

"As much as I'd love to, I need to scan through those files. Uh, Phelix asked me to meet him at the conference. If there's no evidence of the schematics in the data, then I'll use the time to talk you up. If there is...well, I guess I'll do the same, but with Operation Honey Pot in mind. After all, we still need to find out when the meeting is happening. If there even is a meeting. Ugh, I hate this."

"Damn, all that work this morning, and you're back to worrying about Phelix the second I stop making you come. You're going to make me jealous."

I sigh, shrugging. "There's nothing to be jealous of. Phelix is your mate and I'm just... I'm a temporary diversion."

"Oh, sweet Eden. That's where you're wrong. Even when you leave, I'll think of this time we've spent together for a long, long time."

Hope flickers inside me at her words, but they still contain the irrefutable reality of things. Mezli cares for me, but I'm leaving. "Same. I'll think of you, too." *For the rest of my boring, lonely life.*

Mezli smiles softly and touches my cheek. "Well, I'll let you get dressed! I hope you don't find what you're looking for in the data. I hope you're right about Phelix." Her smile flickers, the only sign that she's worried too. "But if you do, I know you can handle this. You're a certified badass spy babe now, after seducing the target and serving as a distraction while I got the files. By the end of this week, we'll be teaching those agents a thing or two about covert operations."

"Yeah, we'll teach them not to recruit unqualified civilians to do their dirty work," I grumble.

She nods emphatically. "Exactly! Just remember that. They're the idiots who are making us do this. If we fail, it's not our fault. Sure, potentially lives are on the line if we screw this up..." Her expression sobers. "Fuck, we better not screw this up."

Mezli's grim reminder helps bolster my resolve as she heads out and leaves me to peruse the files. Enough screwing around—literally and figuratively. It's time to focus and make sure we don't fail this mission.

28

✦PHELIX✦

Conference goers mill around between lectures as I weave my way toward the entrance of the conference hall, uncertain of how my meeting with Eden will go. Nerves kick up inside me as I wait for her, scanning the stream of aliens coming and going on the walkways for her telltale figure. My hand reflexively goes to the datapads in my bag, unable to repress the urge to check and re-sort them. My fingertips slide against the familiar cool metal and for a moment, the tension starts to wane. Then my thumb catches on a dent on the datapad closest to my body.

That's not right. I'd put that one on the other side the last time I sorted them.

Tension ratchets up as I attempt to recall the last time I did this ritual. It was before I left to go to the nightclub, and I could've sworn I left them the same as always, but I wasn't in the best state of mind.

The unease at finding things not in their perfect place doesn't fade as I fix the datapads. Seeing Eden approaching in a cute black jumpsuit that matches her springy curls, I do my best to shove my distress aside and wave to her. Her eyes light up once she sees me, and that does a lot to set me at ease.

I'd worried that after last night things would be awkward, but she smiles at me, a beaming ray of sunshine that warms my heart. "Phelix! I hope I didn't keep you waiting too long."

"No, not at all." I extend a hand in the human greeting. "Good to see you again."

She bypasses the hand and wraps her arms around me instead, setting me ablaze with the press of her lush body against mine. My mind flashes to her lying on top of me as she came over and over on my cock, and when she pulls away, her cheeks are flushed, making me think it brought back a similar memory for her.

"Sorry, just happy to see you again!" she says sheepishly.

I'm baffled by her need to apologize for granting me the chance to feel her body against mine again, but shrug. "I'm happy to see you as well."

She touches my upper arm and her eyes meet mine, conveying a strange mixture of emotion I can't parse. "I know I've already missed too much of the conference, but I was wondering if maybe we could speak somewhere less crowded."

"Is everything alright?" I ask.

She smiles, but that same strange emotion lingers in her gaze. "Yeah! I just wanted to talk to you about something...sensitive." She looks around and leans in to whisper, her warm breath against my neck and her intriguing scent making me shiver. "Medical stuff."

That wasn't what I was expecting. Is she injured? Dammit, I should've been more careful. The thought of causing her pain makes me feel ill.

I try my best to remain calm as I respond. "Of course. Whatever you need."

We find a small seladin bakery with a secluded courtyard for customers, and Eden insists on treating me to a pastry. I want to argue that I should be the one to pay, but that would negate her kind gesture.

When we sit, she gives me another inscrutable smile, and I can't help feeling like she's trying to soften me up before a blow.

"So, um, I wanted to thank you," she says.

I raise a brow, calmly sipping my drink as I anticipate what she wants to tell me. "For what? I should be the one thanking you for what happened last night."

She flushes prettily at the mention of our joining, but she shakes her head. "No. I mean, yes, thank you for that! But also, for what you did for me."

"What I did for you?" I'm still not understanding.

She takes one of my hands and squeezes it. "The medipod. You took a risk helping some unknown human hack into the device."

That's not at all what I was expecting. "You've already thanked me for my assistance. I was happy to help you, especially when the barbaric practices of locking lifesaving medical technology behind a paywall are involved."

I still remember the anger I felt when Dr. Mori sent me a message begging for help to keep her pregnant patient and their future child safe. Working in the biggest neonatal hospital on Nexxa Itat, I'd never considered what it'd be like to not have the funding needed to treat my patients properly. I prided myself on being the best in my field, but Eden opened my eyes. Competence and intelligence aren't the most important factor in medicine—credits are.

It disgusts me. We live in a technological age where things only a few centuries ago that would've been seen as miraculous are commonplace. There are enough resources in the galaxy for all to get the care they deserve, but greed is the most abundant resource of all.

At first, I wanted to run away and go to some destitute colony, serving as a medical missionary to make amends for taking my privileges for granted. It was tempting—play the savior and get away from the asinine nexxit noble politics and the pain of being alone. Tempting, but ultimately selfish. No, I decided to stay and use the resources and power afforded to me by my social status and medical background to reshape things from the inside.

Eden misinterprets my calm dismissal of her thanks. "I know it wasn't a big deal to you, but it was huge to me."

I squeeze her hand back. "Talking to you changed my life, Eden."

"Really?" Her brow furrows in disbelief. How can she not see how important she is?

"Yes," I say adamantly.

I'd tell her about the professional epiphany and identity crisis our conversations triggered, but I don't want her to feel like she did something wrong. Or to realize how much of a pompous ass I've been for the majority of my life.

"Talking to you was like a light in the dark. I was going through the motions, especially after things with Mezli went poorly. You helped wake me up."

It's a dangerous confession to make, but something in Eden begs me to lay all my secrets and vulnerabilities at her feet. Maybe it's a human thing. I'll have to see if I have the same reaction to Mezli's friend at dinner tonight.

I hope I don't. I want whatever this is between me and Eden to be special.

"I—I felt the same way. Talking to you made me feel alive. It's why I ended up here on Spire for the conference. You were the spark that made me yearn for more." Eden's eyes drop to her hands, her cheeks flushing.

"I'm surprised Mezli didn't have anything to do with that."

"What? No... Oh wait, you mean because we work together! Right!" She takes a large gulp of her water. "Uh, we didn't know much about each other, just worked for the same pharmaceuticals company. They assigned her to be my guide of sorts while I'm on Spire. I don't think they expected us to have so much chemistry! Get it? Because we work at... nevermind."

I suppose that makes sense, but I get the feeling she's leaving something out. "How did you end up working for a large company? I know you were eager to do work beyond your job on your home colony, but I'm surprised at how quickly you went from being a rural doctor to being brought out for the conference on the company's credits."

"Oh! I, uh, I may have embellished my application." She rubs the back of her neck. "A lot."

I chuckle at her sheepish look. "Dr. Mori! I'm shocked."

"Hey, we all can't be fancy rich doctors who can fly across the galaxy on a whim and stay in luxury suites! I saw my chance, and I took it. I may be in over my head here, but at least I'm doing *something*."

"Don't mistake my shock for anything bad. I'm impressed by you. Impressed and inspired," I say, genuinely meaning it more than she can know.

"Inspired, huh? You have something you're going to take a chance on?" she asks, quirking a brow.

"I do." Thanks to Eden, I have more than one thing at stake this week. For once in my life, I'm ready to take the leap.

Her cheeks grow pink as I gaze at her. After a moment, she looks away to take a bite of her pastry, and when she looks back at me, a friendly mask has settled over her features. "Good. I'm glad. I want you and Mezli to be happy."

I hate that she's not sharing her feelings. I hate that I don't know if it's because she's not interested in me the way I am in her or if she's trying to protect herself from getting entangled with a mated pair.

I wouldn't blame her if she didn't want me. I'm selfish to hope we could find some sort of arrangement that wouldn't leave one of us out in the cold. But after we shared our bodies in a way I've never experienced before and knowing she's the reason I'm here at all, something deep in my soul yearns to find a way to keep her.

"What about your happiness, Eden?" I ask, trying not to let hope and fear of rejection bleed into my tone.

My heart sinks as her facade settles more firmly in place and she lets out a soft laugh. "I'm happy. How could I not be when I get to spend the week with two gorgeous aliens?"

This is all just a fun, new experience for her. Nothing more. Goddess, I'm a fool.

"Right. Well, I hope I can help you enjoy yourself again during your time here." I give her a cocky grin, then take a bite of the pastry that tastes like ash in my mouth as I swallow down my disappointment.

29

✦ MEZLI ✦

Something is burning when Fina's partner, Maerlon, greets me at the door to their loft. A string of curses ring out from inside and the tall seladin's glowing white eyes flare.

"Better get inside. Fina's freaking out."

"Your fault?" I ask, teasing him.

"No. Paul's." His eyes glow brighter in amusement.

"What's he doing here? I thought this was dinner with your sister and my professional colleagues."

"Your colleagues? Oh right, I forgot you're up to some *fa-shar* nonsense and pretending to be a doctor? Fina tried to explain, but it made no sense."

"It's simple. I'm trying to get back together with my estranged mate, who is a doctor attending the conference. I met a human while there and befriended her because I like to collect them like lost flesstras. Your sister—much hotter than you, by the way—saw us at the conference and invited us to dinner after I said I knew you."

"There's something you're leaving out. That plan is nonsensical," Maerlon says, assessing me with his arms crossed over his chest.

"Speaking from personal experience?" I bite back at him.

He glares at my reminder of his ridiculous behavior when he first met Fina and kept his identity a secret.

I don't feel bad not telling them about the covert mission I'm on, because it doesn't matter anymore. Eden commed me earlier letting me know the schematics weren't in his files. The agents were wrong—unsurprising, given how bizarre this whole arrangement is —and now I'm just waiting for them to get back to us and officially call off the mission. So yeah, tonight's weird, and I don't like pretending that I have a different job, but it could've been a lot worse. Instead, there's a bubbling sense of hope and anticipation about seeing Phelix now that I know he's not a criminal.

I pat Maerlon's arm. "Look, I know you want to protect Fina from my antics, but I promise, this won't harm her. At worst, it'll be an awkward evening. At best, well...that's probably a moot point considering Paul's here."

The handsome human in question appears from the kitchen and scowls at me. I beam back at him with my most saccharine smile. "Paul! What a delight it is to see you again! Did Fina invite you because she felt bad you were spending yet another night alone?"

His brown cheeks darken at my dig. "She invited me because I wanted to meet Eden."

My joviality vanishes. "Why do you want to meet Eden?" I can't keep the possessiveness out of my tone.

"After you told me about the attack, I wanted to talk to her and make sure she's really okay. And, like you said, maybe I'm tired of being alone."

"You can't date her!"

He scowls at me. "First, you tell me all the aliens on dating apps aren't a good match for me. Then you stood me up for our first date. If you want me so bad for yourself, you're doing a terrible job of wooing me."

"Fuck off. Did you miss the part where I'm here to seduce my mate?" He's got a point, but I still don't like him thinking about Eden.

"Will you two please stop arguing and come help me?!" Fina's voice rings out from the kitchen.

I rush in to find Fina on her knees in front of the food replicator, smoke billowing from it. "Shit, what happened here?" I ask, dropping down beside her to investigate.

She coughs and turns to give me a sheepish smile. "I tried to program the food synthesizer to make something special for tonight, and it didn't turn out."

"Why are you cooking? I thought baking was your thing." Fina is an amazing baker, but she's not the best when it comes to using tech to make an actual meal. The last thing she made me was some kind of noodle dish that was somehow dry and soggy at the same time.

She smacks me on the shoulder with a towel. "I was trying to make something nice! It's not every cycle that I meet my partner's older sister *and* my best friend's mate."

"Don't forget Eden!" I say cheerily.

"Remind me, who is Eden?" Fina asks.

"She's my..." Shit, how do I explain who Eden is to me? She's so much more than a friend, and even a lover doesn't feel like enough. She's...special. I settle for a joke, since that's easier than pinning down what Eden means to me. "She's another wayward human. You know I love collecting them."

Fina laughs. "Well, I'm excited to meet her. Even if this food is a disaster."

"If you didn't want a disaster, you should've made Maerlon program the food," I tease. I dodge out of the way as she throws the towel at my face and stands with a huff.

"I offered! She wanted to do it herself," Maerlon says, joining the crowd in the kitchen.

"Okay, fine. I'm a terrible cook! I'll listen to you next time." Fina's eyes water from the smoke and unshed tears of frustration. "Dammit, what are we going to eat? People are coming in less than an hour."

"It's okay. I'll figure it out." Maerlon wraps Fina up into his arms and murmurs soothing words to my distraught friend, brushing the tears off of her cheek. There's a jealous pang in my chest for the intimacy and love they share so easily. I'm happy they've found each other. They both deserve it. Still, it doesn't make me any less envious.

"You're too good to me," Fina says softly, resting her cheek against his shoulder and letting out a long exhale as her stress melts away in his embrace.

"Nope. Just barely good enough for the most wonderful woman in the galaxy."

Ugh, barf. Not feeling quite as jealous now.

I avert my eyes as she goes up onto her toes to kiss him, and catch Paul doing the same, a sad look crossing his face.

I feel bad for the guy. He's been just as unlucky in love as me.

Partially due to me. He wasn't wrong when he said I was sabotaging his dating attempts. At first, it was because I was still pissed about how he broke Fina's heart when they dated. Then it turned into me keeping him open as an option in case I wanted to date him. Shit, I need to stop being such an ass to him and apologize.

Maerlon gives Fina one last squeeze and then pats her lush backside. "Go sit down with your friends, and make sure Paul and Mezli don't kill each other before our other guests arrive."

"Okay. Thank you, my love."

"Anything for you. *L'thris a talla.*"

I roll my eyes, managing to pull an amused smirk from Paul. It's a start.

I grab Fina's hand and guide her into the living area of the loft, plopping down next to her on the sofa. Paul sits on a chair across from us, no doubt still wary about Maerlon getting possessive over Fina. Not that the seladin sweetheart ever would, but when your ex is dating an enormous alien with fangs and glowing eyes, I understand his caution.

Sympathy surges up in me again at how I've treated Paul recently. "Sorry," I murmur.

"What was that?" he asks.

Goddess, I'm trying to be nice for once and he's being an ass! "I said I'm sorry!" I shout.

He winces. Guess he really couldn't hear me. Whoops.

"I'm sorry, Paul," I say a third time, keeping my voice gentle. I'm turning into Eden with all these apologies.

His mouth falls open as he gapes at me like I'm the first alien he's ever seen. It makes me want to smack the shocked look off his face. Fina lets out a small "wow" and that takes me aback. I'm not always mean to him, am I? Shit, seeing his wide eyes, I'm worried he's taken all my teasing seriously.

"You're sorry?" Paul asks, voice hesitant.

Does he really want me to say it again? Goddess, humans are dense sometimes. "Yes. I'm sorry. I shouldn't have treated you the way I did. I know that you've been lonely, and I really did want to go to the embassy opening with you. I really did want to see if there was something between us."

"You did?" His tone is even more incredulous.

"Yeah. I did. I like you, Paul. Once I got over how much a dick you were to Fina, I could see the appeal."

His cheeks flush darker at my admission. "I... I see the appeal of you too, Mezli."

Fuck. How do I tell him, "I think you're hot and a decent person, but I'm not into you anymore because all I can think about is my estranged mate and a sexy human doctor who, oh, by the way, I happen to be playing spies with"? I don't want to hurt his feelings even more, but I can't tell him the whole truth.

"That means a lot to me. I, uh, you know my...mate is coming to dinner tonight?" I ask.

He nods, and thank the Goddess, he doesn't look upset.

"He's why I missed the party at the human embassy. I hadn't seen him in years and we didn't part on good terms and I was too... emotional to go out that night."

Paul reaches out and places a hand on my leg. "It's okay, Mezli. I understand." His eyes flash to Fina momentarily, and then he lets out a soft chuckle. "Figures that everyone I'm into ends up with a hot alien."

"You'll find your hot alien soon, Paul! Maerlon's sister is single..." Fina says, patting his arm.

Paul's thick eyebrows shoot up. "I think Maerlon would kill me if I tried to hit on his sister."

"No, Maerlon likes you! He's a big softie, he wouldn't mind."

"I'll take your word for it," says Paul, glancing over to the kitchen where the huge seladin is humming as he reprograms the food synthesizer.

Fina shrugs. "Okay, if Ulena's too intimidating, then maybe a hot human! Mezli said her friend Eden is beautiful."

"No," I say immediately, scowling.

Fina gives me a perplexed look. "No?"

"I thought we were done with you sabotaging my dating efforts," Paul says with a groan.

"I... I like Eden," I say, face heating for some bizarre reason at my confession. I feel panicky, wanting to flee from my own feelings now that I've said them aloud.

"I thought you said you were into your mate?" Fina asks.

Her sweet, familiar face holds no judgment, which allows me to continue even though my stomach feels like it's full of fluttering insects. "I like both of them. I want both of them."

Paul lets out an infuriating "ah" that sounds like he's holding back his judgmental thoughts, and the urge to smack him rises again. Fina glares at him and he shakes his head. "I'm just wondering why you're acting like that's some kind of dirty secret or insurmountable problem. You like two people. Am I not getting something?"

"Did you miss the part where one of them is my fated, Goddess-chosen mate?"

He shakes his head. "No, I heard that."

"Paul, don't be mean," Fina says, poking him in the shoulder.

"Ow! I'm not! Do they both want something exclusive from you?"

I pause at his question. "I don't know... I didn't ask."

Paul's mouth downturns. "*You* didn't ask? You say everything that's on your mind! So much so that I'm mentally scarred from some of the things you've told me. I don't get it."

"Do nexxit not have polyamory? Is it taboo to have more than one partner?" Fina asks, far more gently than Paul's approach. Somehow it makes the question even more uncomfortable.

"It's not taboo. It's just not done with mates."

"Since when have you ever given a shit about what's done?" Paul huffs.

"I... Fuck you!" It's a childish response, but my brain is going a mile a minute. Is it really that simple? No, it can't be. Eden wouldn't... Phelix would never want...

"Okay, okay, that's enough. We're supposed to be calming down before everyone gets here, not making things worse," Fina says, chastising both of us.

"Sorry. I'm not trying to be a dick. I'm just being honest," Paul says.

"Could've fooled me!" I snap back.

"Ugh! Enough. Paul, you're not an expert on relationships. I'm sure Mezli has her reasons not to talk to them about her feelings." Up until a couple of days ago, Fina was the only one who knew about what happened with Phelix, why I ran away from home, and how hard I've fought to become the *xala* I am now.

I smile at her in appreciation. "Thank you, Fi—"

"And you stop snapping at Paul!" Fina interrupts. "He's trying to help, even if he's too blunt. You, of all people, should understand that."

"Fine," Paul and I grumble in unison.

"Good, now let's go finish setting things up and see if Maerlon needs any help."

We stand, and as Paul moves to go past me, I reach out. He

instinctively flinches, and I suppress a scoff. You slap someone *one* time and they act like you'll strike at any moment.

"Stop it, I'm giving you a hug," I say, wrapping my arms around him.

"Oh. Okay." Paul's warm, solid body feels nice against mine, but it's nothing compared to Eden or Phelix. He sighs and squeezes me back, making me wonder when the last time someone hugged him was.

That settles it. I have two missions tonight. One, figure out shit with Phelix and Eden. And two, help Paul impress Ulena so he can finally get some alien action.

30

✦EDEN✦

Phelix and I spend the rest of the afternoon at the conference attending lectures. I was so excited to learn when I applied for the sponsorship to the conference, but sitting next to him, it's hard to care about the latest dermal regeneration advances or symbiotic organism implants. If he notices me glancing at him almost as much as I'm looking at the panel of lecturers during the talk on the impact of artificial wombs on natural fertility rates among nexxit, he doesn't say anything. Though, he glances over at me with a devilish gleam in his eyes when a bookish aespian in the audience asks a question about insemination during nexxit copulation. I almost melt into a puddle, remembering just how much I learned about that topic last night.

I'm overheated as we leave the conference hall and find our way through the crowded transit system to Sagittarius district, where we're headed for dinner. He cages me against the window of the transport with his body to protect me from the stares and touches of overly curious aliens, and my skin buzzes with the need for him to touch me more. By the time we make it to the multistory building next to a glowing synthetic garden, I know I'm flushed a bright red. I only hope he attributes it to getting overheated from the bustling walkways and not because I'm turned on by his mere presence.

The heat inside me cranks up even more when Mezli comes skipping out of the front of the building and tugs me into a hug, her lips brushing against my cheek as we part.

"Glad you found it alright!" she says, squeezing me before letting me go and turning to look at Phelix. Both nexxit tense, but Phelix acts first. He tugs her against his chest, and Mezli's eyes go wide in surprise. I smile at her as she looks at me over his shoulder, silently urging her to accept his gesture. Her face softens, and she lets her body loosen, her eyes eventually closing as she burrows her face against his neck and squeezes him back.

The intimacy and vulnerability of this moment between them takes my breath away. She fits against his body like a missing puzzle piece, her arms slotting perfectly between his and her petite body melding into his bulky frame. Truly, they're made for each other.

I rub at the bittersweet ache in my chest, forcing myself to stop staring and let them have their moment. I'm so happy for them, and so damn sad that I can't claim a space in their beautiful mosaic.

The moment seems to stretch on forever, though I know it only lasts for a few seconds. Mezli reluctantly moves back, looking dizzy and flushed. "I...uh, nice to see you, Phelix."

"You look beautiful," he says, his voice thick. He'd said the same thing to me earlier today, but I know it means so much more when he says it to Mezli.

She gives him a lopsided smile. "You look pretty damn good, too." She turns and beams at me, grabbing my hand. "And you look as delectable as always."

Phelix looks me up and down, and the buzz that waned while I was feeling sorry for myself comes back in full force. "She does. Good enough to eat."

"Hah! If you two are that hungry, we should head inside for dinner," I joke, trying to dispel some of the tension.

"Right! Follow me." Mezli leads us inside and up an elevator to an upper floor of the building, pausing outside a door near the end of a narrow hall. "I can't wait for Fina to meet you. Well, Fina and Maerlon. And Paul!"

"Paul?" Phelix asks.

I raise a brow, nerves rising. "The guy that works at the human embassy? I thought he was really angry at you."

"Yep! He's not mad at me anymore, don't worry. I apologized for standing him up the other night."

Phelix tenses. "We're having dinner with someone you've dated?"

"No! I was going to go on a date with him, but then I didn't. It's fine. He's great."

Jealousy trickles down my spine, and the sharp exhale Phelix lets out indicates he's not pleased about this development either.

I've never had a problem with meeting new people before, but faced with Mezli's best friend and a guy she's apparently into makes the urge to flee rise. I push down my nerves, and plaster a smile onto my face as Mezli tugs the door open and leads us inside.

✦

"You didn't know what he looked like? Like nothing at all?" I ask between bites of a delicious, tangy salad of unfamiliar vegetables.

Fina laughs, her smile lighting up her face as she nods. "Nope! Nothing." She's sweet and shy and warm and I understand now why Mezli adores her. I don't think it would be possible to dislike her, unless you're a total asshole. Even Phelix seems charmed by her goofy wit and banter with Mezli.

"If she'd known what he looked like, I doubt she'd have developed an infatuation," Maerlon's sister Ulena deadpans. I can't tell if she's joking or not, but I hope it's the former because the two share a lot of similarities in their appearance. Long, glossy silver-white hair, strange glowing eyes, and sharp smiles that indicate their predator ancestry. They're a little frightening at first glance, but there's beauty once you get past the initial shock.

"Don't listen to her," Fina says, kissing Maerlon's cheek. His incandescent eyes brighten in what I'm guessing is a mix of embarrassment and affection.

"At least she didn't get violently ill after she first saw him," Phelix says, and I tense to see how Mezli will respond, but she snorts and reaches out to pat his shoulder affectionately.

"That was just a...misunderstanding."

Paul laughs. "And I thought her slapping me when we first met in person was bad."

Phelix fist tenses on his fork, as it has every time Paul's spoken tonight.

"Why did she slap you?" Ulena asks, eyes darting between Paul and Mezli.

Mezli shrugs. "Oh, another misunderstanding. Paul's a great guy! We've spent a ton of time together since he relocated to Spire, and he's easily one of the top three humans I've met!"

Fina snorts at her joke, and Paul flushes at her attempt at praise, but Ulena just gives Paul another assessing look. "What are his merits? Why would a beautiful woman like you be interested in him?"

Phelix's eye twitches as he stabs into his food with too much force. I can't help my similar reaction, heart sinking when Mezli perks up.

"Oh! He's amazing! He's smart, handsome, and funny, and looks like he could really throw you around, if you know what I mean."

Ulena blinks back at her. "No, what do you mean? Why would you want him to throw you?"

"I wouldn't throw anyone!" Paul pipes up, pressing a hand to his face.

"You're not strong enough to lift her? Humans must be weaker than they appear. Mezli, I could easily lift you," Ulena says.

Mezli shakes her head, and touches Paul's arm. "Oh, he could lift me! He's so strong and...virile!"

Ulena raises a brow. "Oh?"

"*So* virile. I've seen him in tight pants and damn, he's got the goods down there.

"The goods?"

"Enormous cock," Mezli adds, like she's talking about the weather instead of the penis of the man sitting across from me.

I choke on my water at her words. I can't believe she's talking up Paul's dick in front of Phelix.

Maerlon laughs and shakes his head at Ulena, who just nods and goes back to her wine with a tiny smirk.

It doesn't feel like a joke to me. Why is Mezli acting like this? I know I told her Phelix didn't have the files, and we don't need to keep doing Operation Honey Pot, but I thought she wanted to try for something more with him.

Phelix places his fork down onto the table with a bit too much force. His expression is completely neutral as he pushes his chair back and stands. "If you'll excuse me, I need to go send a comm."

Fina nods, a hint of worry in her eyes at his sudden need to leave. "Of course. You can use the bedroom if you'd like."

"No, I'll just go out in the hall." He leaves without even looking at Mezli. Or me, for that matter. It shouldn't hurt, but it does.

She stares at his back as he heads to the door, confusion melding with disappointment and anger in her gaze. Her eyes slide over to me and whatever she finds on my face makes her immediately look away, grabbing her wine and taking a heavy swig.

Ulena must not be great at reading a room, because she looks at Mezli and gives her a fanged smile. "I'm not particularly interested in enormous cocks, unless they're on an attractive woman."

"Oh! Well, nevermind then. More Paul for the rest of us then!" Mezli awkwardly tries to pat the man's hand, but he tugs it away and looks down at his salad like he wishes he could disappear.

I wish I could, too. This conversation has gotten way too uncomfortable for me to bear. I thought Mezli wanted something real with her mate, but I guess I didn't read her right. I need to go apologize to Phelix for convincing him she wanted to make something of their mating.

"I need to go, uh, check on something too." My chair scrapes loudly against the tile floor as I stand, drawing everyone's eyes to me.

Mezli's brow furrows. "Eden?"

"It's, I'm..." I don't bother finishing the thought before I walk away, because tears well in my eyes and I don't want to be the weirdo who started crying at a dinner party with people I just met.

Why did I think I knew Mezli enough to vouch for her? Sure, we've spent the past few days practically attached at the hip, but that doesn't mean anything. She told me herself she worked hard to change who she was. To be the carefree person who doesn't think too hard about things like emotions. God, I'm a moron. Even worse, my naivety got Phelix hurt.

I step out into the hallway, releasing a shaky exhale as the door slides closed behind me. Phelix stands across the hall, back leaned against the wall and face resting in his upper hands. He looks up as he hears me approach, and the pure undisguised heartache in his eyes is staggering.

"I'm so sorry, Phelix. I thought..."

"Don't apologize." His voice is strained and I watch as he attempts to put his cool mask in place, and fails. "It was a foolish notion. A momentary weakness on my part to hope for something I don't deserve."

A tear spills down my cheek. "You deserve happiness, Phelix. You deserve..." Love? Respect? Everything? Me? I don't get a chance to settle on what to say, interrupted as the door behind us slides open again and an agitated Mezli storms out.

"What the heck is going on with you two? Is everything okay? Why are you lurking out in the hall?"

Phelix lets out a humorless laugh. "I didn't want to get in the way of your amazing friend Paul and his enormous cock."

"What's that supposed to mean?" She huffs in anger, blowing her bangs with the force of her exhale.

"It means he came here tonight because he wants to have something real, and you've spent half the meal talking about how incredible and well-hung Paul is. That's shitty, Mezli. He doesn't deserve that. I don't... Ugh, nevermind!"

"You don't what?" she snaps back, eyes wide.

"*I* don't deserve that. I spent this morning in your arms, and that apparently means nothing to you. I mean nothing to you." My face is hot from embarrassment and wet from my tears, and I wish I could just go home and get away from these feelings.

"Eden..."

I shake my head as she reaches out toward me. "Forget it. I don't matter. I'm just a fool who couldn't handle casual sex. It's fine. What's *not* fine is taking your chance at being with your mate and throwing that in the garbage."

"You matter." Phelix touches my arm, startling me out of my rage.

"Of course she fucking matters!" Mezli shouts. "You both do! I'm not interested in Paul. I was trying to set him up with Ulena. I didn't know what I was saying would upset you."

"Clearly," says Phelix in an irritated drawl.

"Fuck you, Lord Nafar. You're really so fragile that me talking about Paul's cock had you running away?"

I open my mouth to defend him, but Phelix replies before I can. "Yes. I'm defenseless when it comes to you. You've held my heart in the palm of your hand from the moment I laid eyes on you, and you seem to delight in turning it to pulp in your careless grip. Of course I'm fragile. I'm a broken, bleeding, pathetic mess because of you."

Mezli blinks back at him, speechless for the first time since I've met her. Silence stretches between the three of us, roiling with tension and heartache.

When she finally speaks, it startles me. "You're a doctor, aren't you Eden?"

"Uh, what?"

"A doctor. Phelix appears to be in need of medical attention. I've wounded him and I don't know how to heal the damage."

Phelix tightens his hands into fists and his sides, starting to shake. "I bare my feelings to you, and you *mock* me?"

"I'm not mocking you! Shit, I don't know how to do this!" Mezli runs a hand through her hair, true vulnerability written across her face.

"Do what?" I ask.

"Make up for the pain I caused. Stop running from my feelings. You name it," she says, gesturing out with her hands. "I don't know how to do this, but I want to try."

"Then quit making jokes and try!" I snap. "You have a mate! He's standing right there, fighting all his experiences and trauma to be open to you. Do you know how many people would kill to have what you have? Most people will never find that kind of partner. I know I certainly won't." A tear rolls down my cheek as I bare my truth. "You're stupid and selfish if you let that slip away," I say bitterly, wiping at my eyes as more tears fall.

"You're wrong, Eden," Mezli says softly. "I meant it when I said you *both* matter. I want both of you so much it makes my insides burn."

My heart flutters like a bird trapped in a cage, but logic forces me to clip its wings. "That's not possible. You don't want me like that. You can't—you're mates!"

"Fuck what I can and can't do. I'm here now and I want both of you. Do you want me? Do you want this?" Mezli asks, her voice trembling as she gestures between the three of us.

"I want this. I don't think I've ever wanted anything more than the two of you," Phelix says with staggering conviction.

"But—I don't—You're meant to be together. I don't fit."

Phelix steps in behind me, caging me between their bodies. "You're wrong. Without you, *we* don't fit together. You're the missing piece."

31

✦PHELIX✦

I don't know who moves first, but suddenly Mezli's lips crash against mine, jarring and wild and so perfectly *her*. Eden is trapped between us as our mouths meet over her shoulder and she tries to slip away, but I pin her against Mezli and break our frantic kiss to claim Eden's lips. Mezli's mouth drops to Eden's throat, and the sweet human keens, allowing my tongue to slip into her mouth. Her back arches, pressing her lush breasts against my chest, and Mezli's lower hands grasp onto my ass, making my cocks extrude so fast I grunt in pleasure-pain.

"This is... Oh god!" Eden cries as Mezli's upper hands cup her breasts and I fist a hand into her short tresses, pulling her head back gently to nip at her throat in tandem with my mate.

"You said you don't fit, but look how wrong you are," I murmur, hips grinding against Eden's soft belly.

Mezli releases her grip on me and spins Eden around to kiss her as I hold our human in place, upper hands grazing her breasts while my lower ones grip her hips, bringing her ass flush with my cocks. I pinch one of her nipples and she cries out.

Mezli chuckles, the low throaty sound going straight to my stiff lengths. "Listen to how needy she is, Phelix. I bet she'd let us fuck her right here in the hall where anyone could see."

Eden gasps and I groan, throbbing at the idea. "Would you let us fuck you like this? Show everyone who you belong to?" I rasp, hand sliding under her shirt to get better access to her tits. It's reckless to even consider, but the idea has too much appeal for me to care. I'm so tired of being in control.

"I... I want..." Eden pants between Mezli's kisses and my assault on her breasts.

"Use your words, doctor," Mezli says, her voice teasing and husky.

The air between us in this cramped hallway chokes me with lust, the heady blend of our mutual arousal and mating pheromones taking away all rational thought.

"I want to watch Phelix fuck you," Eden says.

My hips grinding against her stutter.

Mezli freezes and pulls back from kissing Eden to look her in the eyes. "Don't do that whole 'I don't want to get in the way' bullshit, Eden."

Our human shakes her head vehemently. "I'm not! I want that. It...the thought turns me on. Is that weird?"

She goes to duck her head in embarrassment, but I don't let her, grabbing her chin and turning her face to look at me. "After you told me about you and Mezli together, I had to go into the hygiene room at the conference and jerk off my cocks twice to get some relief from how much it aroused me."

Mezli chuckles at my confession. "You two are kinky freaks. We really are perfect for each other."

Goddess, we are. It feels incredible to acknowledge how well the three of us fit.

"I'll show you how perfect. Turn around and put your hands on the wall," I say in a low command.

Mezli quirks a brow and I expect her to argue about me ordering her around, but she winks at me and does as I asked, popping her ass back toward me as she rests her hands on the wall. She turns over her shoulder with a smirk. "Yes, *Lord Nafar.*"

I groan and palm the cocks trapped in my pants in an attempt to placate them. Eden watches us with desire glittering in her eyes. I know she said she's happy to watch, but I don't want that right now. Mezli unlocked something in me when she didn't fight me and a beast inside me roars to life, needing to claim and bend both of these perfect *xalas* to my will.

"Get on your knees and make her ready for me, Eden."

Her eyes widen, but she eagerly obeys, sliding to her knees between the wall and Mezli's cocked hips. Mezli's lower hands drop to her skirt, and she lifts it up, showing us that she's bare underneath.

"I said, hands on the wall."

Mezli's eyes lock with mine over her shoulder. "Make me."

I'm on her before she can attempt to put up a fight, my upper hands tearing hers from her hips and slamming them against the wall to hold her in place. "Be a good *xala* and spread your legs for me. Or do you want me to make you do that too?" I rasp into my mate's ear.

Mezli shivers and squirms against my grip, but she spreads her legs.

I use one of my lower hands to guide Eden's head between Mezli's thighs, and she follows my lead, licking a long stripe up Mezli's pussy. Mezli cries out as Eden uses her hands to spread her wider and press into her pleasure spots with her thumbs.

Goddess, I'm going to release in my pants at the sight. My grip on Mezli's hands tightens and I quickly use my lower hands to release my cocks. I inhale deeply to push the urge to come down and regain control.

"You going to just stand there with your cocks out and boss us around, or are you going to fuck me, *Lord?*"

She's such a brat and I love it. I want to spend every night for the rest of my life with her mouthing off at me and battling me for control, while Eden sweetly follows my orders like she wants nothing more than to please me. And then, once we're done pretending I'm in charge, I want them to turn around and show me just how little control I truly have.

I don't respond to her with words, letting my cocks do the talking as I line them up with her dripping entrances and ease the tips inside, testing to make sure I don't hurt her.

Her breath hitches and I pull back, using every shred of self-control I have to wait for her to relax before pressing in again.

"Quit teasing me and just fuck me!" Mezli says, trying to press herself back to take me deeper.

"As you wish." I take her at her word and snap my hips forward, sinking my cocks in further.

"Oh, fuck!" Mezli's cry is unrestrained and devoid of any teasing now.

I groan at the tight grip of her channels squeezing me like a vise, unable to move for fear of losing myself already.

Eden's tongue diligently swipes around Mezli's entrance and I moan and buck forward involuntarily when I feel it touch the base of my front cock.

"Shit, make her come before I..." My words break off in a rough grunt as Eden laps at where we're joined again.

I make the mistake of looking down over Mezli's shoulder to see the eager human's face buried between Mezli's thighs, glasses askew and her hand shoved inside her pants as she works herself furiously.

Eden redoubles her efforts on Mezli's pleasure spots, and I slam into my mate, loud grunts punching out of my lungs as my urge to fuck and to come deep inside her overtake me.

Mezli's channels clench hard around my cocks as she comes, gasping both our names. Eden's muffled moan against Mezli's cunt is my undoing, and I feel my release boiling up from inside my slit, my knot preparing to slip inside my mate's sopping pussy.

It's coming, I'm coming, oh Goddess. My vision starts to go white as I go to tumble over the edge.

"Everything alright out here—Oh, shit!" a low, masculine voice gasps from behind me and I turn in horror to see Paul staring at us slack-jawed from the doorway to Maerlon's loft.

Something feral and possessive crashes into me, and the urge to protect and lay claim on these *xalas* roils up inside me and explodes out in a growl. "Mine!"

"Shit, sorry!" The interloper apologizes but stays frozen on the spot.

I want to tear his throat out. My brain catches up with my instinct before that can happen, thank the Goddess. I stop pounding into my mate and curse, pulling away from Mezli as she attempts to tug her skirt down. It's too late for my cocks to get the memo about the interruption, and they throb as my unstoppable climax hits me, cum shooting out of both and splattering all over Mezli's backside and the floor.

"Go away, Paul!" Mezli yells, and the human unfreezes, wincing as he slams the door, leaving us alone again.

She laughs, free and wild as my damn cocks continue to paint her ass and pussy, some of my release even having the audacity to splatter onto Eden's cleavage. I gasp as the final spurts leak out of my cocks onto the floor. Eden looks shell-shocked for a moment, but then she starts giggling uncontrollably. Both of them appear to have lost their minds.

I wince as I tuck my sloppy cocks back into my pants, since despite my release they refuse to retract, knowing I didn't get to knot my mate like my body was screaming at me to do. Fuck, I would have knotted Mezli in the dingy hall where anyone could have happened upon us. I've lost my mind too.

"Did you hear how Paul squeaked when you growled at him? Incredible. I'm never letting him live that down." Mezli's eyes water from laughing so hard.

"No. You're never seeing him again," I grumble.

Mezli scoffs and pats my cheek. "Sure, sure. You'll tear out the throat of any who dare to gaze upon your mates."

Eden lets out a little squeak of alarm at her words.

"Don't listen to her. I'm not that barbaric. I'll simply give him an offer he cannot afford to say no to. Perhaps a lucrative position with my father's business. On the other side of the galaxy."

Eden's eyes are still wide as I offer her a hand to help her up from the floor.

"I'm joking," I say softly. "I didn't mean to alarm you."

She shakes her head. "You didn't, it's not—"

"Damn, you really marked your territory!" Mezli interrupts, oblivious to Eden's whispered words. She swipes a hand through the mess on her ass and thighs, which doesn't do much to help the situation. "As hot as that was, I'm going to need to clean up before we get out of here."

"We're leaving?" Eden asks, taking off her smeared glasses and wiping them on the hem of her shirt.

"Probably for the best after we traumatized poor Paul. You stay out here while I go say goodbye to Fina and Eden and I get cleaned up, killer." Mezli kisses my cheek, then slaps my ass, and I'm so flabbergasted by the casual way she's touching me now that I don't argue as she tugs Eden back into the apartment.

I'm left alone in the hallway, dazed and already aching for my *xalas* to rejoin me so we can continue things in a more private location. My cheeks ache and it takes me a moment to realize it's because of the smile still stuck on my face. Goddess, this is the best night of my life.

32

✦ MEZLI ✦

Coming off the high of my explosive orgasm and my confession to Eden and Phelix, I don't even mind the way everyone stares as I return to the dinner party.

"Sorry about that, we needed to have a quick conversation. Fina, mind if we use the hygiene room for a bit?"

"Uh, sure?" Her reply comes out as a question as she gawks at Eden and my disheveled state. Ulena and Maerlon's nostrils flare, no doubt scenting the jizz I'm covered in.

"Looks like it was an interesting...conversation," Ulena says, raising a knowing brow at us.

"It was! Would've been better without the interruption." I look pointedly at Paul, who has the decency to blush and act like he's very interested in one of Maerlon's paintings.

Eden clings to my side as I lead her into the hygiene room at the back of the loft and she sighs in relief when I lock the door behind us. "God, I'm so embarrassed! They could tell what we did, couldn't they? Your friends are going to think I'm such a freak."

"Did you miss the part of Fina's story where she had a bunch of freaky holosim sex with an alien stranger? They have no room to judge you for having fun in the hallway with your mates."

Eden squeaks in protest, obviously not believing me. I open the door back to the loft and poke my head out, raising my voice so everyone can hear. "None of you are judging Eden for eating me out in the hallway, right?"

She tugs me back inside and smacks my arm, glaring at me. "I believed you about them not caring!"

"Then why did you make that cute little nervous squeak?" I ask, upper hands fumbling for my dress zipper.

"You said 'mates'. Twice now!"

"Oh. I did?" I hadn't realized because it felt so natural.

"Yes!" Her cheeks flush even darker and I know that's not just from the sight of me getting undressed in front of her.

Is she upset with me? I reach over to get the shower started and shrug back at her, trying to push down panic at the idea she's angry I called her my mate. I thought I told her I wanted her, and she agreed.

"Is that a problem?" I ask, dreading her answer.

"It's not accurate!" She frowns at me, crossing her arms.

"You're worried about semantics when I've told you I want to be with you? *Really?*"

"It's not semantics! It's a biological fact. Phelix is your mate. I'm your..." She sighs as she trails off, like it's a forgone conclusion that biology matters more to me than what's in my heart.

It pisses me off. After the way I've opened myself up to her these past few days, after I've let her *see* me, she thinks I'd care about her less than Phelix?

I open my mouth to tell her that, but the sadness in her eyes stops me. Goddess, yelling at her won't make this better. I can only keep showing her I care until she believes me. She's stubborn, so it'll take more than a quick confession of feelings and a hallway fuck.

I reach out and take her hand. "You're mine. If you'll let me have you."

"I want you to have me," she says, voice threaded with restrained hope.

I lean over and kiss her cheek. "Good. As much as I'd like to have you again right now, we should get cleaned up. Don't want to make our poor mat—uh, our Phelix, wait too long for us. He might break down the door and strangle Paul."

She giggles and nods, releasing my hand so I can step into the shower while she grabs a washcloth to clean off her face and chest.

A buzzing vibration on my wrist pulls my focus away from her cleavage to my comm, and Eden's comm chirps at the same time. Glancing at mine, I see it's a message from Agent Tysea.

"Wow, we hear nothing for almost a day about those files and they have to choose now to check in." I can't wait to be done with them. Hopefully, this is the last time they'll reach out and we can spend the rest of this conference week in peace. I don't see what else they'd want from us—we did what they asked and they were wrong about Phelix. Case closed.

Eden expands the message and scans through it, her brow furrowing as she reads.

"Shit, don't tell me they want us to do some other nonsense. Do you secretly have a mate that we need to seduce for non-existent data?" I ask, as I open the message to take a look at what has her concerned.

> Tysea: Analysis of the files downloaded from Nafar's datapads completed. Schematics are in his possession. Proceed with determining the time and location of his meeting. Use any means necessary at your disposal and do not let the target out of your sight.

My heart drops into my stomach. "Fuck."

Eden re-reads the message, frowning at it. "I—I don't understand. There weren't any files that matched the schematics they described in what you downloaded."

"You're sure? There was a lot of data there. Maybe you missed it."

She shakes her head adamantly. "I didn't! I checked three times. Yes, there were medical schematics, but they were all for advanced healing tech. Nothing that could be used as a weapon!"

She sounds so certain. I want to be certain, too. But I'm not. Something isn't adding up, and it's making my skin itch with an impending sense of disaster. "Why would they lie about this, Eden? You're smart, but you must have missed something. You hadn't had a full night's sleep and I've been distracting you. And I know you..." I pause, the sick dread inside me increasing. "You wanted to believe that Phelix wouldn't do something like this."

Her expression flickers when I mention Phelix.

There it is. My skin tightens even more. I want to scrub at it to wash away this mess. Scour my skin until the truth of what's going on doesn't crawl all over me. "You lied," I say, keeping my voice even despite the urge to vomit. "You wanted to be with Phelix, so you lied about the schematics."

"What?! No!"

Eden's disbelief looks genuine, but there's something lurking under the surface. I should know. I was trained since birth to see what people are trying to hide. Taught to root out people's hidden truths and use it as a weapon against them. The only difference now is that the dagger of what she's hiding from me is piercing into my own fragile heart.

That same training washes over me as I step out of the shower and wrap myself in a towel. Everything inside me sinks down, deep into the pit where I store all my Goddess-damned emotions—my affection for Eden, my idiotic hope for something with her and Phelix, my heartache, and my rage.

"It was more than just professional correspondence, wasn't it?" I ask, keeping my tone cold. Dammit, I should've asked her more questions when she told me she knew him. My teeth grind together and emotions roil inside me, dangerously close to the point where there's no more room to keep them from bursting out of me like an overfilled closet.

"I... I guess you could say we flirted. But he stopped comming me and nothing else happened! I didn't say anything because—"

"Because you wanted to protect your crush. Dammit, Eden! You care more about some stuck up, criminal *xalar* than people's lives?"

Not just people's lives—she cares more about Phelix than *me*. I told her I want her to be mine, that I think she's my *mate*, and this whole time she was prioritizing Phelix. Does she even care about me?

Fuck, this is why I don't let people in.

Eden shakes her head. "I didn't lie about the schematics! They weren't there. I swear!"

I scoff. "Goddess, you don't have to keep lying. It's really not a good look. Was sleeping with me your way of trying to distract the dumb, horny slut, or was that just a fun perk of your week covering for Lord Nafar's unsavory dealings?"

"N-no! How could you think that?" She's crying now, and no matter how hard I try to harden myself, it kills me to be the reason she's upset.

Hot tears slide down my own cheeks. Fuck, *I'm* crying. "What else am I supposed to think, Eden?"

"I would never do that to you. I care about you just as much as Phelix. I'm falling in love with you. The data wasn't there. Please, you have to believe me. Something else is going on." She reaches for me, tears spilling down her face and dropping in heavy splotches onto her chest.

I should be elated at the mention of love. I desperately want to believe her. But then she has to keep speaking.

"I'm s-sorry, Mezli!"

Her apology makes the fissures in my heart deepen. I don't want apologies. I wanted someone I could trust. I wanted someone I could love without fear of getting hurt. "Enough! Enough of your trite apologies. They fall from your lips endlessly but are so fucking meaningless. You're sorry? Well, I'm sorry I ever met you. I'm sorry that I was such a Goddess-damned moron to think that your sweet, innocent act was real. I'm sorry that I ever had the misfortune to meet you! You're even worse than Phelix. At least he had the decency to show me how much of an awful person he was from the start."

"Mezli, p-please..." Eden gasps for air between her heavy sobs and my heart shatters the rest of the way.

I curl in on myself, needing to be done with this conversation. I want to shut everything out so that I don't have to feel this way. I can't fight the defensive instinct to push Eden away because it's all I know how to do when I'm hurt.

"Go tell your boyfriend he's been made. I can't do this. Please, just... just go."

She gives me one last pleading look, but there's nothing left in me but anguish. When she listens and heads out the door, I sink down to the floor and let the pain consume me.

BANGING on the door rouses me from my stupor. It takes me a moment to get my bearings, and I push myself up from the squishy, damp bathmat with weak arms. My whole body feels like it was hit by an air taxi.

"Mezli, you okay in there? Eden said you weren't feeling well." Fina's worried voice filters through the locked door. "She looked a little rough, too."

I wipe the snot and tears from my chin. "I'm f-fine—one second, I'll unlock—"

"Mezli, open the damn door!" Phelix shouts from the other side, rattling the door so hard it looks like he might knock it down.

"Why is *he* still here?" I croak out the question, not intending to speak aloud but too confused for it not to slip out.

"I'm still here because my mate has locked herself in the hygiene room and our lover ran out of here sobbing, unable to say anything to me except, 'I need to make this right'. What the fuck is going on, Mezli?"

I stand on wobbly legs, securing the towel around me that had fallen down during my breakdown, and press the button to unlock the door. It slides open to reveal Phelix right on the other side, concern and confusion etched into his stupid, handsome face.

He's a far better actor than Eden, but it doesn't make any sense why he's bothering to keep up their charade. "You know what's going on. Your pretty pen pal told me everything."

He scoffs at me, eyes narrowing. "You've got to be joking. You're ruining the chances of the three of us making something together because you're mad that we spent a handful of weeks talking over comms about hacking into a medipod and mildly flirting? Mezli, we weren't together. You left! I was lonely and broken, and Eden was the first person who made me hope for something to help me mend even a small piece of my heart. But even then, I stopped talking to her because I didn't want to give up on the idea of our mate bond."

"I don't care about that!" I try to shout, but it comes out more as a pathetic croak. "I care that you're a criminal who is endangering lives and apparently are so good at 'mild flirting' that you convinced Eden to cover it up for you."

"He's a criminal?!" Fina pokes around Phelix's broad shoulder, her eyes wide.

Phelix scowls at me. "No. She must be drunk."

"I can't get drunk, you pretentious piece of shit!" I say, shoving against his chest.

Fina pushes past him, ducking under his arm, and moves to stand in front of me defensively. "She's not drunk. She has an implant that neutralizes alcohol in her system. Got it after she met you and you called her a drunken whore. So back the fuck up and explain why the hell my best friend is so upset, or I'm calling station security."

My tender heart mends a small amount at her standing up from me. I may have shit luck in love, but I have the best luck in friendship. I confessed to Fina about my implant after a night she was trying to keep up with me on shots—I finally felt safe enough to let her know that my party girl persona wasn't entirely real, and I didn't want her to get alcohol poisoning because I was trying to look cool.

"Phelix, just go be with Eden," I sigh. "I don't understand why you're still here. The mission is over—you know that I know, so there's no point in me trying to spend more time with you."

"You may not be drunk, but you're still not making any sense. What mission?"

I throw my upper hands up in exasperation. "The one to stop you from selling illegal medical schematics!"

"What?"

As I look at my mate's bewildered expression, a flicker of doubt creeps into my mind. His emotions and thoughts are completely unguarded, and not in the false openness we both are so skilled at. He really doesn't know what I'm talking about. Shit.

33

✦ PHELIX ✦

Mezli and I stare at each other, her friend between us forgotten. My mind tries to make sense of the bizarre turn this night has taken, running over every interaction I've had with her and Eden over the past few days.

Running into Eden in the hygiene room at the conference.

Mezli inviting me to lunch to catch up.

Them propositioning me for sex at the nightclub.

Mezli leaving after we slept together.

Wait, hold on.

Mezli storming off after I knotted Eden and then standing by the closet when we came down to check on her. The closet I had my satchel in.

The next day, meeting Eden at the conference and noticing my datapads were out of order.

My blood goes cold. "You were *spying* on me?"

"Don't act so surprised!" Mezli huffs angrily. "That's what happens when you try to sell dangerous schematics on the black market."

The purple-haired human standing between us gapes at us. "Whoa whoa whoa, black market? Spying?! What the hell have you gotten yourself into, Mez?"

It's a question I have as well.

Mezli glances down at her comm nervously, then tears it off and tosses it on the floor. "Come on, I'm sick of arguing in this hygiene room." She pushes past me and Fina, turning on the fan in the hygiene room and shutting the door behind her. She storms into the main area of the loft, where Maerlon and Paul are cleaning up dishes from dinner. I resist the urge to yell at her to put her clothes back on, still too damn confused to prioritize shielding her from Paul's view.

"Everything okay?" the imposing seladin asks as Mezli plops down on the couch. Fina shakes her head and gives him a look that says she'll explain later.

"I didn't know if they were listening or not. I don't want to get even more shit from those damn agents about how I'm not doing my duty to protect galactic security. If they cared so much, they wouldn't have recruited two civilians to do their damn work for them!"

Agents? Galactic security? Either Mezli had some kind of break with reality or someone is fleecing her and Eden.

"What agents? Who are you working with?" Fina asks. My head is reeling too much to formulate words.

"They're Consortium agents. They recruited me to get close to

Phelix because they suspected him of dealing in dangerous, illegal medical tech. Since Lord Nafar here is a member of the second house of Nexxa Itat—fancy nobility nonsense," Mezli explains to the rest of the room, "—they couldn't go after him without proof of his dealings without risking a political nightmare."

I should've known. I knew something was off, and I didn't listen to myself. I let my fucking cocks and my pathetic heart take control. Everything from the moment I saw her and Eden was a lie. I'm going to be sick.

"And you were all too happy to believe them," I say with a grimace. "To believe some absurd story about me being a criminal. I shouldn't be surprised, but I didn't realize your hatred of me ran so deep. These past few days must've been torturous for you. Forced to flirt and pretend that you had any interest in our mate bond. Forced to fuck the *xalar* you loathed. Your social training is excellent—you fooled me into thinking I could be happy."

The dinner from earlier churns in my stomach, and bile threatens to escape me. How could I have been so blind?

"It wasn't—that's not—ugh, stop being such a melodramatic jerk for a moment and explain!" Mezli says, confusion twisting her features. "Are you saying it wasn't true? They have the files with the schematics!"

I level a cold stare at her. "I'm not dealing in dangerous schematics, nor have I ever done such a thing. I've dedicated my entire career to finding ways to help bring life into this universe. To help sustain our people's population. Why in the Goddess' name would I involve myself with something that would take lives away?"

"I didn't know you, Phelix! When they came to me and said that Eden and I needed to get close to you and verify the data, I didn't think to search your work history. Lives were at stake!" Mezli's voice shakes as she snaps back at me defensively.

Paul clears his throat from the kitchen. "Um, not to confuse things more, but I don't understand why they asked a random human doctor who'd never been away from a small farming planet to do a covert operation."

Mezli shrugs in exasperation. "It was a trade for the Consortium sponsoring her trip to the medical conference. According to Eden, she oversold her qualifications on her application and they thought she'd be more well-suited for the job."

"Huh, you'd think they'd have worked with the human Coalition to find someone more qualified," Paul says, lips downturning as he thinks. "Or at least contact them to vet potential candidates for sponsorship. Part of the treaty that allowed us to establish an embassy on Spire included oversight on those types of things."

As much as I initially disliked this human, his comment helps the pieces snap into place. The Consortium would never have sponsored a random human to come to such a prestigious medical conference without a series of checks. Eden was chosen because they knew about her connection to me. They knew I'd trust her because of our shared ideology.

A humorless laugh escapes me. All of this nonsense. All of this hope and heartache because of corporate greed. "Those 'agents' lied to you. They're not with the Consortium, so they didn't need to consult anyone. If I had to guess, they're mercs working for the company that holds the rights to the life*saving* schematics I have with me, trying to keep me from distributing their tech without a license. You weren't entirely wrong when you said I'm a criminal, because technically what I plan to do with them is illegal. But I can't stand by and allow schematics that should be freely available to everyone to sit behind a paywall while people die. If I can do one damn thing right in my pathetic, privileged life, it'll be taking on the risk of a slap on the wrist and a fine to make a difference."

The entire loft goes silent. I drag in deep breaths to keep myself from sinking into despair. I don't know any of these people. They could easily turn me in to these "agents" or to the actual Consortium, and all of this will have been for nothing. Just another example of how meaningless my life is.

"That's very noble of you and as a member of the Coalition ambassadorial staff, I'm going to pretend that I didn't hear any of that," Paul says. I'm starting to like him.

"Yeah, we didn't hear anything," Fina agrees.

"If we had, we would agree with your decisions. And ask if there's anything we can do to help," adds Maerlon.

Mezli snorts and finally looks me in the eye, after spending my whole explanation staring at the floor. "Well...sh-shit," she says quietly, her voice breaking. "You're a good person."

A choked laugh bursts out of me. "You say that like that's a bad thing."

"It's terrible." Mezli's face falls and tears start to slide down her cheeks. "It means I've ruined my chance at something good. Again."

My chest sizzles with the pain of our truths coming to light, alongside the smallest flicker of hope that her words kindle. Should I let the pain win like it always does, hardening me again and again until my heart is an impenetrable fortress? Or should I let the spark of hope catch hold, knowing how much more it hurts when I'm inevitably burned?

I choose fire.

"Did you feel anything when we were together?" I ask.

Her tears come faster. "I felt *everything*. Too damned much!"

"Too much to try again?"

"W-what?" She blinks at me in disbelief. "Phelix, I *lied* to you. I fucked you and led you on and drove away Eden, who—*shit*—is alone right now, when I promised to keep her safe. Why would you ever want someone like me?"

"I don't know," I say with a weak smile. "All I know is that I've been broken since we met and when we were together, with Eden, I finally felt whole."

Fina lets out a small gasp at my words and then clasps a hand over her mouth, reminding me we have an audience.

I don't care. Some things are more important than pride or decorum.

I stand and move to kneel before Mezli, wiping away some of the moisture from her cheek. "I lied, too. It's crystal clear to me why I'd want to be with you. You're stubborn and reckless and clever and kind and I knew from the moment I saw you, my life would never be the same. We're only ruined if you want us to be."

"I... I don't want that," Mezli says, barely above a whisper. "But I don't think we can do this without Eden. She's our mate, Phelix. I've felt it every time we touched. I sensed it from her smell and her taste. Hell, she was able to take your knot! She was made for us, just like we were made for each other." Her face falls in anguish. "She's our mate and I scared her away."

My heart soars with how right her words feel. I spent so much time explaining away my feelings for Eden that I never gave myself the chance to recognize what was staring me in the face. "You're right. So now we have to prove it to her."

DOZENS of unanswered messages to Eden and three hours of searching later, that romantic sentiment feels much less attainable. No sign of her in her hotel, she's not at Mezli's apartment or my hotel, and there's no record of her scanning in at the conference hall. Nothing. We looked every place she's been to on Spire. It's like she's vanished.

Dread pools in my stomach as we reconvene at Maerlon's apartment, no closer to finding her despite all of us searching.

"Dammit! Why won't she answer?" Mezli groans, typing another message into her comm. "What did she say when she left?" she asks for the hundredth time.

"She said she had to make things right." I still don't understand what she meant by it. I should've chased after her and made her explain. This is my fault.

"Make what right?" Mezli asks. "She didn't do anything wrong! I'm the one that accused her of working with you to hide the schematics. I didn't believe her over those damn fake agents."

"Did you have an established meeting place with them? Maybe she went there." Paul says, trying to keep Mezli calm with his even tone.

"No! They said to contact them and they'd come to us when we had an update."

"Which may mean they have a way of tracing your location," Maerlon says, his dotted brow furrowing with concern.

"Goddess, you're right. She must've contacted them, thinking that there was a mistake with the files and she'd correct them. And whoever the agents really are, they tracked her down and..." Mezli's face pales.

"Made sure she wouldn't cause any more trouble," I finish grimly.

34

✦EDEN✦

I'm the biggest fool in the entire galaxy. Naive to believe that I was special enough to be the only human brought to an intergalactic medical conference. Clueless enough to think that I'd found what I've been searching for with an emotionally unavailable alien and her mate. Now all that foolishness has truly fucked me over.

No one knows I'm here. My family is halfway across the galaxy, and I didn't tell Phelix or Mezli where I was going. Not that I think they'd care about finding me.

My pulse spikes as I think about how screwed I am. I don't know who these people are other than they're clearly not with the

Xi Consortium. They might think it's easier to kill me and dump my body somewhere than deal with the hassle of one random human.

My eyes dart across the tiny, dim room to "Agent" Tysea sitting across from me on a white couch that looks a lot more comfortable than my cold metal chair, reading a datapad with a yawn. They're acting like bringing me here and locking me in with them is boring, and I have to pray that it's a sign they don't have murderous intent.

My predicament could be worse, I guess. The mag-cuffs locking my hands together are in front of my body instead of pinned behind my back. They didn't bother blindfolding me or gagging me, and I'm not tied to my chair. All in all, whoever they are, they're doing a half-assed job of things. Either that, or they're so used to kidnapping people that they're confident there's nothing I can do to stop whatever they have planned. Unsurprising, given how incompetent they've thought I am from the moment we met at the docks.

I fight against the tears that well in my eyes, but it's no use. You'd think I would've cried myself into dust between Mezli's attack on me and the fear of what's going to happen. But they stream out of me in a seemingly endless supply. I'm soaked in tears and terrified sweat and I've never felt more humiliated and alone in my life.

Time passes and my waves of panic and sadness ebb in and out like the tide. Eventually, the fear clears enough for me to assess the situation and I start to get angry with myself.

What the hell am I doing? Am I going to just sit here and accept my fate?

Fuck that. When have I ever let myself give up because the odds were against me? I excel when put in situations where I have to figure things out as I go. Yes, I was an overconfident moron, and that's what got me into this mess. But that confidence is also what's going to get me out of it.

I hope.

I scan the room as subtly as possible, though Tysea isn't paying any attention to me as they swipe through their datapad, feet dangling over the arm of the sofa. The small window to my left isn't large enough that I could fit through it, and the couch Tysea is on sits between me and the only door.

Running isn't feasible. On the off-chance the door is unlocked, I still would have no clue where I am and I'm not fast or athletic enough to try to flee. I'm also not strong enough to overpower them, especially not with my hands bound. I saw them place the key to the mag-cuffs in their pocket, along with my comm, so I'm not sure how I'd get to that.

There's only one option I can see. A risky, extremely dangerous one. When they sat down, Tysea dug a small sidearm out from a holster on their back and placed it on the floor beside them. I thought at first it was meant to intimidate me, but it was really so they could be more comfortable lying down.

God, they really think I'm helpless. It's the only advantage I have, so I need to use it. A plan forms in my mind, and my pulse races as I run through every possible outcome. I'm either about to get shot or get what I need to have a fighting chance.

As quietly as possible, I stand up from my chair and move across the room. Tysea sets down their datapad and sighs when I get a few steps away, pushing themself upright. "Sit back down, human."

I call forth tears and drop to my knees in front of them. "P-please just l-let me go," I say in a tremulous voice that's not hard to fake. I'm terrified.

The ankite gives me a look of annoyance, but I continue. "I'll b-book a transit off of Spire a-and go back to Europa 3 and never leave a-again. I w-w-won't tell anyone what h-happened."

Their features morph as they watch me beg for release,

becoming a creepy facsimile of my own. "I can't do anything until Ashlath decides how to proceed. I don't like keeping you here any more than you do. I had plans this night cycle." They sigh again, and I want to smack the false sympathy off of their face.

"Please!" I cry, reaching forward to grasp feebly at their legs in supplication.

"Don't touch me," they hiss, kicking me away. I grunt in pain as their foot impacts my stomach and I fall over. Wracking sobs erupt from me and I hear them make a disgusted sound. "Pathetic. When you're done blubbering, go sit back down."

I wait for a moment, continuing my heaving cries, then reach out with my bound hands to where the blaster sits right beside where I fell. I grab hold of it, and when Tysea doesn't react, I curl up on my side and shove the small gun down my shirt between my breasts, silently praying that it has some kind of safety on.

When I don't shoot my tits off and Tysea starts humming to themself, I slowly uncurl myself and crawl back to my chair. They don't even look up at me. What an arrogant bastard. This would be the perfect moment to shoot them. I'm far enough away that they wouldn't be able to grab me in time before I got the shot off. My fingers tremble uncontrollably as I bring my hands back up to my chest.

I can do this. I don't want to kill them, but I don't want to die. I can do thi—

I flinch when Tysea's comm chirps, almost tipping the chair over backwards. Tysea's eyes dart up to me and I cover my chest with my hands, hoping it looks like a defensive gesture. They roll their eyes and then read the comm, "Huh. Looks like it's your lucky day."

"Wh-what?" My words come out as a hoarse croak.

"Apparently your partner is even more incompetent than you, and Phelix slipped away from her," Tysea says in an annoyed drawl.

"He did?" I ask. Did Mezli confess what we were doing? Is she in danger now, too?

"Yes. Apparently she found the meeting info on his comm, and then left him alone while she showered, like an imbecile. Truly, the stupidity of you two knows no bounds."

My mind races. "So...you want me to find him?" I dread the thought of seeing him now, but at least it means that I won't stay trapped in this tiny room or have to kill to escape. What was I thinking? I don't even know how to shoot a gun!

"Correct. I guess your feeble human mind is capable of logical thought after all. You need to get him to meet with you. Now. Tell him you found out that Mezli's been spying on him and that's why you left. Convince him to let you come with him to the data drop-off so you can watch his back."

"H-how am I supposed to make him believe me? He's not an idiot."

Tysea glares at me. "I don't know, but you better figure it out or things won't end well for you, Dr. Mori. Try using your filthy human cunt—that seemed to have worked well enough so far."

I wince hard at their cruel summation of what I've done this week. Taking all the excitement and affection and hope and boiling it down to me being a gullible whore. It stings because there's far too much truth to it, but I can't let it distract me. I've been given a chance to escape whatever fate they had planned for me. I found my way into this mess, and I will find my way out.

TYSEA DEPOSITS me back at my hotel room, giving me fifteen minutes to make myself presentable. I commed Phelix on the way here, telling him he wasn't safe and I needed to meet with him. I gingerly remove the gun from between my breasts and set it on the bed, my hands shaking with nerves. I stare at it for a moment, still shocked that Tysea didn't catch me stealing it and didn't notice they hadn't put it back in its holster when we left that cramped room.

Who's the incompetent one now?

With barely any time to celebrate my risky maneuver, I scramble to redo my makeup and dress in something slutty but reasonable enough to wear out in the early hours of the day cycle. A quick glance in the mirror freezes me.

God, who is that woman? I don't recognize this hollow shell of a person, wrapped in pretty packaging. My dreams and excitement carved out of my chest, leaving me dull and lifeless. At least there's still fear. That might be the only thing that helps me to convince Phelix to listen to me. If he holds any affection for me, maybe he'll see how broken I am and try to help fix it.

The thought makes bile rise in my throat. Here I am, lying again to him. Trading my safety for his. I don't know if I can do this...

I'd considered calling out for help when Tysea herded me through the crowded hotel lobby, but their tight grip on my arm held enough threat of violence that I couldn't make myself speak.

I slump to the ground and curse as fresh tears threaten to ruin my makeup. *Focus, Eden! You don't have time to cry.*

This whole situation is so fucked. And for what? Why go through all this effort to catch Phelix in a deal for mundane medical schematics? It doesn't make any sense. If he's caught selling that type of data illegally, surely the crime won't come with more than a fine that he could easily pay. They're obviously not agents of the Xi Consortium, so who the hell are they? Enemies of his family hoping to smear his house's name? Even that doesn't make sense, since they could've found a much more scandalous thing to catch him doing than trying to distribute lifesaving medical tech.

Banging on the door tells me my time is up. My eyes dart to the gun on my bed, and I grab it and shove it in my jacket right before the door swings open. Tysea glares at me and gestures for me to follow. I'll probably never know the why of this situation, so I can only focus on the how. How to convince Phelix to listen to my lies. How to choke back the fear and heartache long enough to make it out of this safely.

WHEN I ARRIVE at the small seladin bakery I visited with Phelix yesterday, my hands are trembling so hard I have to shove them in my pockets to hide the immediate giveaway of my mental state. Phelix is already here, and a sob threatens to tear out of my throat at the warmth and concern that cross his face when he sees me.

I smile shakily and close the distance, feeling Tysea's eyes on me even though they dropped me off a few blocks over. Who knows if they're monitoring me or not? They gave me back my comm once I finished changing at the hotel, but I'm sure they have some kind of tracking installed on it at the bare minimum.

"Ph-Phelix!" I say as cheerily as possible and feel like I've been punched in the stomach when he smiles and immediately pulls me against his solid, soft bulk.

"Thank the Goddess you're alright," he murmurs into my hair, letting out a relieved exhale.

I squeeze him back and, fuck, the tears are here already.

"I'm s-so sorry, Phelix." I try to pull back, but he holds me tighter.

"Do you trust me, Eden?" he asks, voice barely more than a whisper and thick with emotion.

God, I can't do this. This wonderful nexxit has fundamentally altered my life with his guidance and affection, and I can't lie anymore.

"I-I can't..."

He stiffens, but still keeps me against his body. "Please. I know I don't deserve it, but I would do anything to keep you safe."

I shake my head. "I trust you! But I c-can't—"

"Shhh, Eden, it's alright. I know about Mezli trying to spy on me. I need to attend a meeting, and I want you with me. You're the reason why I'm doing it in the first place. You opened my eyes to the injustices of this galaxy, so it's only right that you're by my side."

He finally releases me, and I step back, doing my best to look him in the eyes.

"B-but..." I have to explain to him. Not saying anything doesn't make the deception any less real.

"I need you there with me. Please. I need you," Phelix says, pleading with his eyes.

The soft vibration of my comm on my wrist startles me and I glance down at it.

> Tysea: We have eyes on you. Don't do anything to jeopardize this.

"S-sorry, just an event notification for a panel," I lie, expecting him to see right through me, but he nods. Wide eyed and trembling, I try to ignore his earnest expression. "Okay. I-I'll go with you."

Phelix grips my hand and squeezes it. "I knew I could count on you."

I have a feeling those words will haunt me for the rest of my life, but there's no turning back now.

35

✦ MEZLI ✦

"Well, well, if it isn't the prettiest nexxit on all of Spire. Didn't think I'd be seeing you again."

I smirk back at Hadrell as their cybernetic eye contracts and then scans over my body. No doubt checking me for weapons. Their cropped white hair flops over their natural glowing eye as they finish their assessment of me, and they flash a fanged smile that only makes their angular face more roguish and charming.

"Oh, you know...after I saw you the other night cycle, I couldn't stay away," I say coyly, pressing my upper arms under my breasts to push them together.

Their eyes drop to look shamelessly at my tits and their grin widens. "Is that so? And here I thought you were spoken for by that handsome nexxit and your human companion. You decide to run out on them too?"

I grimace at the unsubtle reminder of how I ditched Hadrell. "I shouldn't have done that. I had a great time. I just wasn't in the place for more."

"And you are now?" They lick their lips with interest. Any other day before this week, a look like that would have me dragging them up their docking ramp and having my way with them in their cramped quarters.

"I am." Their dotted brow raises in surprise, but I shake my head. "Not with you! Sorry, that was misleading."

"If you're not here for fun, then you're here for...?" They ask, mirroring my crossed arms as they look down at me.

"Business."

Their cybernetic eye narrows to a pinprick of light. "Really? A pampered princeps like you needs help from a Y'thir?"

"Yes! Wait, how do you know about my title?" I squeak in surprise.

They grin at me again, knowing they have the upper hand. "Your mothers have a contract out on you, to find you and bring you home. I didn't realize who you were until after I left the station last time and was checking through a jobs database, otherwise I may have tried harder to keep you by my side."

"You've got to be fucking kidding me," I mutter. Anything I could give Hadrell would be inconsequential compared to the bounty my mothers would've offered to bring their wayward daughter home. I stumble back a step, and their hand darts out to stabilize me before I fall on my ass.

"Relax," they say with a soft chuckle. "I didn't come here for you. I may be space trash, but I don't kidnap people."

"Oh thank the Goddess," I exhale as they release me. "Listen, I don't have a lot of time. I need you to pretend to be a data smuggler."

"That's not exactly a stretch for me." They cock their head. "What's the catch?"

"It's a bunch of convoluted nonsense, but basically some greedy assholes with a big medtech conglomerate are trying to entrap one of my mates, and they kidnapped my other mate. I need you to pretend to be the person Phelix is meeting with so we can turn the tables back on them."

Their natural eye softens when I mention my mates. Yes, I knew they'd love that angle. Seladin are a bunch of romantic saps. "This doesn't make a whole lot of sense, but if your mates are in danger, I won't refuse you."

"Good! I'll explain on the way. Thank you, Hadrell. I'll give you my entire life's savings if this works. Shit, I'll pay you my mate's entire savings."

"I assume one of your mates is the nexxit I met the other night. I didn't catch his family name—who is he?" They ask flippantly, like they assume that won't mean much.

"Phelix val Nafar," I say with nonchalantly.

"*Es'het*, of the second house of Nexxa Itat?" They grin at me in delight. "Looks like I'm getting a new ship."

PHELIX

EDEN TREMBLES the entire transit ride to Perseus district and my chest aches with the need to comfort her. She's been through so much these past few days and her tender, inquisitive nature has been trampled by everyone she's encountered. I want to tell her we know what's going on. That Mezli and I have a plan and that everything will be okay. But she keeps glancing at her comm and looking over her shoulder and I know the bastards that are manipulating her are too close by. If they're reckless enough to kidnap a human and attempt to entrap a member of Nexxa Itat nobility, that could translate to violence. I would rather die than have any harm come to either of my mates. The one small relief is that Mezli isn't here. If I had to worry about both of my mates, I think I'd have a nervous breakdown.

I take Eden by the hand when we arrive at our stop, guiding her through the bustling mid-morning walkways to the fake meeting spot. "Almost there. Just let me do the talking. This shouldn't take long."

"Phelix, I..."

I pull her in and kiss her, not wanting her to endanger herself at the last second. I use my lips and the press of all four hands against her soft, delicate body to convey that she's safe. That I understand and I don't care about anything that she's done. That I just want to be with her and Mezli.

An imposing, hooded figure on the other side of the secluded courtyard clears their throat and Eden startles, stumbling back and clutching my arm. "Do you have the package?" they say in a voice that sounds like a stereotypical criminal from an old spy vid.

"Uh, yeah." I fumble with my satchel and pull out a datapad at random. It doesn't matter which one I hand them—they're all filled with vids of baby flesstras and recipes for homemade *skrllpt*.

Eden tries to maintain her grip on me, but I extract myself and walk to meet the tall, mysterious person. Whoever Mezli got seems convincing enough, if a little melodramatic in their presentation.

"Wait!" Eden says, her voice frantic. But it's too late. Two ankites enter the alleyway, one with orange-yellow skin coming in behind the fake buyer and a shorter pale green one behind Eden. The shorter of the pair gives me a smug once over, pushing Eden to the side to get closer to me. My fists clench with the need to destroy them for daring to lay a hand on her and for all the emotional trauma they've put both my mates through.

"Dr. Phelix val Nafar, it's good to finally meet you," they say evenly. "You're a lot less impressive in person. No offense."

"What's going on? Who the fuck are these people?" the fake buyer asks, spinning around to find a blaster pointed at their chest. "Whoa, whoa! I don't want any trouble."

Eden gasps, seeing the weapon. My stomach lurches even though I anticipated they might show up armed. Thinking about facing down a blaster is much less terrifying than actually seeing one brandished a few feet away.

The orange ankite holding the gun frowns at the fake buyer. "Should've thought about that before you decided to trade in illegal medtech. You and your associate have a choice. Turn yourself into the authorities and hope you don't get sentenced for too long a stay on a prison colony, or pay reparations to our employer and give us the names of the others in your network."

"What if I don't like either of those options?" the hooded figure asks in a rough growl, and I want to yell at them to shut up.

The ankite points the blaster at their chest. "Then you can take the third option of a bolt to the chest and your body dumped in a nearby garbage compactor."

"All of this over some fucking schematics? You're threatening to kill us just for trying to save lives?" Eden asks in disbelief.

"Be quiet, human, or I'll make you." The pale green ankite next to her scowls, and she cries out as he shoves her to the ground.

"Those schematics, and stopping the unauthorized distribution of them through their 'philanthropic' organization, are worth more than your pathetic life."

Fury rises in me. "If you touch her again, I will destroy you."

They scoff. "Human pussy must be incredible to make you threaten me when I could literally kill her and you before you even touched me."

"It's pretty damn great, but scum like you won't get the chance to experience it. Not when you're stuck on that prison colony you mentioned before." My heart stops when I hear Mezli's voice. What the fuck is she doing here?

She steps out of the shadows with a cocky grin. No. No no no no no. She shouldn't be here. Now both of my mates are in danger and I'm useless to protect them.

"Don't give me that look, Lord Nafar," Mezli says. "I wasn't about to let you two have all the fun without me." She winks at me, and I'm so upset and stunned that I miss the rapid flash of our fake data smuggler disarming the ankite next to them, and aiming the weapon back at them.

"What was that about being able to kill us before we even touched you?" The fake contact's over-the-top gruff accent is gone, replaced by the calm, cool tone of a professional.

"To the void with you!" The ankite next to Eden curses, reaching behind their back for their weapon. Their brow furrows as they find their holster empty, and they spit out a curse, whirling around just in time for Eden to pull a *blaster* out of her jacket and aim it at them.

Divine Goddess, how did she get that?!

The ankite scowls at her and lunges, but they're far too slow. Eden drops her aim to their leg and squeezes the trigger with a shout. The ankite stumbles, crying out in pain as a bolt of energy strikes their thigh. Eden scrambles away and looks at her hands in horror.

"Fucking hell, Eden! You're a badass!" Mezli exclaims as she helps our mate to her feet. Mezli gently takes the gun from Eden's trembling hands and levels it at the injured ankite in case they try to do anything stupid.

"Shit, what the hell were you thinking?" I curse, rushing over to my mates. "You could have died. You both could have..." Hot tears spill down my cheeks, matching those on Eden's shell-shocked face.

Mezli reaches out and pats my arm with one of her lower hands. "There, there, sweet Phelix. Your mates have everything under control. Everything okay over there, Hadrell?" she calls over to the hooded figure with their blasters still trained on the ankite.

My mouth falls open as they push their hood back and I realize it's the seladin from the other night.

Hadrell laughs at my shocked expression. "Of course. You got this covered? I can't be here when station security arrives."

"Yeah. They should be here any second. I'll comm you with payment details." Mezli's confidence in the face of blaster fire and life-threatening situations is somewhat terrifying, but oddly arousing. She's magnificent. Both my mates are.

The seladin nods. "You better." They turn to leave, but pause. "Oh, congratulations on your mating. I expect an invite to the ceremony when you make it official."

Mezli snorts and waves them off, and they disappear right before a swarm of station security converges on us.

Everything is a blur as they take over, cuffing the mercs, confiscating the blasters, and taking us to a nearby security station to question us. This part I expected—Paul used his connections at the human embassy to report Eden's kidnapping and her unauthorized smuggling onto the station. He kindly left out any details on the absurd spy shenanigans she and Mezli had engaged in, or my less-than-legal data distribution plans.

When they finally clear us to leave, giving Eden a small fine along with the paperwork required to make her visit to Spire authorized, I'm exhausted. But we can't rest yet. Now that it's just the three of us, we need to talk.

36

✦EDEN✦

Overwhelming fatigue hits me as I step through the door to Mezli's apartment. My mind flashes to the first time I was here. I'd just arrived on the station and my head was abuzz with thoughts of covert operations as the "agents" brought me to meet with my partner. That Eden was so clueless, it hurts to think about. All of her optimism and enthusiasm were drained by the last few days, leaving this new, exhausted version of me behind.

Phelix and Mezli bypass the small living room, leading me gently to Mezli's bedroom. Mezli sweeps the pile of outfits still left there from before we went out to the club to the floor—god, was that only two days ago?

"Lie down," Phelix rumbles as he guides me to the bed.

EMILY ANTOINETTE

I want to argue. I want to explain why I lied, explain that I never meant to hurt him, and explain that I don't blame Mezli for how she reacted. But all that comes out of me is a feeble croak of acknowledgement before I sink down onto the mattress.

Mezli sits beside me and strokes my arm, while Phelix moves to my feet to take off my boots, rubbing them once they're bare.

Tears leak out of me at their comforting touch. They're acting like they cherish me, even after all that's happened. "I need to..."

Mezli lets out a soft chuckle. "If you say you need to apologize, I'm going to have to punish you. No more apologies!" She looks over at Phelix pointedly. "From either of you."

"If that's what my mates desire, I'll never feel sorry again," Phelix says, his mouth tilting as he teases her back.

"The only one here that hasn't apologized for their actions is me," Mezli says with a sigh. Her hand stops caressing my arm, and she looks at me intently. Gazing down at me, she reminds me of an angel—or a very persuasive devil. Either way, it makes my chest expand like I've been holding my breath and she's fresh air.

"I should've believed you. I should have trusted your word over those damn fake agents. I should have trusted you, and Phelix, and that the connection we have means more than my fears and baggage. I didn't, and I'm sorry. It won't happen again."

"Mezli, it's okay." I push myself up so I'm propped against the pile of cushions at the headboard, and Phelix comes up to sit beside her, wrapping two arms across her back.

"It's really not. I hurt you. Even worse, I promised I'd protect you while you were here and I didn't. I told you to go, knowing how dangerous Spire might be for you, even without those fake agents."

"You're not the only one who's made mistakes," Phelix says matter-of-factly.

She smiles weakly back at him as he brushes away some of her tears. "No shit, Lord Nafar."

"Definitely not," I add, scooting in and resting a hand on Phelix, closing up our triangle.

"Does that mean you'll forgive me?" she asks. "I'd understand if you both wanted to get the fuck off Spire and never see me again. I'm a lot to deal with. Too much, most people would say."

"Good thing there are two of us," Phelix says. "The mighty Princeps of House Frye deserves nothing less than two mates."

"When you put it that way..." She pulls him in and kisses him. Tender, open, and so soft, unlike the forceful, almost punishing kisses she's given Phelix thus far.

I don't want to burst this bubble of affection, but I can't stop myself from speaking. "Are you sure?"

They pull back from their kiss, the weight of both their gazes making it hard to breathe. "Sure about what, sweet Eden?" Mezli asks.

"Sure that you want me involved with you, even though you both are mates. I... I don't know if I could handle coming between you or feeling like you'll always matter more to each other because of your mate bond. I've waited so long to find someone to love. It'll hurt to not be with you, but I'll survive." I swallow down the lump in my throat and let out a weak laugh. "I have a lot of practice being alone."

They exchange a meaningful look, and nervous flutters erupt in my stomach. I don't want them to confirm the reality of our situation, but it's better to know now. I can go home, cry for a few weeks —or months—and then attempt to move on.

Something inside me revolts at the thought of never seeing them again and I can barely keep fresh tears at bay.

Phelix speaks first. "We realized something after you left. Something that should've been obvious if we weren't so absorbed in our own drama and fragile emotions. You say you'd come between us, that you wouldn't matter as much to us. But you're wrong. There is no 'us' without you, Eden."

"You could figure things out without me," I say, internally screaming at myself for arguing against them wanting a relationship with me.

"What Phelix means is that you're our mate." Mezli holds a hand up to me when I open my mouth to argue again. "And not just in a 'we love you and we want to be with you' way—though that's true, too."

A small squeak of surprise escapes me at her casual mention of *loving* me.

She grins at my reaction, and Phelix smiles with tender devotion at both of us. "You're our mate. Like, our Goddess-given mate. I don't know how or why, but you are. Both Phelix and I can feel it. We were just too hard-headed to see the signs at first."

"You feel it when we touch, right? That electric wave of arousal and sense of comfort and rightness?" Phelix asks, stroking the top of my thigh and igniting that exact feeling within me.

"That's just attraction, though..." I say.

Mezli laughs and shakes her head at me. "No. Trust me, I've been attracted to and intimate with many people. It's different. It's like something inside both of our bodies connects on a cellular level." She brushes a curl away from my face, sending pleasant shivers down my spine. "If that's not enough for you, might I remind you that you took Phelix's knot? That's only possible because you're our *mate*."

"Oh..." My response feels silly, but I'm having a hard time coming up with words to express my confusion and exhilaration. How is it possible that the first people I've shared myself with are my mates? The odds are astronomical. Absurd. Like something out of a ridiculous fairy tale, not something that happens in real life.

"How is this possible?" I finally ask. "I'm not a nexxit."

"I don't know, some mystical divine shit or whatever," Mezli says flippantly.

Phelix rolls his eyes at her and considers my question instead of waving it off, which I appreciate. "Mate bonds for nexxit are said to be granted by the Goddess. A divine sign of her approval and blessings. But we've known for centuries that there's something on a biological level that recognizes and signals that someone is your best chance at creating offspring. I've studied the extensive research on them, since my work involves finding ways to improve our low fertility rates. Studies have proven that mated pairs have a much higher reproductive success than non-mated ones, however, what exactly causes that has eluded us to this day."

"That makes it even less likely that I'm your mate," I say, sighing. Believing the mate bond came from some divine source made it sound more plausible, despite me not being a spiritual person. Divinity leaves room for the potential of something magical. Science is based in fact. "We're not reproductively compatible," I say with a sigh. "If a mate bond comes from a biological imperative, then what we feel isn't coming from that!"

"It's not just for reproduction," Mezli says. "My mothers are mates and there wouldn't have been a way for them to conceive without the aid of technology. Same sex mates are just as blessed by the Goddess."

"If it's a divine force, why would your Goddess pair a random human with you? I'm no one special. Why *me*?"

"It's random. Everything in the universe is random and we just do our best with our feeble minds to make sense of it. You can either let it upset you or you can embrace it. Trust me, I get it if you're upset to be stuck with us. I felt the same way when I found out my mate was this stuck up jerk," Mezli says, gesturing to Phelix.

He laughs, sounding so unrestrained and oddly delighted by her gibe. It's this, rather than their words, that makes whatever remaining resistance I had to believing them melt away. A few days ago, he'd be snapping back and hardening his shell. When he doesn't, when he enjoys her barbs, I realize both of them are relaxed and happy together, not in spite of my presence, but *because* of it. They fit together because they have *me*. Silly, naive, smart, inquisitive, supportive, empathetic me. I matter to them just as much as they do to me. I belong with them.

"You're my mates?" My voice is filled with awe as I allow that truth to settle in my heart.

"We're your mates. If you want, we can take a DNA sample and send it off to a mate finder, like our parents did for us. I bet you a million credits that it'll confirm what we already know."

"Neither of us have a million credits," I say, laughing the idea off.

"Then we'll bet a million of Phelix's credits!" Mezli says, winking at him.

The romantic side of me wants to wave the offer off, but the scientist in me can't resist. "I... I'd like that. Not because I don't believe you. I just...want to be sure."

They both smile in reassurance, not upset by my need to have confirmation.

"Wait. You have a million credits?" My mouth falls open as my brain processes that information. I knew Phelix is a noble and that he's rich, but didn't really consider the realities of that.

Phelix ducks his head and grimaces like that's a bad thing. "Yes. I have more than that. Is that a problem?"

"Only if you go back to acting like a rich, entitled prick," Mezli says, but there's no bite to her tone. "And oh, by the way, it's not going to be a big issue since I, uh, promised a lot of credits to Hadrell for their help..."

Phelix's brow quirks. "How much?"

"A lot," Mezli says in an uncharacteristically nervous squeak.

He sighs, but doesn't look the least bit upset with her. "Whatever it was, it was worth it. I'd give up all my money to keep my mates safe."

My stomach flips at his mention of mates, but unlike before it's from excitement instead of nerves.

Mezli snorts, dimming some of my arousal from his romantic words. "That's sweet, but I give you one month max of living like me and Eden before you went crawling to your family for money."

He scoffs right back at her, but then his expression turns serious. "I'm not enough of an asshole to pretend that money doesn't make life vastly more simple. But it never made me happy. I'd willingly trade my wealth if it meant I could be with you two. If it meant I could stop being so...alone."

The vulnerability and honesty of his words resonate deeply with me, and I can see they hit home with Mezli too. The three of us have felt alone in our own ways for so long. Phelix hardening his heart against the judgment of his peers and rejection from his mate, cutting himself off from others so he wouldn't have to feel the pain of it again. Me, wasting away my youth on a planet made for those who have already lived full lives. And Mezli, surrounding herself with friends and lovers but never letting anyone see her true self. We're all broken in our own ways, but together we can mend and become something beautiful.

Mezli wipes away a tear and pulls Phelix against her, wrapping her arms around him and holding him tight. I mold myself against his back, and she releases him to hold on to my arms instead, so he's surrounded on both sides. We stay like this for a while, melting into the comfort of each other's touch.

Eventually, Mezli lets out a soft chuckle. "Let's avoid getting into any more trouble so you don't have to give up more of your money. I miss not having to worry about making rent."

OUR EXHAUSTION quickly catches up with us and we end up falling asleep on Mezli's bed, squished together. When I wake up, my neck is stiff from my awkward position, but my heart is overwhelmingly full. The soft buzzing of my comm against my wrist wakes me, and I extricate myself from the tangle of limbs and head into the small living room to answer the vid comm.

The holo screen expands in front of me and my parents' smiling faces appear.

"Hey sweetie! Hope we didn't interrupt you during a lecture... Oh!"

My mom's smile quickly morphs to curiosity, and she trails off as she looks past me to what's behind me. I turn to see that my positioning gives my parents a clear view through the open door into the bedroom. Where there are two nexxit sleeping, and I'm dressed in a fluffy purple robe that is many sizes too small.

I squeak and move so my back is to the kitchen rather than the bedroom. "I'm good! Great! Just getting ready after uh, after a..."

"Late night?" Dad volunteers with a knowing eyebrow raise that makes me want to spontaneously combust from sheer embarrassment.

"Y-yeah. I..." *You're thirty years old, Eden. You don't have to hide that you had sex from your parents like a naughty teen.* "I met someone."

"Two someones, from what I could see," Dad adds and my mother can't contain her snort of laughter.

"I'm so happy for you, Eden! As long as you were safe, we don't judge how many aliens you 'meet'" Mom uses air quotes on the word "meet" and winks.

Oh god, please kill me.

"I'm not going to meet a lot of aliens! They're the only ones. They're... really special."

"Ah." Dad says blandly. "You're not coming home," he adds and Mom nods in agreement.

My eyebrows shoot to my hairline. Why wouldn't they let me come home? "W-what? I thought you didn't care if I slept with—"

"No, no angel. Relax. I meant you're not coming home because you've found your people."

My mind reels at how certain and final she sounds. I was so wrapped up in the drama with the fake agents and figuring out what I meant to Mezli and Phelix that I hadn't thought about what that meant for me beyond the next few days.

"What? No, I'm coming home!" I say quickly, though as soon as I do, I feel sick.

Dad, the king of understated reactions and emotions, actually rolls his eyes at me. "It's time, Edi-chan. With or without these special aliens you've met, it's time. We've kept you cooped up for far too long. It's time for you to fly."

"But you need me! I can't just leave you."

"Your father and I will be fine. We're healthy and comfortable. The colony has the funds to hire another medic to replace you."

I shake my head, tears welling in my eyes as I speak aloud my fears to my parents for the first time. "What if you get sick? I need to be there to take care of you. What if you need help? What if—

"Eden." Mom cuts me off, stern even as she wipes a tear away.

"You can't let 'what-ifs' control your life. And you can't stop the inevitable. Staying stuck on Europa 3 to take care of us and throwing away your life in the hopes of extending ours a few more years isn't worth it."

I'm crying now, sucking in shallow breaths as I watch her tears fall. "Mom..."

She shakes her head, and I realize that me being stuck and unfulfilled is painful for them, too. "I won't allow it. You're not coming back."

I swallow down my argument. This is what I've yearned for, but I never expected it to be so terrifying. "O-okay. Thank you."

"We love you, Edi-chan," Dad says, wiping away a rare tear of his own.

"I love you, too. I'll be okay." I say, more to reassure myself than them.

"We know you will. Now, go have some fun with your 'special' aliens."

"They're uh, actually, they're my mates."

This is the news that finally shocks my parents, both of their mouths falling open in shock. "What?!"

37

✦ MEZLI ✦

Raised, unfamiliar voices pull me out of sleep. Phelix is solid and toasty against my back, his cocks extruded and hard against my ass and his hands gripping my hip and arm like he's afraid I'd try to get away from him while he's asleep. My front is much colder and I reach out with a groan to pull Eden back against me, but am met with empty space.

I roll out of Phelix's grip, rubbing the sleep out of my eyes as I blearily get to my feet. Eden's voice is clearer now that I'm waking up a bit, and the voices sound human. She must be on a vid comm. I'm still in my dress from the night before last, too lazy to get up and get undressed once the three of us merged into a sleepy cuddle pile. Which is good because when I step out into my living room,

I'm greeted by a large holoscreen projection of two humans who must be Eden's parents.

"Oh! Mezli!" Eden startles as I come up beside her, wrapping one arm around her waist and draping another over her shoulder before leaning in to kiss her cheek. Her face is warm from the flush my casual affection in front of her parents causes, but I don't care. I want her back in bed with us as soon as possible and this is as chaste as I can make myself be.

"Morning, sweet Eden," I purr, letting my hand around her waist slip down to grab her ass cheek. I smile brightly at the elderly humans on the holo projection. "You must be my mate's parents. It's so lovely to meet you. I've heard so many wonderful things about you."

Her father smiles back, his eyes crinkling softly the same way Eden's do when she laughs. Her mother beams back at me, Eden's same sunshine radiating from her. I breathe a small sigh of relief that they're not freaking out at the sight of an alien draping herself on their daughter.

"It's so nice to meet you, Mezli! Wow, Eden, she's *gorgeous*," Eden's mother stage whispers.

"Mom!" Eden says in a high-pitched whine.

"What? She is! A great match for my perfect daughter."

"Edi-chan says you're one of her mates," her father says. "That you were destined to be together or there's some kind of biological link between you two and another nexxit. I have to admit, it sounds...strange."

I nod. "I understand why it would be odd, especially for humans who don't typically mate bond. I don't know how or why Eden is my mate, but I feel like the luckiest *xala* in the universe to have found her. We both do."

"I'm glad you realize that," her father says, his eyebrow quirking in amusement as I give Eden a squeeze and she flushes even more.

"Mezli and Phelix are wonderful, too." Eden's voice is dreamy and her mother practically squeals in delight at her daughter's obvious happiness.

"Speaking of Lord Nafar, I'll go grab him so he can say—"

"Mmm, where did my gorgeous mates go? I'm starving for you," Phelix rumbles in a low voice that makes my nipples harden.

I turn over my shoulder to see Phelix emerge from the bedroom, rubbing the sleep out of his eyes—completely nude. His cocks are fully erect and already weeping with need, and he brings a lower hand down to palm one lazily as he steps into the living room.

"Ah!" Eden squeals, quickly turning so the holo screen is facing away from our mate.

"What's wrong?" Phelix asks, dropping his hand from his dick with a concerned frown.

"Eden's on a vid comm with her parents."

"Oh fuck," he curses, scrambling back into the bedroom, banging into the doorframe with another expletive.

"He looks...nice," Eden's mom says, looking a bit dazed after getting an eyeful of his dicks.

"Oh, he's alright I guess," I say, rejoining Eden by her side. "We only keep him around for his equipment, if you know what I mean," I add with a wink.

Her mother blinks a few times before bursting out into a warm laugh that sounds so much like Eden's it makes my heart squeeze with affection. "I can see why."

Eden's dad raises a gray brow at his wife, and she just laughs even harder. "Well, I look forward to meeting him when he's a little more, uh, prepared."

"I don't know, he looks pretty prepared for something," her dad deadpans, immediately making me fall in love with him.

"Hah! Your parents are such a delight. Now I know where Eden gets her charm from."

"Yeah, sure, uh, I should probably go!" Eden says, desperate to move away from the topic of Phelix's junk.

"Alright, sweetie! We'll talk later. I love you!" Eden's mom says, waving her hand at us.

"I love you, too!" Eden cuts off the comm feed and lets out a loud groan.

"I'm so sorry!" Phelix calls from the bedroom. "I didn't know you were on a comm. Give me just a moment and I'll come out and apologize."

"Too late, they already saw the goods and gave you the seal of approval," I shout back, earning a chuckle from Eden.

"Not exactly how I imagined introducing my mates to my parents," she says with a sheepish smile.

"I think it went pretty well! They seemed okay with you being mated to two hot aliens. We'll make them adore us when we come visit you," I say, squeezing her shoulder reassuringly. At least it's meant to be reassuring, but her smile falters.

"Uh, you won't need to visit," she says hesitantly.

"What? Of course I'm going to visit. I'm going to make our rich mate buy a private ship and shuttle us back and forth to Europa 3 every damn week. You're stuck with us, so stop coming up with reasons why we can't be together!"

"What's that about me buying a ship?" Phelix asks, emerging from the bedroom in one of my robes, which strains at the shoulders and barely does anything to cover up his delicious girth.

"You don't need to buy a ship!" Eden says shaking her head.

"Yes, you do!" I argue.

"No, you *don't*. I'm not leaving!"

I blink back at her, my frustration evaporating in an instant. "You're not?"

"That's what I was talking to my parents about. They commed me to tell me I should stay on Spire. Said they didn't want to see me wasting my life away on Europa 3. We didn't talk about logistics and I don't have anywhere to live lined up after my hotel reservation ends, but I'll figure it out. I'm nothing if not resourceful."

Phelix chuckles at her fierce determination. "You're entirely capable of figuring things out, but I assure you, you don't need to worry."

"Yeah, you can live with me!" I say, head already spinning with all the fun possibilities of living with Eden. Making breakfast together, forgetting about the breakfast and eating each other instead...

"You can live with *us*," Phelix says firmly.

I frown. "This place is kinda small for three people, but we can make it work if I get rid of some of my fabric stash and maybe remove the coffee table... Hold on. You're staying? What about your job on Nexxa Itat? What about your family?"

"My family will be delighted I've settled down with my mate and stopped being the dark blot on our house's pristine reputation. And you think I can't find a job here? I'm sure both Eden and I will be able to secure positions on Spire if I reach out to some contacts. It'll be easy since most of them are here for the conference."

"So confident," I tease. It would've bothered me in the past to hear him so sure that things would work out for him. Knowing him better now, I understand he knows things will work out because he's smart and determined, not just because he's an entitled jerk. "It's kinda sexy." I step closer to Phelix and run a hand down his exposed chest, stopping at the robe's tie with a smile.

His cheeks darken ever so slightly, but he smiles back. "Is that so?"

"God, yes. It's very hot," Eden says, stepping in to press herself against my back, resting her chin on my shoulder.

My body tingles with pleasure touching them both, and an urgency to feel even more of them surges through me. "I need you both. Bedroom. Now."

Eden's breath hitches at my command, and Phelix's jade eyes glitter with an intense arousal that matches my own.

I tug Eden after me, awkwardly attempting to undo my dress zipper as we stumble into the bedroom and Phelix's mouth lands on mine in a hot kiss. Phelix helps me, slipping my dress down off of my shoulders, then tugging off Eden's clothes. I nip at Phelix's lower lip and shove at the robe he's crammed himself into, but his arms get stuck and he ends up tangled up in it.

He huffs out a laugh, and I melt. Every time he shows us this soft, unguarded side of himself, I fall more in love. I was such an idiot to see what he presented at face value and assume that was who he truly was. Seeing him bared for me, both figuratively and literally, as Eden untangles him and he's standing before us in all his naked glory, makes me feral for him. With Eden on display beside him, I lose control.

"I want you to fuck us," I say, voice thick with my need. My pussy is already soaked and ready, and from the way Eden gasps at my lips on her neck and my hands on her tits, I bet she's wet too.

"Who do you want me to fuck first?" Phelix asks. "I'm so turned on I can't guarantee I won't knot whoever I'm inside. I'm sorry."

"I want to watch you knot Mezli while she eats my pussy," Eden says, sounding shy about her dirty talk.

"No. I want you to fuck *us*." I repeat, my channels clenching at the thought. "You've got two cocks and two mates and I want us to both come with you inside us at the same time."

"F-fuck, okay," Phelix says, the aroused flush on his cheeks spreading down his throat, and his cocks bobbing with excitement.

"How would we even do that?" Eden asks, her eyes wide.

"Lie down on the bed and I'll show you, love," I purr.

She obeys me beautifully, her gorgeous tits and stomach jiggling as she lays down with her knees up, spreading her legs without me even needing to ask. Her pussy is already slick with her arousal. Wet, pink, puffy, and so pretty that I can't resist crawling between her legs to taste her.

"Goddess, Eden. You taste incredible." I linger there, teasing her clit with my tongue and working two fingers inside her. I hear the slick sound of Phelix fisting his cocks, and knowing he's watching us makes this even hotter.

When Eden's just about to come, I pull away and she whines in frustration. "I told you. I want you coming on our mate's cock."

I slide my body up to rest atop hers, savoring the drag of my sensitive nipples up her silky skin, and claim her lips. She moans as she tastes herself on me, and I wrap my legs around hers to pin them wider, grinding myself against her as my need for more builds.

"Get over here, Phelix." I order as I press my body down on top of Eden, tilting my hips so that my pussy is more exposed.

Eden squirms under me, and the sensation of holding her down makes me even wetter. I pin her arms above her head with my upper hands and nip at her neck. "Be a good girl and lie still while our mate fucks your tight little cunt. He's going to fill that pretty pussy up until you scream."

"Y-yes, fuck I want it so bad. I'll be good," she moans.

Phelix takes that as his cue to line himself up with us, the bed

EMILY ANTOINETTE

thankfully making us the right height for this strange configuration to work. The slide of his blunt cockhead against my entrance makes me groan. It takes him a minute to get his cocks positioned right, and for a moment I think it's not possible but then Eden gasps and I bite down a moan as his thick cock presses into one of my channels.

"Oh fuck. Shit," he curses as he slides as deep as he can at this angle. It rubs against a spot inside me that makes sparks dance up my spine and this time I can't stop myself from crying out.

"Don't you dare come yet," I say between gasps as he shudders above me but maintains control.

He pulls back and thrusts again, harder this time, making my breasts slide against Eden's tits. She arches her back into me as he does it again, setting a steady pace of slow, maddening thrusts.

"Fuck, you feel so good," Phelix groans, sounding as broken and desperate as I feel.

"I'm going to come, o-oh god," Eden gasps.

"Not yet, baby. You'll come when I tell you to," I say, needing us to come together.

"I'll try," she says in a needy whine, but I know she won't hold out long.

That's alright, because I only need a few more hard thrusts from Phelix to find myself on the edge too.

"Come for me, Eden," I gasp out as Phelix pounds inside us and my orgasm crashes into me.

Eden cries out, writhing against my body, and stars dance behind my eyes at the sheer pleasure of my release and knowledge of hers.

"Sh-shit, can I?" Phelix asks in a choked voice.

"Knot her, Phelix," Eden answers before I can reply.

I gasp as Phelix pulls out and quickly repositions to thrust both of his cocks into me. They jerk inside me, and the first jets of his release pushes me over the edge again. He doubles over my back with an animalistic grunt, leveraging me back onto his cocks until his knot pops inside me, stretching me almost to the point of pain.

I start to panic as wave after wave of pleasure hits me with each pulse of his bottom cock releasing inside me. Fuck, I didn't know it felt like this. Goddess, it's too much, I can't.

"I, ungh, I—" Tears of ecstasy and the overwhelming release of decades of repressed need and emotion flood out of me, dripping down onto Eden's neck as I sob into her sweet-smelling skin, coming again.

"Shhh, we've got you." Eden's arms slide up to stroke along my sides and hips. "You're doing so well."

Phelix's hands stroke down the backs of my thighs in gentle and loving tandem with Eden's soothing touch, even though I can feel him shudder through his own unending climax. "You're so perfect, taking my knot inside you. Letting me fill you up with my cum," he murmurs, his words washing over me.

Both of them anchor me, guiding me through the blissful torment of pleasure with their words and touch. I give in and let myself go, knowing they'll be there to bring me back to myself.

38

✦PHELIX✦

Hours of fucking, whispered words of affection, and planning for the future later, I force myself to leave Mezli's bed, despite my mates' protests and attempts to convince me to stay. But my comm buzzed with a reminder of my meeting today, and after all the drama this week, I need to see this commitment through and close this bizarre chapter of my life.

Smuggling schematics isn't for me. I'm too well-known and I can't endanger my mates again. I'll find another way to make a difference. Maybe I'll finally use my name and social acumen for something worthwhile, and convince the wealthy and bored to fund medical initiatives. Not nearly as sexy or dramatic as dealing in restricted data, but I'll live.

My contact arranged our meeting at a cafe in Sagittarius district, and my nerves ease realizing we'll be surrounded by plenty of bystanders instead of in some seedy alley where I could get mugged.

I approach the designated table in the back left corner and find its occupants' face hidden behind a menu.

"Have a seat, Dr. Nafar," they say, their voice sounding familiar. When they set the menu down, I realize why. A seladin with short white hair sits across from me, their cybernetic eye tracking over me, while their glowing white one stays locked on my face, and they flash me a sharp smile.

"You're..."

"Mezli's friend. Sorry for all the secretive *fa-shar* nonsense. You can never be too careful, dealing with nobles. No offense."

"Uh, none taken. But...there must be a mistake—I'm supposed to be meeting with a representative of a medical aid network, not a pirate."

They laugh, leaning forward to whisper conspiratorially. "My dear doctor, who else do you think would be capable of smuggling and delivering illegal medical tech?"

"Ah." My face heats at my naive assumption. "Right."

"Don't worry. Your data is in safe hands and your reputation will remain pristine. Thank you for your contribution to the cause, doctor. If you'll pass over the schematics, I'll let you get back to your mates," they say with a knowing wink. With a seladin's enhanced sense of smell, I must reek of Eden and Mezli.

"It's that simple?" I ask, expecting something far more dramatic. I hand over the datapad and they casually slip it into a bag at their feet.

"Yeah. Usually crazy medtech mercs don't get involved, but

there must've been a leak in your personal data that got you flagged."

"Shit, I did have a security breach on my personal comm, but didn't even consider it would be an issue. I figured it was just some rival house trying to dig up dirt on my family. I upgraded my security parameters, but I guess it was too late. I'm so sorry."

They shrug. "Don't apologize to me. From where I'm sitting, everything worked out pretty damn well. You reunited with your mate, connected with your other mate, delivered lifesaving med schematics, oh, and made me fifty times the payday I was expecting to earn while I'm on the station. Speaking of which, I'll take my payment in credits. Or if you happen to have a private ship, I can take that off your hands instead."

I curse internally at how much Mezli promised to this charming mercenary, but keep my expression placid. "You know, I just purchased a private ship for the trip back to Nexxa Itat that I won't be needing anymore. It's yours. But that means the debt is settled. Don't come around trying to bleed more money out of me or my mates. It won't end well."

They nod and reach out to clasp my arm. "Deal. The only other thing you owe me is an invite to your mating ceremony. Which judging by the state of you, won't be too long from now." Their expression softens, revealing a glimpse of longing behind their charming veneer. "Lucky bastard."

I laugh, tension bleeding out of me at the relief of being done with this whole mess. "Yeah. I really am."

✦

5 months later

"Company is arriving in less than an hour, and we still need to— ah!" Eden cries out as Mezli works the thick dildo in and out of our mate's ass, clenching around it greedily despite her protests. The sight is obscene and beautiful. I could happily watch my mates play with each other for hours, but like Eden said, we have somewhere to be.

Mezli leans down and sucks Eden's clit and she goes off like a firework, hips rocking up and body writhing futilely as I hold her in place against my chest with my upper arms and keep her legs spread open with my lower ones, kneading her heavy breasts through her orgasm. Our Eden loves to be held down and forced to receive her pleasure over and over, and this is her second orgasm.

"Is she ready?" I ask, grinding my stiff cocks against Eden's back in an attempt to relieve some of the pressure inside me. I won't last long after watching Mezli stretch her open, but with the time constraints, for once that's a good thing.

Mezli looks up at me from between Eden's legs, her face glistening with our mate's wetness. "Oh yes. She's been such a good girl, letting us stretch her asshole. Letting us get her ready to take all of you. Now it's time for her reward."

When Eden mentioned having both my cocks inside her during dirty talk a couple of months ago, it shocked my release out of me as I was pounding inside Mezli. I didn't think it was possible given how small and tight she is, but she brought it up again outside the bedroom, having hatched a plan to make it happen with Mezli. According to Fina, it's very much possible, and while I didn't need to know the details about what kinky holosim activities Mezli's best friend gets up to, it was reassuring to know I wouldn't harm Eden making the fantasy a reality.

We've worked for the past month to get Eden ready. Mezli decreed that tonight's the night we give it a shot. Maybe not the best timing, considering that we have to meet with all our parents in less than an hour for the first of the official mate bonding ceremonies this weekend. But how could I say no when I walked in to find Mezli feasting on our mate's cunt and whispering about how good I was going to fill her? How I was going to knot her ass, even though that would *definitely* make us late.

I release my hold on Eden after pressing an open-mouthed kiss to her lovely neck, licking some of her sweat and unique sweetness from it. Mezli switches places with me, moving behind Eden to rest against the headboard and hold her against her chest, whispering things that make our pretty human flush darker and gasp.

She's already slick from her arousal, lube, and some of my front cock's muscle-relaxing cum that Mezli worked into her earlier, but I coat my cocks with more lubricant just to be safe. Just seeing her spread wide, both holes eager and ready to be filled for me and her soft stomach and breasts on full display, makes my cocks throb and my knot threaten to swell even though I'm not even inside her yet.

"Mmm, you ready for my cocks?" I murmur, teasing the heads against her.

"Yes," Eden whimpers.

"I'm not convinced she wants it," Mezli says, giving me a feral grin over Eden's shoulder before pinching her nipple hard.

"Ah! Please, I want it."

Goddess, there's not much more in the universe I love more than Mezli making Eden beg. I still don't know what I did to deserve these *xalas*, but I'll work every day to prove that I'm good enough for them.

I raise a brow at Mezli, looking for her go ahead. "Is that enough to convince you? She sounds so sweet when she begs, but she'll sound even better when she screams for us."

"Ask for it one more time, pet, and then we'll give you what you want," Mezli purrs into Eden's ear, snaking a hand between her spread thighs to tease around her swollen clit and brush the head of my top cock, making me groan.

"Please fuck me! God, I want it so bad, please," Eden moans.

"Good girl. Fill her up for me, Phelix."

I notch my cocks against her holes, taking a few attempts to get the positioning right, and groan as both cockheads sink in a fraction.

Eden cries out, and I freeze, but she shakes her head and whines. "No, no, please don't stop. Keep going!"

Mezli chuckles, continuing her slow teasing of our mate's clit even though my soft stomach traps her hand between me and Eden's pussy. "You heard the *xala*. Give her more."

Sweat beads at my temples as I press in further to Eden's impossibly hot, tight channels, holding myself from thrusting in and instead waiting for her body to relax and let me in, bit by bit. We're both panting by the time I'm as fully seated as I can get, my knot resting against her ass cheeks.

"Oh fuck, oh fuck, it's so much," Eden says in a breathy whimper, her pussy and ass clenching down on my cocks as Mezli works her clit and nipples and sends her over the edge. It's almost painful how she squeezes me, her body milking my cocks making my knot throb with the need to shove inside and fill her with my cum.

I pull back and thrust with more force, watching her tits and stomach bounce as I start to pound inside her. She gasps and cries out a mixture of expletives and our names, but she doesn't use her signals to tell us to stop, so I rut into her like a *xalar* possessed.

Eden comes again and Mezli grabs the back of my neck, pulling me in to crash her lips against mine over Eden's shoulder. Feeling her tongue fuck into my mouth is my undoing and I use the last shred of my sanity to pull back with a shout, both cocks bucking and throbbing as my cum shoots out over Eden's gaping holes and belly as Mezli keeps her spread open for me.

"Fuck!" I grunt as my fists work a seemingly unending supply of my release out of me, pearlescent pink cum glistening against Eden's beige skin. Mezli swipes two fingers down, gathering up some of my release and brings it up to Eden's lips, who greedily sucks on them as they both gaze into my eyes. "Fuck," I say again, at the beautifully filthy picture they paint.

Mezli kisses Eden on the cheek and whispers praise in her ear, releasing her when I finally stop spilling my seed. Eden moves off, lying in a daze on her side, granting me access to my other mate's cunt, already sopping with her arousal. I dive between her legs and devour her, hands pressing into her pleasure spots in the way I've learned gets her off the hardest.

"Shit, Phelix!" Mezli keens, holding my head against her as she grinds against my face and takes her well-deserved pleasure. Her hands tighten in my hair to the point of pain, but I savor the feeling of her demanding my service with her characteristic ferocity. It doesn't take her long before she's coming, soaking my face and chin as she lets out a low moan.

I work her with my tongue and hands until she releases me and shoves me off playfully. Sitting up, I catch the end of a kiss she shares with Eden, and my chest seizes with so much love and devotion to my mates that it takes my breath away.

"That was... Thank you," I say weakly, wrung out from my release.

Mezli lets out her own weak chuckle. "I'd say that experiment went quite well, don't you, Dr. Mori?"

Eden grins, her body languid and relaxed in a way she only is after getting thoroughly fucked. "Fuck yeah."

I lean over to kiss her sated smile, but jolt back when my comm chirps angrily from the bedside table.

"Whoops," Eden says sheepishly as I look at the amount of time we have to get decent and make it to the arboretum for the family welcoming ceremony.

Mezli shrugs. "Eh, they can wait. My mothers are just thrilled that I'm finally making our mating official. If we piss Phelix's mom off in the process, even better."

"Yeah, make her wait! My parents won't care either," Eden adds.

I snort at their disdain for my mother. They've been fiercely united against her since I shared her cruel remarks about my size and appearance one late, emotional night cycle about a month after we moved into our current apartment. Neither of them wanted me to invite her to our mating ceremony, but I insisted. I'd rather deal with her unpleasantness for a weekend than a lifetime of her ire. Plus, my father will be there to temper the worst of her criticisms.

"I care about respecting *your* parents. Now get up and take a shower so we're not late," I say, giving Mezli's pert ass a light swat.

"Make me, Lord Nafar," she teases, sticking her tongue out. Eden giggles as I growl and scoop our mate up and throw her over my shoulder, carrying Mezli to the shower as she squeals her delighted protests.

My cocks are already hard and ready again, and when Eden joins us in the shower and exchanges a wicked look with Mezli, I know there's no way we're not getting to the ceremony at least an hour late. It doesn't matter when we make this mating official. We've already bonded, heart and soul. This is our own private ceremony as our bodies join together again, filling the broken parts of ourselves with each other's love.

EPILOGUE

PAUL

A boisterous cheer erupts in the ballroom as the happy mated trio exchange kisses, flushed and love-drunk on each other.

I down the rest of my fizzy amber cocktail to hide my grimace, then politely clap along with the rest of the party guests. Eden's parents insisted on adding a human wedding reception to the weekend of non-stop events celebrating her mating with Mezli and Phelix.

The parade of mated bliss has dragged on for almost two whole day and night cycles, and that's only the events where friends are encouraged to attend. Two days of watching them as they recite words of devotion, share their hopes for the future with friends and family, and even bathe in a pool of water gathered from a Goddess-blessed spring back on Nexxa Itat. I was thankful to be in the back of the crowd for that one—watching the three of them washing each other's bodies up close would've been a bit too much for me to handle.

Both Eden and Mezli insisted I come to the ceremonies, though I've felt out of place the entire time. Eden wanted me in attendance because I helped her skip past the red tape typically involved with immigration to Spire, and Mezli wanted me here because we're friends now. Like, real, supportive, "comm if you need help and I'll drop everything" kind of friends, instead of her just gleefully tormenting me. I care about both of them, and Phelix tolerates me, so I couldn't say no.

Now here I am, surrounded by love and joy and all I want to do is go back to my crappy loft and wallow in my loneliness in peace. Maybe cry myself to sleep. Anything would be better than being surrounded by a crowd of happy people while I die inside a little with each toast to the mates.

I know I sound like an ungrateful, jealous bastard. I really don't mean to be. I'm happy for Mezli and Fina, and know that we're much better as friends. But when you've been alone long enough and all of your friends have found people to share their lives with, it starts to grate on you. Little by little, their affectionate glances and casual touches wear you down until you're raw. Then even the smallest display of love stings like salt in a wound.

Ugh, when is it going to be my turn? I'm not a bad guy. Sure, I didn't end things with Fina very maturely, but that was a long time ago. I've worked on myself. They say you have to love yourself before you can love someone else, but I call bullshit. I know plenty of insecure, imperfect people who've found love just fine. Mean-while, I've spent the past five years in therapy working through childhood trauma to become someone ready and open to receiving love, and...nothing.

It's not like I'm not trying. When I first arrived on Spire, I was more than a little intimidated by dating aliens, but that was almost a year ago. I'm far more used to aliens now, and find many of them attractive. I've spent weekend after weekend swiping through Syzygy looking for dates and hanging out at bars. None of the ones I matched with were looking for more than the novelty of fucking a human. I already went through my slutty phase while I was getting over breaking up with Fina, and I'm too old and scared of alien STIs to do that nonsense again. I want a connection, not a fuck buddy.

When I got sick of being propositioned by horny aliens, my friends offered to help. Maerlon tried setting me up with his coworker, Jezrit, but five minutes after sitting down to dinner, he bluntly told me he wasn't attracted to me. Mezli insisted I go on a date with one of her old flames, a massive vuloi named Grespan. We went out a few times, but then he met my pretty blonde coworker from the embassy and that was the end of that.

It's hopeless. I'm doomed to spend my life single, attempting to cobble together enough scraps of platonic affection from my friends to get by.

God, when did I get so bitter? I wave the nexxit serving drinks off when she stops by to see if I want another. Resting my face in my hands, I take a deep breath and try to push my melancholy mood away.

"Having a bad night?" a velvety voice asks from beside me.

"Uh, no, I'm fine, I just—" my words stop abruptly as I look up to give a fake smile to the alien speaking to me because—*damn*. The seladin sitting next to me has a roguish flop of white hair that partially obscures one glowing eye, granite skin with glowing markings that frame their sharp cheeks and jawline, and a green cybernetic eye. They're wearing a shimmering jumpsuit, and my eyes follow the path of the neckline that's cut down to their waist, exposing a thick sliver of their torso.

I tear my gaze back to the stranger's face, cheeks burning as they let out an amused laugh that sends a shiver of arousal down my spine. "You're just...?"

"Oh, um, just a little tired. It's been an eventful weekend!" I give them as much fake cheer as I can muster.

"I bet. Sometimes nexxit mate bonding ceremonies last for a week, so I'm glad the happy throuple went easy on us."

"Hah, yeah." I don't remember seeing this intimidatingly hot alien before, but I've had my head up my ass the whole weekend, so I wasn't exactly on the lookout for seladin babes.

Their cybernetic eye narrows, scanning across my face. I squirm under their assessment, waiting for them to find some hidden flaw inside me that's keeping romantic interest at bay. They frown slightly, confirming my pessimism.

I wait for them to excuse themself, but they stay. After a moment longer, they speak again. "I've always found mating ceremonies a bit depressing. Like, yes, we get it. You're in love. Good for you. Now go fuck and stop shoving it in my face that I'm alone."

My brows shoot up, and a shocked laugh escapes me.

"Was that too harsh?" they ask, laughing along with me.

"Nope, not at all. Couldn't have said it better myself," I say, giving them my first real smile of the entire weekend.

"Nice to meet a kindred spirit. I'm Hadrell. They/he pronouns," they say, extending a hand in the human fashion and flashing me a fanged grin.

I move a little too slow to take their hand in mine, momentarily distracted by thoughts of what it would feel like to have those teeth pressed against my skin. I grab their hand and shake it with too much force. "Paul! I'm Paul. He/Him. Nice to meet you!"

"Can I get you a drink, Paul?" he asks, leaning in a bit like he's about to tell me a secret. I lean in without thinking, drawn by their magnetic presence, until my thigh is pressed against theirs and I can smell their earthy cologne.

"They're free so, uh, sure. Another drink sounds good." I don't know why this stunning seladin is flirting with me, but I'll soak it up for one more drink and then politely excuse myself.

His face lights up and he places an elegant hand on my thigh and squeezes it casually. My cock immediately perks up, because I'm that hard up for physical touch. I flush and they laugh again, removing their hand to wave over to the bartender. I want to grab their hand and place it back on my leg. It felt so good.

Shit. Maybe I could make an exception for my rule of not having casual sex, just for tonight. It's been a rough, long weekend and a hookup with a sexy alien might help me relieve some of my tension. Or at least distract me from my sadness for a bit. What could it hurt to let this handsome seladin take me to bed?

A BLARING ALARM GOES OFF, shocking me awake. I groan and hold my hand up to shield my eyes from some of the harsh overhead light. My head is pounding and when I try to sit up, I get so dizzy I have to lie back down.

Fuck, how much did I drink?

"Well, that's not ideal," a groggy voice murmurs, and I realize two things: One, I'm definitely not in my own bed, and two, I'm not alone.

SPACE FOR MORE

I attempt to sit up again, but the room we're in lurches, sending me tumbling off the bed and onto a hard metal floor.

"*Es'het*, are you okay?" A head pops over the edge of the bed, and last night's hazy events grow slightly clearer. I can't remember their name, though.

"I'm... Shit, my head hurts. Where are we? Did we, uh..."

The seladin grins down at me, looking far too composed after how much we drank last night and with the alarm still ringing out around us. "Did we drunkenly go back to my place to cuddle and commiserate about our loneliness, then fall asleep after you cried into my chest? Yes."

"Oh god." Shit, I can't even do an alien hookup right. "I'm so sorry."

"Don't be. I cried, too," he says with a wink. "Though, I should probably apologize to you. You asked where we are. The answer is my ship."

"Your ship?" A memory of the seladin making a joke about it not being about the size of the ship but how you fly it comes back to me. "You live on a spaceship?"

"I do. Why? Don't I look the part of a dashing space adventurer?"

"Right now, you look like a blur. My head is still spinning. Can you turn off that alarm?" I ask, putting my hands over my ears to try to muffle some of the jarring noise. My comm buzzes with my usual notification that I need to leave for work. "Shit! I have to go."

Their smile fades and they rub the back of their neck sheepishly. "Uh, I'm afraid that's not possible. That lovely alarm that's blaring? It's an alert that we're making a hot exit from the station."

"What?!" In my panic, I manage to use the edge of the bed to pull myself up to standing, and am greeted by a large viewport and the sight of the massive space station quickly receding from view.

"Hope you're up for some excitement," they say with a weak laugh that's punctuated with a flash of light and another violent lurch of the ship.

My head spins even more as I realize that was the ship taking fire. I'm on a ship with a stranger, potentially about to die because they're some kind of *pirate*, and we didn't even have sex! I swoon like a goddamn damsel in distress, feeling their strong arms catch me before darkness takes me.

Want more Space for More? Sign up for my newsletter to get an exclusive bonus story.

AUTHOR NOTE

Hello alien lovers! Thank you for reading Space for More. If you're reading this far, I hope you enjoyed it!

Space for More shares the same humor, emotion, and spice, but has a lot more angst than Space for Love. Because of this, I know some Space for Love fans may not like it as much, but that's okay! I wanted to write this book as my take on fated mates— one where the characters have to work on their bond instead of it just magically fixing their flaws and resolving past trauma. Eden, Mezli, and Phelix are all complicated characters who at their core just want to love and be loved. So while their journey to finding their HEA was a lot more drama-filled, the destination was the same deep, loving bond I want for all of my characters.

Writing this book was a learning process. My naive baby author brain didn't consider the difficulty of writing three main characters with equal importance both to the story and to the romantic relationships they all share. However, I knew I wanted to write a FFM romance since those aren't common in alien romance (and it made my bisexual heart happy). I'm nothing if not stubborn once I get an idea, so I persisted!

Huge thanks to Kass and Lyonne, who read my extremely rough first draft and gave me the courage to not give up on this story. Thank you to my amazing beta readers, Aimee, Angelina, Arielle, Furvias, Holly, May, Melissa, and Violet. Your encouragement and (often hilarious) feedback meant so much to me. And of course, thank you to all my lovely ARC readers!

Thanks again for reading and for your support!

ABOUT THE AUTHOR

Emily loves cozy, emotional, and spicy romances with a monstrous twist. When she isn't musing on the merits of doting, dominant monsters, she reads an obscene amount of romance novels, and cultivates her eccentric recluse persona.

Printed in Great Britain
by Amazon

41025060R00189